ROYALLY ENDOWED

EMMA CHASE

EverAfter Romance
A Division of Diversion Publishing Corp.
443 Park Avenue South, Suite 1008
New York, New York 10016
www.EverAfterRomance.com

Cover Design: By Hang Le
Photography: Thomas Watkins
Cover Model: Vincent Azzopardi

For more information, email info@diversionbooks.com

First EverAfter Romance edition August 2017.
ISBN: 978-1-68230-777-9

Also by Emma Chase

THE ROYALLY SERIES
Royally Screwed
Royally Matched

THE LEGAL BRIEFS SERIES
Overruled
Sustained
Appealed
Sidebarred

THE TANGLED SERIES
Tangled
Holy Frigging Matrimony
Twisted
Tamed
Tied
It's a Wonderful Tangled Christmas Carol

To sweet crushes and slow burns.

PROLOGUE

Logan

Some men think with their cocks.

You know the type. Quick smooth-talkers, shifty eyes always scanning for a nice pair of legs, a set of full tits, or a tight arse they can pant after.

Other blokes think too much with their brains. You know that type too. Annoyingly careful, slow-moving, constantly parsing their words like they already know whatever they're saying is going to come back and take a bite out of them.

I'm not either of those.

I always go with my gut. When it clenches with a warning, I act—no hesitation. When it tugs and nudges, I pause and reevaluate. When it twists and writhes, I know, guaranteed, I've cocked up big-time.

My gut is my best friend, my conscience, my most lethal asset.

And it has never let me down.

It's my gut that drags me to her door. That roots me in place as I knock. That gives me the words—pleading, unfamiliar remorseful words—I'll gladly say to make this right.

To get her back.

Because while my gut is brilliant, sometimes I can be a real fucking idiot.

Yesterday was one of those times.

"Ellie. It's me—open up, we need to talk."

I sense movement on the other side of the solid oak door—not in sounds or shifting shadows beneath it, but more of an awareness. I can feel her in there. Nearby and listening.

"Go away, Logan."

Her voice is tight, higher-pitched than usual. Upset.

"Ellie, please. I was a twat, I know . . ." I'm not keen on begging from the hallway, but if that's what it takes . . . "I'm sorry. Let me in."

Ellie is difficult to anger, quick to forgive; she just doesn't have it in her to hold a grudge. So her next words fall like an axe—cutting my legs right off from under me.

"No, you were right. The princess's sister and the East Amboy bodyguard don't make sense—we'll never last."

Did I actually say that to her? What the fuck is wrong with me? What I feel for her is the one thing in my life that makes sense. That matters.

But I never told her that.

Instead . . . instead, I said all the wrong things.

I brace my palm against the smooth wood, leaning forward, wanting to be as near to her as possible. "Elle . . ."

"I've changed my mind, Logan."

If a corpse could speak, it would sound exactly like my Ellie does now. Flat, lifeless.

"I want the fairy tale. I want what Olivia has . . . castles and carriages . . . and you'll never be able to give me that. I would just be settling for you. You'll never be able to make me happy."

She doesn't mean that. They're my words—the insecurities I put on her—that she's hurling back in my face.

But God, it fucking hurts to hear. Physically hurts—stabbing deep into the pit of my stomach, crushing my chest, grinding my bones. I meant it when I said I would die for her . . . and right now, it feels like I am.

I grab the doorknob to walk inside, to see her face. To see that she doesn't mean it.

"Ellie—"

"Don't come in!" she screeches like I've never heard her before. "I don't want to see you! Go away, Logan. We're done— just *go*!"

I breathe hard—that's what you do when pain wrecks you, breathe through it. Then I swallow bile, straighten up, turn around and walk down the hall. Away from her. Just like she wants, like she asked. Like she screamed.

My brain tells me to move faster—get the hell out of there, cut my losses and lick my wounds. And my heart—Christ—that poor bastard's too battered and bloody to express anything at all.

But then, just over halfway down the hall, my steps slow until I stop completely.

Because my gut . . . it strains through the hurt. Rebels. It shouts that this isn't right. This isn't her. Something's off.

And even more than that . . . something is very, very wrong.

I glance up and down the quiet hall—not a guard or a maid in sight. I look back at the door. Closed and silent and still.

Then I turn and march straight back to it. I don't knock, or wait, or ask for permission. In one move, I turn the knob and step inside.

What I see there stops me cold.

Because whatever I was expecting, it sure as fuck wasn't this.

Not at all . . .

CHAPTER 1

Logan

Five years earlier

"You wanted to see me, Prince Nicholas?"

Here's a confession: when the powers that be first offered me a position on the royal security team, I wasn't interested. The idea of following around some self-important aristocrats who were in love with the sound of their own voices—and the smell of their own arses—didn't appeal to me. The way I saw it, guards were only a step above servant-boys—and I'm no one's servant.

I wanted action. A blaze of glory. Purpose. I wanted to be a part of something that was bigger than myself. Something noble and lasting.

"Yes, Logan—have a seat."

I'd distinguished myself in the military pretty quickly. And Winston—the head of Palace Security—had taken notice. They were looking for very particular qualities in Prince Nicholas's personal team, he'd said. Young lads who were quick on their feet, loyal and ferocious when required. The type who'd be just fine bringing a knife to a gunfight—'cause he wouldn't be needing a fucking knife or gun to win.

After only a few weeks, I had a different take on the

position. It came to feel like a calling, a duty. Important men make things happen, get things done—they have the power to make life easier for the not-so-important people.

I protect them, so they can do that.

And the young prince sitting across from me, behind the desk in the library of this luxurious penthouse suite—he's an important man.

"How old are you, Logan?"

"My file says I'm twenty-five."

If Saint Peter was a fisher of men, I'm a reader of them. It's a skill that's essential to this occupation—possessing a gut feeling for what someone else's intentions are. The ability to read a man's eyes, the shifting of his feet—to know what he's capable of and just what kind of man he is.

Nicholas Pembrook is a good man. To his core.

And that's a rare thing.

More often than not, important men are prime scumbags.

His mouth twitches. "I know what your file says. That's not what I asked." He's also not a fool—and he's been lied to enough in his life that he's got an ear for things that don't ring true.

"How old are you really?"

I look him in the eye, wondering where he's going with this. "Twenty-two."

He nods slowly, massaging his thumb into the palm of his other hand, thinking. "So you signed up for the military at . . . fifteen? Lied about your age? That's young."

I shrug. "They weren't real discerning at the recruitment office. I was tall, solid and good with my fists."

"You were still a child."

"I was never a child, Your Highness. Any more than you were."

Childhood is when you're supposed to muck up, figure out who you are, what you want to be. You're given permission to be a jackarse. I didn't have that privilege; neither did Nicholas. Our paths were set before we were born. Opposite paths, sure—but whether you grow up in a shack or a palace, the expectations and demands of those around you tend to snuff out innocence pretty damn fast.

"Why'd you leave home so young?"

Now it's my turn to smirk. Because I'm not a fool either. "You know why. That's in the file too."

I'm good at identifying scumbags because I come from a long line of them. Criminals—not especially successful ones. Petty, scrounging, desperate enough to be dangerous—the kind who'll smile to your face, pat you on the back, then stab you as soon as you're not looking.

My grandfather died in prison—he was in for murder committed during an armed robbery. My dad will die there too, hopefully sooner rather than later—he's in for manslaughter. I've got uncles who've done stints for a whole range of criminal activities, cousins who've been killed in broad daylight in the middle of the street and aunts who've pimped out their daughters without a second thought.

By the time I was fifteen I knew if I stayed in that shit-hole, I'd start to stink. And then I'd have only two options: prison or the cemetery.

Neither one of those worked for me.

"What's this really about? All the questions?"

It's always better to cut to the chase, deep and quick.

His gray-green eyes focus on me, his face probing, his shoulders slightly hunched, like an elephant's sitting on them.

"Now that I have Henry in hand, the Queen wants us back in Wessco, in two days. You know this."

I nod.

"I want to bring Olivia home with me, for the summer."

For a time, I was on the fence about the pretty New York baker. She put ideas in Nicholas's head, made him reckless. But she's a good lass—hardworking, honest—and she cares about him. Not about his title or his bank account. She couldn't give a shit about those and probably would prefer him without them. She makes him happy.

And in the two-odd years I've worked with the Crown Prince, truly happy is something I don't think I've ever seen him be.

"Is that wise?" I ask.

Olivia Hammond is a sweet girl. And the Palace . . . has a knack for turning sweet to sour.

"No. But I want to do it anyway."

And the look on his face—it's raw and exposed. It's yearning. From the outside looking in, you'd think there's nothing a royal could want that he can't have. Nicholas has private planes, servants, castles and more money than he can spend in a lifetime—but I can't think of a single instance when he did what he wanted, just for the hell of it. Or when he let himself do something he knew he shouldn't.

I admire him, but I don't envy him.

"Olivia wants to come, but she's worried about leaving her sister alone for the summer. Ellie's young, still in school and . . . naïve."

She's got a wild streak in her too. As bright as the pink in her blond hair, which has been joined by blue, then green, during the two months we've been in New York.

"I could see her attracting trouble," I comment.

"Exactly. Also, Ellie will have to run the coffee shop on her own, with just Marty for help. Olivia's father is—"

"He's a drunk."

I'm good at spotting them too—can smell them from a mile away.

"Yes." Nicholas sighs. "Look, Logan, you've been around long enough to know that I don't trust easily, or often. But I trust you." He pushes a hand through his black hair and meets my eyes. "Which is why I'm asking you. Will you stay in New York? Will you help Ellie, watch over her . . . make sure she's safe?"

She seems like a decent girl, but I already said I wasn't a servant—and I'm also not a nanny. Protecting the royal family is a duty I've chosen; keeping tabs on an American teenage girl is a fucking headache waiting to happen.

Nicholas glances out the window. "I know it's a lot to ask. It's not your job; you can say no. But there's no one else I would choose . . . no one else I can depend on. So, I'd consider it a personal favor if you say yes."

Ah . . . hell.

I have a brother. To say I wish I didn't would be an understatement. And not in the same way Nicholas wishes his royal snot of a brother would grow the hell up, or how Miss Olivia seems put out by her younger sister at times. The world would be a better place if my brother weren't in it—and that's a stance shared by others.

But if I had a choice, if I could assemble a brother from the ground up, I would build the man sitting across from me right now.

Which is why, even though I'm going to bloody regret it, it takes only a moment before I give him my answer.

"James has a boy back home—about a year old, so he'll want to go home with you. Tommy'll be happy to stay—the Bronx is like his own personal harem. Between the two of us, and two more men, Cory and Liam maybe, we'll keep the girl out of trouble and the business afloat for the summer."

Nicholas's face splits into the biggest smile and relief lights up his eyes. He stands, holding out his hand to shake mine, pounding my shoulder with gratitude.

"Thank you, Logan. Truly. I won't forget this."

If nothing else, this summer will be . . . different.

CHAPTER 2

Ellie

I'm an old soul when it comes to music. I blame my mother. One of my earliest memories is of her singing me to sleep with a Led Zeppelin lullaby—"All of My Love." When she baked in the kitchen of my family's coffee shop that's named after her, Amelia's, her boom-box would be bumping. Sometimes she'd mix it up, but more often than not, it was the throaty, soul-stirring, high-octane tunes of female artists that spilled from the speakers into my and my big sister's ears. It left an impression.

I mean, once you hear Janis Joplin go full-out Bobby McGee, you don't go back.

This morning, just after four a.m., I've chosen "Gloria" by Laura Branigan. It pounds against my eardrums—upbeat and peppy. And today, I could use some pep.

Olivia left for Wessco yesterday and I'm so happy for her—really, genuinely, screechingly happy. She deserves this—to be waited on hand and foot, to be pampered and adored by a gorgeous, filthy-souled, golden-hearted prince. Liv deserves the whole world, even if it's only for three months.

But, I'm going to miss the hell out of her.

There's also the small detail that . . . I haven't slept in twenty-four hours. Not a blink. And if past is prologue, there are going to be a lot of sleepless nights in my future. I'm a high school senior—I have exams to study for, projects to complete, extracurricular activities to activitize, lifelong memories to make—and now I have a business to run.

Who the fuck has time for sleep?

I jack up the volume on my phone and scoop a tablespoon of instant coffee grounds into my mouth—washing the bitter, spiky granules down with a gulp of black, cold coffee. We don't serve instant for the coffee shop. Instant coffee is disgusting.

But it serves a purpose. It's effective—efficient. I love caffeine. *Love it.* The high, the rush, the feeling that I'm Wonder Woman's long-lost cousin and there ain't shit I can't do.

I would mainline it, if that were actually a thing.

I would probably become a meth-head if it weren't for the rotting-teeth, ruined-life, most-likely-dying-by-overdose elements of it all. I'm a high school senior, not an asshole.

After swallowing my nasty liquid-of-life, I get back into the song—shaking my hips and shoulders, flipping my mermaid multicolor-streaked blond hair back and forth. I spin on my toes, I twerk and shimmy, I may even leap like a ballerina—though I'll deny it—all while filling the pie dishes on the counter with ooey-gooey, yummy, freshly sliced fruit and rolling out the balls of floured dough for the top layer of the two dozen pies I need to make before we open.

My mother's pies—her recipes—they're what Amelia's is known for and the only reason we didn't go under years ago. We used to need only a dozen, but when news of my sister's romance with the Crown Prince of Wessco hit, the fangirls, royal-watchers, mildly interested passersby and psycho-stalkers came out of the woodwork . . . and right to our door.

Business is booming, which is a double-edged sword. Money's a little less tight, but the workload has doubled, and with my sister gone, the workforce just got cut in half. More than half, actually—more like a third, because Olivia really ran the show. Up until recently, I was a total slacker. That's why I was adamant she go to Wessco—why I swore I could rise to the occasion and handle things while she was gone.

I owed her and I knew it.

And if I'm going to actually keep up my end of the deal, I really need to move my ass with these pies.

I sprinkle some flour on the dough and roll it out with the heavy, wooden rolling pin. Once it's the perfect size and thickness, I flip the rolling pin around and sing into the handle—*American Idol* style.

"Calling Gloriaaaaaaaaaaaaaaaaaaaaa . . ."

And then I turn around.

"AHHHHHHHHHHHHHHH!"

Without thinking, I bend my arm and throw the rolling pin like a tomahawk . . . straight at the head of the guy who's standing just inside the kitchen door.

The guy I didn't hear come in.

The guy who catches the hurling rolling pin without flinching—one-handed and cool as a gorgeous cucumber—just an inch from his perfect face.

He tilts his head to the left, looking around the rolling pin to meet my eyes with his soulful brown ones. "Nice toss."

Logan St. James.

Bodyguard. Totally badass. Sexiest guy I have ever seen—and that includes books, movies and TV, foreign and domestic. He's the perfect combo of boyishly could-go-to-my-school kind of handsome, mixed with dangerously hot and tantalizingly mysterious. If comic-book Superman, James Dean, Jason Bourne and some guy with the smoothest, most perfectly pitched, British-Scottish-esque, Wessconian-accented voice all melded together into one person, they would make Logan fucking St. James.

And I just tried to clock him with a baking tool—while wearing my Rick and Morty pajama short-shorts, a Winnie-the-Pooh T-shirt I've had since I was eight and my SpongeBob SquarePants slippers.

And no bra.

Not that I have a whole lot going on upstairs, but still . . .

"Christ on a saltine!" I grasp at my chest like an old woman with a pacemaker.

Logan's brow wrinkles. "Haven't heard that one before."

Oh fuck—did he see me dancing? Did he see me leap? God, let me die now.

I yank on my earbuds' cord, popping them from my ears. "What the hell, dude?! Make some noise when you walk in—let a girl know she's not alone. You could've given me a heart attack. And I could've killed you with my awesome ninja skills."

The corner of his mouth quirks. "No, you couldn't."

He sets the rolling pin down on the counter.

"I knocked on the kitchen door so I wouldn't frighten you, but you were busy with your . . . performance."

Blood and heat rush to my face. And I want to melt into the floor and then all the way down to the Earth's core.

Logan points toward the front of the coffee shop. "The door wasn't bolted. I thought Marty was going to replace the broken lock?"

Relieved to have a reason not to look at him, I turn around and get the lock set out of the drawer—still in the packaging. "He bought it, but we got swamped the other day and he didn't have time to install it."

Logan picks it up and turns it over in his hands. "I'll take care of it."

"Do you need a screwdriver?"

"No, I have tools in the car."

I lean my elbow against the counter, looking up at him. Logan's really tall. And not just because I'm a minute five foot one. He's like, tall-tall. Long—like a sexy tree. And solid—broad across the chest in his black dress shirt. Strapping.

"You're like a Boy Scout, huh?"

It's my attempt at flirting—probably only slightly less effective than *Dirty Dancing*'s "I carried a watermelon."

He does the mouth-quirk thing again.

"Not even close."

There's a bad-boy edge in the way he says it—a heavy hint of the forbidden—that gets my heart pounding and my jaw eager to drop.

To cover my reaction, I nod vigorously.

"Right, me neither . . . Never been a—"

Too vigorously.

So vigorously that my elbow slips in the flour on the counter and I almost knock myself unconscious. But Logan's not only big and brawny—he's quick. Fast enough to catch me by the arm and waist to steady me before I bash the side of my head against the butcher block.

"Are you all right, Ellie?"

He leans down, looking at me intently—a look I'll see in my dreams tonight . . . assuming I can sleep. And, wow, Logan has great eyelashes. Thick and lengthy and midnight black. I bet they're not the only part of him that's thick and lengthy.

My gaze darts down to his promised land, where his pants are just tight enough to confirm my suspicions—this bodyguard may have a service revolver in his pocket, but he's got a magnum in his pants.

Yum.

"Yeah, I'm good." I sigh. "Just . . . you know . . . tired. But I'm cool . . . totally cool."

And I shake it off, like I actually am.

He nods and steps away. "I'll fix the lock now. And I'll give you the key afterward. Keep it with you; don't lose it. From now on, you lock the door behind you when you leave, and you keep it locked when you're home by yourself. Understand?"

I nod again. Livvy must've been talking to him. It's not my

fault keys abandon me. I put them in a specific spot, so I'll know where they are for later—and I swear to God, they sprout legs and run away.

Slippery, little Houdini bastards.

After I take the last pie out of the oven and set it on the cooling rack, I fly upstairs to get dressed for school. I don't have the time or the wardrobe that some of the girls at my school have, but I make the most of what I've got: dark jeans, a sheer pale-pink short-sleeved top with a white tank underneath, black flats and a black leather jacket I found at the consignment shop last year.

I like jewelry, I like to jingle when I walk—like a human music box. So, it's cheap rings on every finger, cheaper bangle bracelets on my wrists and a long silver dangly necklace.

I don't contour my face or fill in my blond eyebrows with dark brown pencil like Kylie Jenner—I'd end up looking like that freaky female serial killer if I tried. But I do use under-eye concealer—practically a whole tube of it—plus a little mascara and light pink lip gloss.

When I hop down the back steps a few minutes before six a.m., Logan is done with the lock and talking to our waiter Marty in the kitchen.

Marty McFly Ginsberg isn't just our employee—he's my and Livvy's big brother from another mother. If our mother were black, Jewish, gay and cool as shit. Marty's the bomb-dot-com.

"Hey, Chicklet." He hugs me. And the man doesn't scrimp on his hugs. "How are you doing? Did you hear from Liv?"

I nod. "Did she send you the pic of her room?"

Marty sighs. "Like she died and went to Nate Berkus heaven." He brushes a green-tipped strand of my hair away. "How were things around here last night?"

"Fine." I yawn. "I haven't slept yet, but that's not news."

Marty grinds the coffee beans, fills two filters and starts brewing the first of many pots of coffee. "How's your dad holding up?"

"Fine, I guess. He didn't come home."

It's not a frequent thing, but it's happened often enough that it's not a big deal. At least not to me.

Logan slowly turns my way. "What do you mean?"

I shrug. "He's still not home. He was probably upset about Liv leaving, got tanked and passed out on Mulligan's bar or one of the benches between here and there. It happens sometimes."

The bodyguard's eyes seem to spark—like a fire's been lit inside him. "Are you telling me you spent the night in the flat upstairs, all by yourself, with an unlocked fucking door on the ground floor?"

"Yeah. But I had Bosco with me."

Bosco is our shih-tzu-Chihuahua mix. He's not exactly guard dog material—unless his plan is to startle intruders to death with his so-hideous-he's-cute face. And if a burglar happens to try stealing hot dogs from the fridge, he'll never make it out alive. Bosco would rip a throat out for a hot dog.

"It's not a big deal, Logan."

Logan looks at Marty and a secret, He-Man-Boy's-Club look passes between them. When he turns back to me, his face and voice are hard. Definitely pissed off.

"We'll take shifts—me and the lads. We can stay down here in the diner if you're uncomfortable having us in the flat, but someone will be here with you, round the clock, from now on. You won't be alone again. Yeah?"

I nod slowly, feeling warm fuzzies in my veins, like my blood is carbonated.

"Okay."

So this is what it's like to have someone to watch over me.

Don't get me wrong—my sister would take a bullet for me

and still beat the shit out of the person who fired the shot. But this is totally different.

Hotter. More Tarzan-y. More comforting. I'm this tough, handsome guy's priority. He'll care about me, protect me . . . like it's his motherfucking job.

Because—it is.

I know from Liv that Nicholas finds the constant protection stifling. But to me, it just feels . . . really nice.

A truck rumbles up the back alley.

"That's the Danish delivery," Marty says. "If he tries pushing squashed-to-shit pastries on us again, I'm going to have to bust some skulls." He cracks his knuckles. "I'll be back."

As he goes out the back door, my friend Marlow slips through it, into the kitchen.

"Hey, bitch. You ready to go?"

"Yeah, five minutes."

Marlow's from a wealthy family. Her dad's a hedge-fund manager and kind of a dick. Her mom is very beautiful and very sad, and I've never seen her without a glass of Pinot Grigio. They don't send Mar to a private school, even though they can afford it, because they want her to have "grit." Street smarts.

I don't know if it's the result of the public school system or if it just comes natural to her, but if I were to bet on the girl most likely to run the world? I'd put my money on Marlow.

"The front door is locked—what's up with that?"

"Logan fixed the lock," I tell her.

Her bright red, heart-shaped mouth smiles. "Good job, Kevin Costner. You should staple the key to Ellie's forehead, though, or she'll lose it."

She has names for the other guys too and when her favorite guard, Tommy Sullivan, walks in a few minutes later, Marlow uses his. "Hello, Delicious." She twirls her honey-colored, bouncy hair around her finger, cocking her hip and tilting her head like a vintage pinup girl.

Tommy, the fun-loving super-flirt, winks. "Hello, pretty, underage lass." Then he nods to Logan and smiles at me. "Lo . . . Good morning, Miss Ellie."

"Hey, Tommy."

Marlow struts forward. "Three months, Tommy. Three months until I'm a legal adult—then I'm going to use you, abuse you and throw you away."

The dark-haired devil grins. "That's my idea of a good date." Then he gestures toward the back door. "Now, are we ready for a fun day of learning?"

One of the security guys has been walking me to school ever since the public and press lost their minds over Nicholas and Olivia's still-technically-unconfirmed relationship. They make sure no one messes with me and they drive me in the tinted, bulletproof SUV when it rains—it's a pretty sweet deal.

I grab my ten-thousand-pound messenger bag from the corner.

"I can't believe I didn't think of this before. Elle—you should have a huge banger here tonight!" says Marlow.

Tommy and Logan couldn't have synced up better if they'd practiced:

"No fucking way."

Marlow holds up her hands, palms out. "Did I say banger?"

"*Huge* banger," Tommy corrects.

"No—no fucking way. I meant, we should have a few friends over to . . . hang out. Very few. Very mature. Like . . . almost a study group."

I toy with my necklace and say, "That actually sounds like a good idea."

Throwing a party when your parents are away is a rite-of-high-school passage. And after this summer, Liv will most likely never be away again. It's now or never.

"It's a terrible idea." Logan scowls.

He looks kinda scary when he scowls. But still hot. Possibly, hotter.

Marlow steps forward, her brass balls hanging out and proud. "You can't stop her—that's not your job. It's like when the Bush twins got busted in that bar with fake IDs or Malia was snapped smoking pot at Coachella. Secret Service couldn't stop them; they just had to make sure they didn't get killed."

Tommy slips his hands in his pockets, laid back even when he's being a hardass. "We could call her sister. Even from an ocean away, I'd bet she'd stop her."

"No!" I jump a little. "No, don't bother Liv. I don't want her worrying."

"We could board up the fucking doors and windows," Logan suggests.

'Cause that's not overkill or anything.

I move in front of the two security guards and plead my case. "I get why you're concerned, okay? But I have this thing— it's like my motto. I want to suck the lemon."

Tommy's eyes bulge. "Suck *what*?"

I laugh, shaking my head. Boys are stupid.

"You know that saying, 'When life gives you lemons, make lemonade'?—well, I want to suck the lemon dry."

Neither of them seems particularly impressed.

"I want to live every bit of life, experience everything it has to offer, good and bad." I lift my jeans to show my ankle—and the little lemon I've drawn there. "See? When I'm eighteen, I'm going to get this tattooed on for real. As a reminder to live as much and as hard and as awesome as I can—to not take anything for granted. And having my friends over tonight is part of that."

I look back and forth between them. Tommy's weakening—I can feel it. Logan's still a brick wall.

"It'll be small. And quiet—I swear. Totally controlled. And besides, you guys will be here with me. What could go wrong?"

Everything.

Everything goes fucking wrong.

By ten thirty the dining room of the coffee shop is wall-to-wall people standing shoulder-to-shoulder. And I don't know any of them. There are empty beer bottles and liquor bottles all over the tables and the kitchen smells like a weed dispensary.

How do I get myself into these situations? Why does this happen to me? And where the hell is Marlow?

A sailor pushes past me.

Yes, an actual fucking sailor—like Popeye—in full dress whites. And it's not even Fleet Week!

"Do you see him too?" I stutter to Logan, who's glowering so hard beside me, his face may actually freeze in place. And he'd still be sexy as hell.

"I told you this was a bad idea," Logan growls.

I stomp my foot.

Because I am a grown-up. Almost.

"You're not supposed to say that! You're not supposed to say, 'I told you so'—it's rude!"

"I don't give a fuck what's rude; you need to listen to me. Do what I say from this point on, understand?"

It's on the tip of my tongue to ask what he'll do if I don't. Spank me? Tie me up? Handcuff me to his side? If those are the consequences for disobeying Special Agent Sexy-Face, I'm about to become a very naughty girl.

Before I can pose the question, a crash from the kitchen pulls me out of my sultry kink-laced fantasy and back to my sucky reality.

The music is so loud, the wooden chairs are vibrating and it's only a matter of time before a neighbor calls the cops. I'm tired and—son of a bitch—they're eating the pies! I spot three—no, four—people standing, talking and shoveling tomorrow's pies into their mouths with their hands. *Dickheads!*

"You're right. I'm calling it. Let's pull the plug."

Logan's dark brown eyes roll to the ceiling. "Finally."

I twist my hands together, working it all out in my head. "So, maybe you could do that whistling thing with your fingers to get everyone's attention? And I'll stand on a chair and say, 'Thank you all for coming. This has been great. I hope you—'"

That's when I realize Logan's not listening. Because he's not standing next to me anymore. He's over by the sound system—cutting off the music, then cupping his hands around his mouth. "Get the fuck out!"

Subtlety, thy name is not Logan St. James.

"You could help, you know."

After the party cleared out, Logan had sent Tommy home—said he would take the night shift and one of the other guys would relieve him in the morning. That he wanted to make sure everything was "set to rights."

I get the feeling Logan isn't too good with delegating.

"Why would I do that?" he asks, leaning against the wall, sliding his thumb across his phone screen. "I told you not to have a bloody party."

Thank Zeus I did my homework right after school, in between filling orders in the kitchen. I have an exam fourth period tomorrow, but I can study at lunch. At the moment, I'm on my hands and knees, scraping and sweeping up the sticky, squashed pie pieces that are stuck to the floor. The recycling bins are filled to the brim with empties, the kitchen is clean and the tables are wiped down. The floor's last thing left.

"It would be the gentlemanly thing to do."

"I'm not a gentleman and I don't sweep fucking floors."

"Nice."

He quirks his head to the side like he's going to say something else, but before he can, my dad walks through the door.

After two full days.

He lumbers in, not quite staggering, but unsteady on his feet, looking straight ahead.

Like Logan, my dad's tall—broad—and he's handsome in a rough, working-man kind of way. The type of guy who showers after work, not before. Or, at least, he used to be.

Now, especially when he's coming off a bender, he tends to hunch, making him look bent and older than he is. His flannel shirt is wrinkled and dirty and his black-gray hair hangs in his eyes.

"What's this, Ellie?" he slurs.

And the weird thing is—I hope he yells at me. Grounds me. Takes away my phone. Like a normal parent would, a regular father . . . who actually cared.

"I, uh, had some people over. It got a little crazy. I'll clean everything up before we open tomorrow."

He doesn't even glance my way. Just gives a small, short nod that I notice only because I'm watching so closely.

"I'm goin' to bed. I'll be up to help Marty when you leave for school."

Then he clomps between the tables and through the swinging kitchen door, to the back steps that lead to our apartment upstairs.

I bow my head and go back to cleaning the floor.

A few minutes later without looking up, I tell Logan, "You don't have to do that, you know."

"Don't have to do what?"

"Worry. You're all tense, like you think he's going to hurt me or something. He can barely exert the energy to speak to me—he'd never hit me."

Logan looks down at me with those deep, dark eyes, like he can see straight through me, read my mind.

"It doesn't have to be his fists. There's all kinds of ways to hurt people. Isn't there?"

Usually, it doesn't bother me. I don't let it. But the last few days haven't been usual. And big, giant aching tears well in my eyes.

"He hates me," I say simply. But then a sob rattles in my chest, shaking my shoulders. "My dad hates me."

Logan's brows draw close together, and after a moment, he takes a deep breath. Then, with a grace that's surprising for a guy his size, he walks over and sinks down onto the floor next to me, legs bent, forearms resting on his knees, back against the wall.

He leans in close and whispers so gently, "I don't think that's true."

I shake my head and swipe my cheeks. "You don't understand. I was sick. The night my mom was killed, I had a sore throat, cough. I kept complaining about it. The pharmacy down the block was closed for renovations, so she took the subway."

When you grow up in a city, your parents have the mugging talk with you at a young age. The one about how no amount of money or jewelry is worth your life. So, if someone wants those things, just hand them over. They can be replaced—you can't.

"He wrote us a letter a few years ago from prison—the guy who did it. He said he was sorry, that he didn't mean to shoot her, that the gun just . . . went off."

I glance up to find Logan looking and listening intently.

"I don't know why anyone thinks stuff like that is supposed to make people feel better. That he was sorry. That he didn't mean to do what he did. It didn't for us. If anything, it just proved that she was in the wrong place at the wrong time. And that . . . if I didn't exist, the love of my dad's life would still be here. I'm not being dramatic—it's just a fact. And that's why he can't even look at me."

We're quiet for a few minutes. Me, leaning back on my calves, Logan looking straight ahead.

Then he rubs his neck and asks, "You know how they say that New Jersey is the armpit of America?"

"I always thought that was shitty. I like Jersey."

"Where I grew up—East Amboy—it's like the taint of Wessco."

A quick laugh busts out of my throat.

"There was this guy—Wino Willie—everyone called him that. He'd spend the whole day begging, walking the streets looking for loose change in the gutters. Then he'd buy the biggest, cheapest bottle of liquor he could get."

The steady sound of Logan's deep voice, the lilting accent, is calming. Soothing, like a dark lullaby.

"But he wasn't always Wino Willie. Once, he was William. And William had a pretty wife, three little kids. They were poor, we were all poor, and they lived in a tiny, one-bedroom flat on the fourth floor of a building that was falling apart—but they were happy."

His voice drops.

"William worked the night shift at the supermarket, unloading trucks, stocking shelves. And one night, he kissed his pretty wife goodbye, tucked his kids into bed and went off to work. And when he came home . . . everything that he loved, everything he lived for, was nothing but ash."

I gasp, small and quiet.

"There'd been a fire, bad wires, and they all got trapped in that tiny flat and died. All except one. The oldest, Brady—he was about the same age as me. He was able to jump out a window before the smoke got to him. He broke bones up and down his leg, but he lived. Now, you'd think, having lost everything else, William would've held onto that lad with both hands. Never let him go, never let him out of his sight."

Logan shrugs. "Instead, as soon as Brady was out of the

hospital, William called social services, signed away his rights, and gave up his only living child."

He shakes his head, his voice softening as he remembers.

"When they came to take him, it was the saddest thing I ever saw. Brady on the pavement, hoppin' around on crutches, cryin' and beggin his dad to let him stay. Willie never even turned around. Never said goodbye. Just walked on . . . and started lookin' for change."

"Why?" I demand, pissed off and hurt for a kid I never met. "Why would he do that?"

Logan looks into my eyes. "To punish himself—for not being there when the people he loved needed him. For failing them, not protecting them—it's the worst sin a man can commit. If a man can't keep those most precious to him safe . . . he doesn't deserve them."

"But it wasn't his fault."

"The way he saw it, it was."

His voice is soft around the edges. Gentle.

"I've seen your dad's face when you're near, Ellie—he doesn't hate you. Right or wrong, he hates himself. You remind him of everything precious that he didn't keep safe. He's drowning so deep in his own hurt, he can't see yours or your sister's, or how he's adding to it. He's weak and sad and focused on himself, but that's on him—you know? It's got nothing to do with you."

It doesn't fix things. It doesn't make anything better. But hearing those words from someone on the outside—who's got no skin in the game, no real reason to lie—makes it . . . not quite as hard.

And that's when I feel the exhaustion. It hits me like rushing floodwaters—hard and fast and knocking me on my ass all at once. My bones feel like they're seventy years old instead of seventeen. Well, at least what I imagine seventy will feel like.

I cover a yawn with the back of my hand.

"Go on up to bed, lass." Logan stands, brushes off his pants and picks the broom up from the floor. "I'll finish here."

I drag myself up too. "I thought you don't sweep fucking floors?"

Logan winks. And, right there in that dim little coffee shop, he steals a piece of my heart forever.

"In your case, I'll make a fucking exception."

He starts sweeping up, but when I get to the kitchen door, I pause. "Thanks, Logan. For everything."

He looks at me a moment, then gives an easy nod. "No need to thank me—just doing my job."

CHAPTER 3

Logan

Over the next two weeks, we settle into a routine. I take the early-morning shift with Ellie at the coffee shop, and then I give Marty a hand in the kitchen fulfilling orders, washing dishes—once Tommy goes with her to school. It's not noble work, but it's busy, fast-paced, and the time goes quickly. I stay till dinnertime, when one of the other boys—Cory or Liam—shows up for the night watch.

I like routines—they're steady, predictable, easy to manage. It's the same, day in and out.

Except for the songs. The ones Ellie blasts in the kitchen at four a.m., while she's baking. Those are always different, like she's got an infinite playlist. A few she seems to like more than others, putting them on repeat. Today it's "What a Feeling" from that eighties stripper movie. Yesterday it was "I Want You to Want Me" and the one before that was "Son of a Preacher Man."

And she's always dancing. Skipping around like sunlight sparking off a mirror.

Once, I asked, "Is the music necessary?"

And she just smiled that sweet smile and replied, "Music makes the pies taste better, silly."

This morning, though, Ellie's looking especially weary, with dark circles—almost bruises—beneath her baby-blue eyes. And there are books and notes spread out on one side of the counter that she glances at, mumbling to herself while she prepares the pie shells.

"You study a lot," I say.

She chuckles. "I have to—I'm in the home stretch. It's down to me and Brenda Raven for valedictorian. I've already been accepted to NYU in the fall, but graduating first in my class would be a yummy cherry on my academic sundae."

At first glance, Ellie Hammond comes off as kind of . . . ditzy. Like she's got a little too much air between her ears. But nothing could be farther from the truth. She's not an airhead; she's just . . . innocent. Trusting. Happy. Probably the most chipper young woman I've ever known.

"Did you go to college?" she asks.

"No."

A counselor told me I was dyslexic when I was nine. It was a relief to know I wasn't just a dumb fuck. She taught me how to get by, but even now reading doesn't come easy.

"I was never real talented in school."

I move closer to the counter, putting my hand on the handle of the rolling pin she's using.

And Ellie freezes, like a delicate blond deer.

"I'll do it," I say. "So you can study. I've watched you make enough of them to manage."

And she looks up at me like I just offered her the world on a platter. "Yeah?"

"Sure." I shrug, ignoring the hero worship in her eyes. "I'm just standing here."

I don't like to be useless.

"Ah . . . okay. Thanks." She opens a drawer and hands me a white apron. "You should put this on, though."

She might as well be holding a roach.

"Do I look like the kind of guy who'd wear an apron?"

Ellie shrugs. "Have it your way, Mr. I'm-Too-Sexy-for-My-

Apron. But that black dress shirt isn't going to look so sharp when it's covered in flour."

I snort. But leave the bloody apron on the counter. Not a chance.

There's an odd satisfaction to baking that I'd never admit to aloud. It occurs to me as I slide the last of two dozen pies onto the cooling rack on the center counter. They look good—with golden, flaky brown crusts—and they smell even better. Ellie closes her big textbook and shuffles her papers away with a bright white smile taking up half of her face.

"God, I needed that. Now I can make this exam my bitch."

She's relieved. And I feel satisfaction in that too.

We head out to the front dining room and take the chairs down from where they sit, upside down on the tables. Her gaze follows my every move—she tries being sneaky about it—skittering her eyes away when I glance back, but I've been checked out by enough women to know what's going on. Ellie's interest is weighted with curiosity and fascination, like the press of soft, seeking hands against my skin. She opens the window shade, revealing the crowd of customers that's already gathered on the pavement. It's smaller than it was a few weeks ago—now that the public knows the Crown Prince of Wessco has left the building, and the country.

Ellie goes back to the kitchen . . . and screams bloody murder.

"Nooooooo!"

Adrenaline spikes through me and I dart to the kitchen, ready to fight. Until I see the cause of her screaming.

"Bosco, noooooo!"

It's the rodent-dog. He got into the kitchen, somehow

managed to hoist himself up onto the counter, and is in the process of demolishing his fourth pie.

Fucking Christ, it's impressive how fast he ate them. That a mutt his size could even eat that many. His stomach bulges with his ill-gotten gains—like a snake that ingested a monkey. A big one.

"Thieving bastard!" I yell.

Ellie scoops him off the counter and I point my finger in his face. "Bad dog."

The little twat just snarls back.

Ellie tosses the mongrel on the steps that lead up to the apartment and slams the door. Then we both turn and assess the damage. Two apple and a cherry are completely devoured, he nibbled at the edge of a peach and apple crumb and left tiny paw-prints in two lemon meringues.

"We're going to have re-bake all seven," Ellie says.

I fold my arms across my chest. "Looks that way."

"It'll take hours," she says.

"Yeah."

"But we have to. There isn't any other choice."

Silence follows. Heavy, meaningful silence.

And it's as if we have the same thought, at the exact same time.

I glance sideways at Ellie, and she's already peeking over at me.

"Or . . . is there?" she asks slyly.

I look at what remains of the damaged pastries, considering all the options. "If we slice off the chewed bits . . ."

"And smooth out the meringue . . ."

"Put the licked ones in the oven to dry out . . ."

"Are you two out of your motherfucking *minds*?"

I swing around to find Marty standing in the alley doorway behind us. Eavesdropping and horrified. Ellie tries to cover for us. But she's bad at it.

"Marty! When did you get here? We weren't gonna do anything wrong."

Covert ops are not in her future.

"Not anything wrong?" he mimics, stomping into the room. "Like getting us shut down by the goddamn health department? Like feeding people dog-drool pies—have you no couth?"

"It was just a thought," Ellie swears—starting to laugh.

"A momentary lapse in judgment," I say, backing her up.

"We're just really tired and—"

"And you've been in this kitchen too long." He points to the door. "Out you go."

When we don't move, he goes for the broom.

"Go on—get!"

Ellie grabs her knapsack and I guide her out the back door as Marty sweeps at us like we're vermin.

Out on the pavement, it starts to rain—a light, annoying mist. From the corner of my eye, I see Ellie pull her hood up, but my gaze stays trained ahead of us. If your eyes are on the person you're supposed to be protecting, you're doing it wrong.

I take note of who else is on the street, reading their body language—pedestrians on their way to work, a homeless guy on the corner, a businessman smoking a cigarette and yelling into his phone. I stick close to Ellie, keeping her within reach, scanning left to right for potential threats or anyone who might make the poor decision to try and get too close. It's second nature.

"Do you need to head to school?"

"Not yet. It's finals week, so I have free study periods first and second."

Without needing to look, I text Tommy that I'll get Ellie to school—he should meet us there.

The rain grows stronger and there's a flash of lightning in the gray sky.

"Is there somewhere particular you want to go?"

I don't want her getting ill from the rain.

"I know a place." And her little hand wraps around my wrist. "Come on."

By the time we pass through the stone arch of the Metropolitan Museum of Art, it's full-out pouring, the water coursing over the entrance steps in a hundred little rivulets. Inside the marble-floored foyer, it's warm and dry. Ellie shakes the water from her hoodie and wrings out her long, multicolored hair and I catch her scent. It's sweet—peach, orange blossoms and rain.

"My mom used to bring me and Olivia here all the time."

I reach for my wallet, but Ellie flashes a student ID and slides two vouchers to the ticket taker. "I have guest passes," she says, "and they have early-access hours for students."

I've never been to a museum—not as a patron, anyway. The royal family has attended more museum events and galas than I can count, but my attention wasn't on the exhibits. I walk beside Ellie from one cavernous room to the next, and she chatters away the whole time, like her mouth's incapable of being still for too long.

"Did you always want to be a bodyguard?"

"No," I grunt.

"What did you want to be?"

"Something I was good at."

Her head tilts, looking up at me. "How did you end up being Nicholas's guard?"

"I was in the military. I was good at it—got picked for special training."

"Like, James Bond, Navy SEAL kind of stuff?"

"Something like that, yeah."

Ellie's head bobs as she thinks. Her golden hair is drying

now, and there's a soft wave to it. She stops in front of an Egyptian display, and the reflection of light off the sarcophagus casts her features in warm-toned shadows.

"Did you ever kill anyone when you were in the army?"

I'm careful with my answer. "What amendment in your Constitution protects people from self-incrimination?"

"The fifth."

I nod. "I'll go with that. Final answer."

Her long, pale lashes blink at me. "So that's a yes. Damn, Logan, you're like a badass killer."

I snort. "Didn't say that."

"You didn't say you're not."

A few steps later she adds, "I don't think I could ever kill someone."

"You'd be surprised what you're capable of in certain situations."

"If you had killed someone . . . would you feel bad?"

I run my tongue over the inside of my cheek and go with honesty, no matter how it might come off. "No. I wouldn't feel bad at all. Some people need killing, Ellie."

I open the door for her and she hums as she passes through—into a fashion exhibit room, all low lighting and seductive red walls.

"So what's with the dark clothes?" she asks as we walk down the hall. "Is it like a mandatory dress code they taught you at Bodyguard School?"

I look down at her. "You ask a lot of questions."

"I like to know things." She shrugs. "I'm a people person. So, what's with the clothes?"

I finger the navy tie around my neck—the one I remember her liking.

"Knights have armor; we have dark clothes. We're supposed to blend in."

"Inconceivable! You're way too fuck-hot to blend."

33

I hold back a smile. She's a flirty little thing—daring; she doesn't know how to hide her feelings, and wouldn't even if she did. If Ellie were older, if we were different people, I'd be giving serious thought to flirting back. I like to give as good as I get, in all things.

Out of curiosity, I ask, "What do you want to be? When you're done with school?"

She sighs, long and deep.

"That's the million-dollar question, isn't it?" Her head toggles back and forth. "If I wanted financial security, I would go into accounting. Become a CPA. I'm good with numbers, and businesses will always need auditors."

I open another door for her to the next exhibit. "It sounds like there's a 'but' coming."

Her mouth sparkles with a smile. "Buuuut, accounting isn't really me."

"What is 'you,' Ellie Hammond?"

"I want to be a psychologist. Talk to people, help them through their problems. I think that would make me happy."

Something tugs in my chest as I look at her—good-hearted lass. I want that for her; she deserves to be happy.

Ellie stops walking and turns to the display in front of her. It's a bed—four-poster canopy, ornate and curtained with intricate, gold-trimmed, royal-blue and purple fabric. She reads the description off the plaque on the wall. "*The bed of His Majesty King Reginald the Second and Queen Margaret Anastasia of Wessco.* That's Queen Lenora's parents, right?"

"Yeah."

She gazes back at the bed with a longing sigh. "Wow. I can't imagine living like this every day. Servants and castles and crowns—how perfect would that be?" She points at the opulent bed. "Queen Lenora could have been conceived on this bed, right here!"

I flinch at the thought.

"Let's not speak of it."

Ellie laughs—a twinkling kind of sound. As we move on to the next display, she asks, "What's the weather like in Wessco?"

I glance up at the glass ceiling where the rain still batters against the pane. "Like this. Mostly gray, kind of cool—it rains a lot."

"I love the rain," she says on a breath. "It's so . . . cozy. Give me a rainstorm and a warm fire going in the fireplace, a soft blanket and a cup of tea in a sturdy brick house—I'd never want to leave."

She paints a very pretty picture.

Ellie stops in front of a painting of the Crown Prince of Wessco, Prince Nicholas Arthur Frederick Edward Pembrook. It's his official portrait, commissioned when he turned eighteen. He's wearing his military uniform, looking regal and dignified. But because I know him, I see the resignation in his expression and the flatness in his eyes.

Like a hostage with no hope of being released.

She stares at the portrait, and her voice turns hushed. "He's going to break my sister's heart into a thousand pieces, isn't he?"

I take a moment before I answer.

"Not intentionally. And not only her heart."

CHAPTER 4

Ellie

One week later

My brain hurts.

But it was worth it. The all-nighters. The cramming. The stunting of my already stunted growth from too much caffeine—all worth it. Because it's over now.

I've crossed the finish line. Planted my flag on the mountain peak. Snapped the last Lego into place.

The only problem is . . . there's no crowd to roar. I have no one to share the news with. Liv's asleep on the other side of the world, Marty's on a date, my dad's "out," a.k.a. wasted at a bar somewhere, and Cory, my friendly neighborhood security detail for the night, was snoring away at the coffee-shop table.

People probably can't tell this about me, but I'm a sharer. I need to spread the word, like I need water or air or microwave popcorn.

Which is why I'm doing something stupid right now. I didn't even tell Marlow, though she would've totally approved, the vixen.

I'm going to Logan's apartment. I know it's dumb, but I just can't stop myself any more than a magnet can stop its stupid slide toward its one true opposite.

A few weeks ago, at the museum, I could've sworn I felt . . . something. A connection. Logan wore my favorite tie—that's gotta count for something, right?

Logan gave me the address to the apartment he shares with the other security guards in case I needed it. And I'm standing there now. It's a decent building—no doorman, nothing too fancy, but not a dump, either. I knock on the door of Apartment 409. I look up and down the hall, shuffling my feet, hearing "Silver Springs" by Fleetwood Mac in my head.

Then the door opens, and it's not Logan I see, but Tommy Sullivan—like I've never seen him before. Shirtless, with low-slung jeans hanging haphazardly off his hips and a cigarette between his lips.

Tommy's a hottie. Not the same kind of Adonis perfection that Logan is, but still a fine-looking boy.

"Ellie!" He smiles, seemingly happy to see me. Tommy's always happy. He takes the cigarette from his mouth. "What are you doing here, pet? Is everything all right?"

"Yeah, no, everything's fine. Is Logan home?"

Tommy raises his eyebrows, questioning, but doesn't ask. Instead he turns his head toward the interior of the apartment and shouts, "Lo!"

He leans out the door. "I'd invite you in, but it's no place for a girl like you. We're all indecent here."

And doesn't that just get my cheeks glowing—and my imagination working overtime.

Then Logan is filling the doorway, looking surprised.

But I barely notice his expression.

Because Logan is shirtless too. And in the immortal words of Joey Lawrence . . . *whoa.*

Smooth, taut skin covers his shoulders and chest—bronze, except for the stunning swirl of colorful tattoos that spread across one shoulder and all the way down one arm.

His arms are big, bulging with muscle—cut, tight. He has

abs—lots and lots of abs—rock hard and rippling like I've only seen on those insane exercise-program infomercials.

It's a beautiful body. A man's body.

He glances up and down the hall. "What's wrong?"

"No, I—"

"You're here by yourself?"

He sounds annoyed and I start to think maybe this wasn't just a stupid idea, but possibly the stupidest idea I've ever had. And through the years, I've had some doozies.

"Yes, I—"

"Where's Cory?"

Even if Cory had been awake, he's not the one I wanted to share my news with. And I didn't want him coming with me here. Because I wanted to talk to Logan—alone.

"He's back at the coffee shop."

"You snuck past him?" Logan asks, like he doesn't believe it.

"Not exactly."

He folds his arms. "Then how did you get here without him? *Exactly?*"

I try to come up with a good excuse for Cory's sake . . . but lying has never been my thing.

"He fell asleep."

Wrong answer. Logan's eyes grow hot and intense.

"He seemed really tired. Don't be mad, Logan."

He pushes a hand through his dark hair, and for a moment I'm caught up in how soft and thick it looks. How it would feel between my fingers.

And then a voice calls from inside the apartment—a voice that doesn't belong to one of the guys.

"Come on, Logan. It's your turn to deal."

She comes into view and she's not just "buxom"—it's like the word was *invented* for her. Big, shiny red hair, flawless skin, legs as long as my whole body encased in tight, might-be-painted-on jeans, a teeny waist and big boobs covered by an even teenier black tank-top.

She looks like the head manager at Hooter's in man-only heaven.

Her green eyes slide from Logan over to me, then back again. "Oh, sorry—I didn't realize you had a visitor." She smiles. "Is this your little sister?"

You know the sound a balloon makes when it's dying?

That's my heart—right now.

He puts his hand on her bare arm and the weirdest combination of sadness and violence consumes me. I want to cry . . . and bite his hand off like an outraged chimpanzee.

"Go back in. Tell Tommy to deal."

Deal? Are they playing strip poker?! *Kill me, kill me, die, die, die . . .*

After she fades back, I shuffle my feet. "Sorry to interrupt."

"It's fine." He says softly, "What do you need, Ellie?"

"Nothing. Never mind. You should go back to your . . . friend."

Logan shakes his head. "She's Tommy's friend."

But what is she to him? More than a friend? A fuck-buddy? A lover?

My stomach spins. I'm such an idiot.

"That's good. Friends are good." I hook my thumb over my shoulder. "I'm just gonna head out. Skedaddle."

'Cause nothing says mature, sophisticated woman like "skedaddle." *Christ on a Ritz cracker, somebody nail my tongue to the wall.*

"Ellie—"

But I'm already turning, skipping the elevator and heading right for the stairs, trying to appear dignified while bleaching the image of Logan touching that woman from my mind.

"Later, Logan."

"Fuck . . ."

And the sound of the slamming door chases me down the stairwell.

Out on the street, the air is humid and the cars are loud, honking. It's after eleven p.m., so the sidewalk isn't too crowded, but it's busy enough that I should be able to give Logan the slip if he tries to follow me.

Or I would be . . . if I were dealing with an average guy.

"Ellie! Hold up!"

There's nothing average about Logan St. James.

I make it one block before he's standing right in front of me, blocking my way. He's got a shirt on, but it's only half-buttoned.

"Why'd you run away so fast?"

I shrug, tapping a quick beat against my outer thighs. "You know how it is—places to go, people to see."

Logan bends his neck forward, lowering his head, catching my eyes and holding on tight.

"Why'd you come here? Tell me the truth."

"It's not a big deal . . ." I sigh, feeling small and stupid.

"Tell me anyway."

I look down at the cracked sidewalk. "Remember the other day, that last exam I was studying for?"

He snorts. "Yeah—physics, wasn't it?"

"I got my grade back." I slip the paper out of my pocket, holding it up. "I aced it."

And for the first time, I say out loud, "I'm valedictorian."

Logan gazes at the paper for a long moment. And when he takes it, I feel the brush of his finger against mine.

"Look at that," he says with awe. "That's brilliant. Smart girl." His large hand moves to my shoulder, squeezing. And I feel it everywhere. Warmth tingles through me, from the top of my ears to the tips of my toes.

"Congratulations, Ellie."

My mouth stretches so far into a smile, tears spring up in my eyes. "Thanks. I just . . . I wanted to tell someone."

Him. I wanted to tell *him*.

Because he's gorgeous, but even more than that—he makes me feel wanted. Valued and important, like I'm someone worth protecting. Knowing this man would give his life to shield me, guard me from pain or danger—it's a heady thing. An arousing, stirring thing.

I lost my virginity to Aaron Myers after the winter formal last year. I'd known Aaron since I was a kid, he's a good guy. But it wasn't true love, it was just something we ended up doing, and it was nice. A good memory.

But now, I wish I had waited. For Logan. I know it's stupid and would never happen, but if in some upside down, alternate universe, it did happen—he would make the earth move for me. I feel more alive just standing next to him, than I have around anyone else. I can only imagine, dream, what it would be like to be held in his arms, to feel the power of his body, his passion and tenderness, surrounding me, inside me.

"I'm glad it was me." His hand squeezes again. "Let's walk you home."

"You don't have to."

As much as I love being around Logan, I don't want to be annoying. Don't want to become a nuisance to him.

"Aye, I do. It's not safe."

I roll my eyes to the skyscrapers. "I grew up in New York— it's my city—I know it better than you do. We're in Tribeca, for God's sake . . . it's not dangerous."

"You're a young, beautiful girl, Ellie. The whole world is dangerous for you."

And, of course, among all those words, the one I latch onto is . . . *beautiful*.

Because I'm still an idiot.

Half an hour later, we walk into the coffee shop, where Cory's blond head still rests on his arms on the table. Logan walks straight to him and kicks the leg of the chair—almost knocking him over.

Cory startles awake, sputtering, "What—who?" Then he rubs at his eyes. "What's the deal, Lo?"

"The deal," Logan says in a deadly calm tone that makes me shiver, "is you're gonna get your arse back to the flat, pack up your shit and go home. You're done."

Oh crap.

"No, Cory—you don't have to do that—it's not your fault." I tell Logan, "It's not his fault."

But Logan doesn't even look at me. He's staring daggers at poor Cory. Jagged, bloody daggers.

"You're gonna want to move now, mate, or you won't like how I'll move you."

Cory frowns down at the table. Then he pushes out of the chair, so hard it falls back, and stomps out.

Logan locks the door behind him.

"Why did you do that? I'm the one who snuck out. It's my fault."

Logan points toward the door. "Did you bash him on the head? Drug his tea?"

No.

"Then it's his fault—and he knows it."

"Couldn't you give him a second chance?"

"No. Not in this job." He moves closer. "We have to be focused and ready—alert at all times. It only takes one fuck-up to get someone hurt, or killed. What if he'd fallen asleep while your sister and the Prince had been here?" There's an edge to his voice. "What if something had happened to you?

And there it is, again. The wonderful warmth that suffuses my limbs. Logan makes me feel precious with every word he says—and every breath he takes.

CHAPTER 5

Logan

The day of Ellie's high school graduation is sunny—one of those bright, clear days when the sky is the color of a robin's egg and the air is both cool and warm. I'm driving the black SUV from the parking deck near our flat to Amelia's, to pick up Ellie and Marty and her dad. Tommy's in the passenger seat. After about ten minutes on the road, he looks at me suspiciously from the corner of his eye.

"Is that REO Speedwagon?"

I hit the signal and make a left turn.

"What?"

"You're humming 'Can't Fight This Feeling' by REO Speedwagon, if I'm not mistaken."

Huh. Didn't even realize it.

My hands slide over the steering wheel as I shrug. "Ellie made me this playlist . . . it's actually not half-bad."

Tommy slips his sunglasses down his nose and stares at me above the frames.

"Who the hell *are* you, right now?"

I glance at him, frowning hard. Then I flip him off.

He laughs and pushes his sunglasses back into place. A minute later, the wanker tilts his head back, and belts out "Keep on Loving You."

And I look for a spot to pull over so I can stuff him in the trunk.

Ten minutes later, I park in the alley behind the coffee shop and Tommy and I head into the kitchen through the back door.

We're welcomed by the sound of Ellie yelling . . .

"Fuck my ass!"

And I choke on my own spit. "What did you just say?"

She turns from standing in front of the sink, eyes wide and stuttering. "I don't . . . I mean, I've never tried . . ."

My eyebrows jump to my hairline.

"It's just an expression!"

Tommy mutters under his breath, "American girls have odd expressions."

Ellie holds up a white, strappy little shoe. "My heel broke. And I don't have any other shoes that go with this dress! I'm royally screwed."

I gesture for the shoe. "Give it here." I turn it over in my hands. "I have some bonding liquid in the car—I can fix this."

She gives me an adoring look. "You're my hero, Logan. I could kiss you, right now."

And the way she says it—all breathy and eager—makes me think she's not just using an expression.

I'm not a fool; I know Ellie's crushing on me hard. I'm aware of how she looks at me when she thinks I'm not looking: so idolizing it feels like I'm on a pedestal fifty-feet tall. Other times, her stare is so naked with desire it hits me like a punch to the gut.

Because as alluring as Ellie is . . . she's also young and way fucking off limits.

Since we're only here for the summer, there's no need to

embarrass her by talking to her about it; I'll keep pretending I don't know what's going on.

"You're looking downright lovely, Miss Ellie," Tommy says.

And she does. In her simple, light pink dress, her slender arms bare, her colorful hair long and shiny and curled at the ends, she looks like . . . a princess. All she needs is a crown.

"Thanks, Tommy."

Marty walks through the swinging door from the dining room and his giant bundle of silver and dark blue balloons—engraved with all forms of graduation congratulations—sways frantically.

"Got enough balloons?" I ask.

Ellie giggles. "They're from Olivia. I think she feels bad that she's not here—but she shouldn't."

Tommy checks his watch. "We need to get going. You can't be late for your own graduation."

"And I have to get a prime seat for the speech," Marty adds.

Ellie's been working on her valedictorian speech for the last three days, around the clock. She slides her arms into her white graduation gown, then uses the glass cabinet door as a mirror to pin her cap on her head. Damn, she's a beauty.

"Where's your da?" Tommy asks.

And the playful spark that's always in Ellie's big blue eyes . . . fades right out of them.

"He's sleeping. He's not coming."

Marty clears his throat, giving me a disgruntled look, but keeps his mouth shut. And we all head out to the car.

I swing around to the trunk and quickly fix Ellie's heel, then hand it to her through the backseat window. "Tommy's gonna drive you over—I'll catch up." The coffee shop is closed for the day. "I'm gonna do a once-over, make sure everything here is locked up tight."

She slips heart-shaped sunglasses onto her face. "Okay—

but don't be late. You guys are the only cheering section I have. I expect to hear some serious *woot-fucking-woots*."

I nod. "Wild horses couldn't keep me away."

"Get up."

Eric Hammond is lying on his back in bed, still wearing last night's gray T-shirt and trousers—stinking like the floor of a pub. He doesn't budge when I call out again, and I have neither the time nor the patience to fuck around.

"Hey." I smack his cheek—holding back from punching him in the mouth, because knocking him out won't speed things up.

"Hey! Let's go—get up."

"What?" He inhales, snorting, and slowly his eyes focus on me. "What the hell are you doing in here?"

I move to his closet, sliding the hangers over, looking for a suit.

"Your daughter's graduating today. I'm making sure you get to where you need to be."

"Ellie?" he says, confused.

"Oh, you're aware she's your daughter? I wasn't quite sure you knew."

"That's today?" he asks, rubbing his face.

I find a dark gray suit and a white dress shirt, still in plastic from the cleaners, that look like they'll fit him.

"It's today. She's valedictorian."

He rubs at the salt-and-pepper whiskers on his chin. And hangs his head. "Damn it. *Damn it.*" He lifts his head, meeting my eyes, his voice a sandpaper whisper. "Logan, right?"

I nod.

"You must think I'm a real piece of shit."

My jaw tightens. "It doesn't matter what I think."

"You don't understand." He opens the drawer at the bedside table and takes out a frame, staring at it—talking to it, more than to me.

I look at Eric Hammond and I can see the man he used to be. Strong and straight—noble, even. Before the weight of life bent him in half, turned him into the sad sack of bones he is now.

"You're wrong," I say softly. "I do understand."

Then my voice turns fierce.

"I just don't care. Not about you." I point towards the door. "I have stood by and watched you break that girl's heart every day for the last six weeks, and I'm not watching it anymore."

It's my job to keep Ellie Hammond safe. All of her. Her body as well as her sweet little soul. And I'm damn good at what I do, but more than that, I *want* to protect her. Because she's kind and smart and precious . . . and *fuck* . . . somebody has to care enough to keep that safe.

"So you're going to get out of that bed and clean yourself up and for the next few hours, you're going to pretend she matters."

He nods and when he sets the frame on the bedside table, I'm able to see the photograph. It's a family picture—a child-sized Olivia with crooked teeth and wild hair; her father standing behind her, sober and happy, and in his arms, her sister with baby cheeks and white-blond hair. And it's like a punch to the gut when I see the woman beside him—gazing up at him, smiling. A woman with short blond hair . . . and Ellie's beautiful face. They look almost exactly alike.

"She does matter," Eric Hammond whispers, running his thumb over the image of everything he once had.

There are photographers outside Ellie's graduation. Not a large group, just three, but they're there. I guide Mr. Hammond towards the door of the gymnasium, where a student volunteer is waiting to exchange our tickets for paper programs.

The journalists shout questions as we pass:

"Mr. Hammond, is Prince Nicholas coming to the ceremony?"

"How do you feel about Olivia's pregnancy? Is the baby the Prince's?"

"Mr. Hammond, when's the wedding?"

Eric's good about it. Doesn't react, doesn't even turn his head. As I lead him to his seat, he asks quietly, "Olivia's not really pregnant, is she?"

"No."

"Is it always like that? The reporters?"

The corner of my mouth pulls up. "Usually, it's a hundred times worse."

I stand in the back during the ceremony, eyes on the crowd, watching the late arrivals and early exits of the people coming and going. When Ellie gives her speech, I know the moment that she spots her dad, sitting beside Marty. Her words pause—just slightly—and for a second her face is slack with disbelief. And then she smiles. So happily.

And even though we're inside, the day seems even sunnier.

Marty says he'll walk back to his place after the ceremony and says his goodbyes outside the school. But when Tommy goes to get the vehicle, Ellie's dad says he prefers to walk back to the coffee shop—it being such a nice day and all.

So I text Tommy to meet us at the diner and then follow Ellie and Mr. Hammond from a decent distance—giving them space for privacy, but staying near enough to reach them if I have to.

Ellie takes her gown off and drapes it over her arm, swinging her diploma and hat in one hand. About halfway home, the pavement clears out a bit and I hear Mr. Hammond talking low and seriously to his youngest daughter.

"You looked beautiful up there today, baby."

Ellie gives a short, self-conscious laugh. "Thanks, Dad."

And then he looks longer, his eyes growing sober and wet. "You look beautiful every day. Just like your mom."

Ellie's chin dips. "I'm sorry. I know that upsets you."

And her saying that seems to upset him even more. Mr. Hammond pauses at a tiny park, a patch of green with a few benches and a pathway that connects to the next street. He guides Ellie to a bench and sits down, and I hear him say there are things he needs to tell her.

I don't listen after that. I stay alert and focus on the surroundings. I keep them in my sight, but I block out the conversation—because that's part of the job too. The only way this works without making people crazier than a box of frogs is if those I'm protecting can still carve out some piece of privacy for themselves.

No matter how up-close and personal we have to be, some things just aren't our bloody business.

After a while, Ellie stands while Mr. Hammond stays sitting.

"I've already lost your sister. I don't want to lose you too," he tells her, sorrowfully.

And there are tears leaking from Ellie's eyes when she hugs him, even while she begs, "Don't cry, Daddy. You haven't lost

Olivia and you're not going to lose me. We love you and we know how hard it is . . . how sad you are."

And then I hear Eric Hammond's deep voice, as he wipes at his face with a tissue and reaches out to pat Ellie's arm. "I'm gonna try, baby. I promise, things will be different from now on."

I won't hold my breath. It's a promise often made but, more often, broken.

They walk back over to the pavement, side by side, and that's my cue to fall into step behind them. As they continue home, Ellie looks back at me—but I don't make eye contact, I turn my head to the street. Because I don't want her to think I know or care about what just passed between her and her father—I don't want her to feel embarrassed.

As they walk up to the front of Amelia's, a blaring red Volkswagen Beetle convertible with Ellie's friend Marlow behind the wheel pulls up and double-parks in the middle of the street. She honks the horn and cups her hands around her red lips—the same shade as the car.

"Let's go! Weekend at Bernie's!"

Based on what I overheard, their classmate Bernie Folger is hosting a graduation party at his parents' shore house in Wildwood, New Jersey. Before she can ask, I'm already telling her, "You can't go alone."

That's when Tommy steps out of the diner door onto the pavement.

"Tommy can come with us!" Marlow shouts. "I'll even let him drive, 'cause I'm a fucking sweetheart like that."

Tommy meets my eyes—and we both nod. Ellie hugs her dad goodbye and turns to me, shyly shuffling those white strappy heels.

"Well . . . I'll see you tomorrow, Logan."

Then she's scurrying to the car and climbing into the back. On his way to the car, Tommy swings past me, tapping my arm. "Mr. Hammond has a visitor. Inside."

He slips into the driver's seat and the three of them take off.

I open the door for Mr. Hammond and follow him into the coffee shop. And that's when I catch sight of the redheaded visitor Tommy mentioned.

The 4th Earl of Ellington rises from his chair.

He smiles the only way he knows how—warmly—while extending his hand. "Mr. Hammond, my name is Simon Barrister. It's a pleasure to meet you. I'd like to speak to you about a business venture that may be lucrative for both of us."

Eric Hammond shakes the Earl's hand. "What's your business, Simon?"

And Lord Ellington's blue eyes sparkle. "I'm hoping that it will be . . . pies."

CHAPTER 6

Logan

Ten months later

A royal a wedding is a major event on any day, but when the royal getting married is the former Crown Prince who gave up the throne for an American girl he couldn't live without? It's a madhouse.

For men like me, it's a high-octane event—my senses are sharp, on high alert. The place is packed with press, aristocrats, dignitaries, celebrities galore. This is what we do—these are the moments that our training and strategizing prepare us for.

Security is planned out months in advance in a war room—like preparing for a battle. Everyone knows his role; everyone has a position. Tonight, my focus in on Prince Nicholas. Although he's never far from Olivia's side, there's another man who's assigned to her—Tommy. Olivia, now a princess and a duchess, shimmers like a pretty disco ball—all white silk and jewels. And Nicholas's smile shines brighter than the tiara on her head.

"Happy" has left the building—and tonight, at the dinner celebrating his royal matrimony, the prince is nothing short of ecstatic.

Though my eyes are scanning the room, I know where the

couple is at all times. So when Nicholas raises his hand and calls me forward with his fingers, I react right away.

"Sir?" I bow.

"We're going to retire to our rooms shortly, but Olivia is concerned about Ellie."

I've been keeping tabs on her too—all night.

At this moment, she's at the bar, undeniably delectable in a champagne-colored silk gown that hugs her in all the right places.

Or . . . the bloody wrong ones, as far as I'm concerned.

One eager-eyed, posh lad after another is offering her drinks, asking her to dance or trying to impress her with their lofty pedigrees.

Fucking sods.

And she's putting the eighteen-year-old legal drinking age in Wessco to good use. Marty's there, laughing and drinking beside her—and her father too—though he's not imbibing. Despite my doubts, he hasn't touched a drop for ten months—not since Ellie's high school graduation. He's working his program, going to meetings even here in Wessco, staying sober. Good for him—for all of them.

"Ellie's been assigned security; they'll make sure she's all right."

I checked on who was covering her for the night, to see for myself that they were top-notch.

Olivia glances at her sister. "But you know her better—she'll listen to you. If she goes out after my dad goes to bed I'd feel better if you were with her."

I meet Nicholas's eyes. "We won't be leaving our rooms for the evening . . .," he winks at his bride, "possibly for days. We'll both have peace of mind if you're on Ellie detail."

I hold up a hand. "I'll take care of it. Don't give it a second thought."

"Tell me, Ellie Hammond," Henry says, "are we legal yet?"

Ellie grins, lifting her martini glass. "Eighteen, officially."

Prince Henry, Nicholas's younger brother and now Crown Prince of Wessco, lifts a brow. "Good God, you're practically a cougar." Then he sighs, looking at her. "Pity, you're also practically related to me now. And while many of my ancestors wouldn't let that slow them down, incest really isn't my bag."

Ellie nods once. "Bummer."

"But," Henry holds up a finger, "that doesn't mean we can't have a fantastic time. I'm going to show you the best bits of Wessco. The good, the raunchy and everything in between. What do you say?"

She's bubbling with excitement. "I say, count me—"

"Out." I step up to them. Firm and final.

"Your sister wants you to go straight back to your room," I tell Ellie.

"She'll be with *me*," Henry says.

As if he doesn't realize that makes it so much worse.

"Your brother specifically said not to leave Ellie with you."

Henry looks offended and searches around the room for his royal sibling. "That tosser . . . no trust anymore." He shakes his head. "Lucky for us, my brother and her sister will be completely preoccupied with their own entertainments. What they don't know won't hurt them."

This is a dicey situation. On the one hand, Prince Henry is my boss—he outranks Nicholas now. On the other hand, he's reckless, self-destructive and irresponsible—and his shiny new title hasn't diminished those traits. So, there's no bloody way in hell I'm leaving sweet Ellie in his care.

"I beg to differ, Your Highness."

And a look comes over his face, a slight bit of shock at being challenged mixed with a shadow of respect. Because while Henry has multiple moral deficiencies, a failure to view himself and his own shortcomings isn't one of them.

He's a royal fuck-up, but he owns it.

"I'm taking her to The Horny Goat, Agent St. James, not charging into battle. You and the rest of security are welcome to accompany us. We'll have a few drinks—or a few dozen—sing some songs and all will be well."

"Oh, that sounds like so much fun!" Ellie claps her hands. And she turns those heartbreaking eyes on me. "Can we go? Please?"

A simmering amusement rises in Prince Henry's expression as they wait for my answer. Because he's also a shit-stirrer. It's what he does—what he lives for: stirring up all the shit, then sitting back and watching everyone slip in it.

"Come on, Logan," Ellie whines pleadingly.

Henry loops his arm around her shoulders with a taunting grin. "Yeah, *come on, Logan.*"

Bastard.

Two hours later, Ellie Hammond, the younger sister of the new Duchess of Fairstone, and the future King of Wessco are on a karaoke stage at The Horny Goat pub. Together. Bouncing around and singing "I Wanna Be Sedated" by the Ramones.

There goes the fucking kingdom.

Thank Christ that Evan Macalister, The Goat's owner, managed to keep the press out. After the song ends, the pair return to the bar, hailed by the shouts of Henry's lads. A tall, curvy brunette has been attached to the Prince's hip all night—she latches to his side, whispering in his ear.

I've kept a tally of the alcohol Ellie's consumed—three martinis at the dinner reception and four whiskeys neat at the pub. She downs a fifth one like water.

"You're a Viking!" Henry encourages her.

"Vikings!!!" Ellie shouts.

When the Prince calls the bartender for another, I push my way through the crowd to Henry.

"She's had enough," I tell him quietly.

"She's fine." He waves his hand at the air.

"She's just a girl," I insist.

Ellie takes exception, poking my arm with her finger and slurring. "Hey! I resent that. I'm a matter adult. Mattur. Ma-*ture*." She tilts her head, gasping. "Oh my God, I just realized that except for one letter, mature and manure are the same word! That's so weird."

I turn back to Prince Henry, raising my eyebrows.

"Like I said . . . more than enough."

He leans across the bar towards Ellie, holding up two fingers. "Ellie, how many fingers do you see?"

Ellie squints and strains, until finally she grabs Henry's hand and holds it still.

"Four."

"Brilliant answer!"

"Was I right?" Ellie asks hopefully.

"No—if you'd gotten it right, I'd be really concerned." Then he bangs the bar with his palm. "Another round!"

That's when Ellie slides clear off her stool. I catch her before she hits the floor, but just barely. And then I glare at Henry.

"Mmm . . . perhaps we have reached our quota for the evening." He puts his hand on Ellie's arm, lifting his chin a little as he says, "It's always important to be able to actually walk out of the pub on our own two feet. Dignity and all that."

Ellie's head lolls on her neck until she rests it on my shoulder, her puffs of breath brushing my throat. "M'kay."

The palace is quiet as the threesome—Henry, Ellie and Henry's female companion—stumble down the halls to Ellie's suite, giggling and whispering as they go. I get the door for them and they collapse onto the chairs and sofa in the sitting room.

Henry watches Ellie and his eyes seem clearer than when they were in the pub. "Who's up for cards?" he asks, checking his pockets. "I've got a deck around here somewhere."

His brunette pouts unhappily. "I'm getting tired, Henry."

And it sounds like his shagging for the night is in jeopardy.

He gestures towards Ellie. "I can't just leave her. She could Janis Joplin in her sleep—Nicholas would literally kill me, and I'd have no choice but to let him."

Ellie shakes her head mournfully. "Janis Joplin—what a voice."

And she starts to cry.

"It's just so sad."

She covers her face with her hands, sobbing now. "She loved Bobby McGee so much!"

Fucking hell.

When I'm done with Henry, there won't be much left for Nicholas to kill.

To keep myself from committing a capital offense, I volunteer, "I'll watch her, Your Highness. I'm on shift all night, and Prince Nicholas wanted to make sure I looked after Ellie specifically."

His eyes dart to me then back to Ellie.

"I don't know . . ."

Ellie raises her head, her crying jag finished for now, then stumbles up next to me and wraps herself around my arm—sighing against it, smelling it, practically humping it.

"You can leave me with Logan, Henry. He's my hero."

Henry cocks his head suspiciously. "Is that so?"

"Totally." Ellie sighs, petting my arm. "My pretty, pissed-off guardian angel."

Jesus Christ.

The blond prince holds my eyes—judging my worth—the way men do. I don't look away; I don't blink. After a moment, Henry nods, smacks his palms on the arm of the sofa and hoists himself up.

"Well, that's good enough for me."

Ellie claps her hands.

"Yay!"

And almost falls into the fireplace.

I guide her into an antique chair.

Henry makes a show of bowing to Ellie, picking up her hand and kissing the back.

She giggles. "Thank you for tonight."

He drops down to his knee. "Did you have fun—the best time of your whole life? I have a reputation to uphold, you know."

Ellie nods, all giddy and loose-limbed.

"It was the very best! I love it here and you're going to be an awesome king."

And a strange look falls over Henry's face. Sad, wistful. "You're a good-hearted girl, Ellie. You should leave this place as soon as you can."

The next time he blinks, that jester's smile is back in place. Henry holds out his fist. "Welcome to the family, sweets."

Ellie tries to fist-bump back . . . but misses and almost pops Henry right in the nose.

Laughing, Henry holds Ellie's wrist and taps their fists together.

Then he stands, nods in my direction, loops his arm around the lady and strides out of the room.

"Hey Logan?"

"Aye?"

"When's your birthday?"

"June seventh."

"Oh."

"Hey Logan?"

"Mmm?"

"How old are you?"

I answer without thinking. "Twenty-three."

"Huh. Hey Logan?"

It's been going this way for half an hour. Ellie sits on the paisley antique sofa, staring into the empty fireplace, with me beside her. I took her shoes off a while ago but she's made no move towards the bed. It's better for her to sit upright anyway.

"What's your favorite color?"

"I don't have one."

"Everyone has one."

"Blue."

"Light or dark blue?"

Again, I answer without thought. "Light blue."

Blearily, Ellie turns her head to me, her long lashes blinking slowly.

"My eyes are light blue."

My mind stutters for just a moment.

"So they are."

In the time I've known Ellie Hammond, been near her, I've tended to look everywhere but at her—that's the job. But at this moment, just a few inches away, there's nothing to see except her.

And so, I look.

Her neck is elegant, her shoulders straight and small-boned. Her skin is smooth and creamy, with a natural rosy flush to her cheeks. Her brows are fair and arched, her eyes round and deep-set—intelligent with a touch of mischievousness. And she has freckles . . . an adorable dusting of light freckles kissing the bridge of her dainty nose.

"Hey Logan?"

"Yeah?"

"I don't feel so good."

And there it is. I've been expecting this.

"Yeah. Don't worry. As soon as you puke your stomach inside out, you'll be feeling loads better."

Her petite features scrunch. "That doesn't sound like fun."

"No."

For a few moments, the only sound in the room is Ellie's quick, harsh breaths.

And then, "Hey Logan?"

"Yes?"

"Where's the bathroom?"

She covers her mouth and her whole body convulses in a heave. Quickly, I lift under her arms, helping her stand, and guide her to the loo. As she steps over the threshold, she lurches towards the open toilet, hands braced on the seat, and a deluge of rejected alcohol spews from her stomach.

I gather the strands of her hair and hold them back, rubbing gentle circles between her shoulder blades and murmuring reassuring words. Though I don't make a habit of it, I've been where she is—more than once—and it's god-awful.

After another few rounds, it seems her stomach is finally empty. I pass Ellie a ball of tissues and she coughs, wiping her mouth and resting back against the wall.

I reach over to flush the toilet and Ellie groans.

"Don't—it's so gross. I'm so gross."

"Stop," I chide—because she's ridiculous.

After a time, she leans her head my way, still covering her mouth with the tissues. "Can you hand me my toothbrush and toothpaste, please? And a glass of water."

I nod, doing as she asks. Ellie's toothbrush is light pink—

the same color as the paint on her toes and fingernails. After she brushes and rinses her mouth, I put the items next to the sink.

"Can you manage the walk to the bed or do you want me to carry you?"

She closes her eyes with a grimace.

"I can do it."

I help her off the floor, holding her steady as she teeters across the room. "It's hot." She moans. "I'm so hot."

Then she steps back and wiggles out of the snug silk gown, letting it pool around her feet, standing in nothing but tiny cream knickers and a matching lace bra. I avert my eyes, but not before the image of smooth legs, flat stomach, a snug heart-shaped arse and perky perfect breasts are branded permanently onto my brain.

Ellie's nipples are dusky pink—an exquisite deep mauve—and part of me feels like a filthy bastard for knowing that.

Another part . . . feels something different entirely.

My throat convulses in a swallow because for the first time, Ellie Hammond doesn't seem like a girl to me at all.

She crawls onto the large bed, her fine arse in the air, and collapses in the center. I grasp the edge of the blanket sitting at the foot of the bed and fold it over, covering her—for both our sakes.

"Hey Logan?"

"Yeah?"

"Will you lie down with me?"

Lie down with a half-naked woman who's looked at me more than once like I'm an ice-cream cone she can't wait to lick up and down? What could go wrong?

Henry's damning eyes glare at me from inside my mind. "I don't think . . ."

"Please—just hold my hand," she begs, and her voice is so small. "If you're holding onto me, you'll stop the spinning."

And it's like I'm being wrenched in two—pulled in two

different directions. The numb, hardened, calloused side tells me to say no, that this is a dangerous, fucking pointless move. But the other, more youthful side—that's tender and impractical—wants to give this girl anything she wants.

Ellie moans softly and she looks so pretty and miserable, I can't deny her.

I slide onto the bed and lie on my back, staring at the golden swirls in the fabric canopy above us, counting sheep and reciting the steps to assembling a rifle—anything to distract me from the tempting forbidden fruit beside me.

Ellie tugs her arm out from under the cover, reaching for me, and I don't hesitate to engulf her small, soft hand with my rough one.

"Thank you." She sighs, her closed eyelids relaxing just a bit.

She shifts closer, resting our joined hands on my stomach, pressing her soft, supple little body against mine. My cock stiffens, stirs.

Down, boy, I tell the savage beast.

"Go to sleep now, love," I say quietly. "You'll be fine. I'm right here."

"And you'd never let anything bad happen to me, would you?"

I close my own eyes and swallow again—feeling something unfamiliar and unnamed tighten in my chest.

"Never."

But a minute later, when I glance over at Ellie, her eyes are open, watching me—the blue of her irises is darker, deeper in this light.

"You're always doing this," she whispers.

"Doing what?"

"Saving me."

I smile, just a bit. "I don't mind."

"Because it's your job?" she asks.

"Yes."

"And because maybe, sort of, you kind of like me too? Just a little?"

A chuckle scratches my throat. "Just a little."

She wets her lips, those eyes still holding me close.

"And maybe because, when you save me it feels like . . . I belong to you? Even just a tiny bit?"

I know what I should say, but I can't bring myself to do it. She'll never remember this anyway. So instead, I let the tip of one finger trace her lovely face slowly, running from her temple to her jaw. Like I have the right to touch her. Like she belongs to me.

"That's right, Ellie."

She closes her eyes on a sigh. And they stay closed so long I think she's fallen asleep. Right up until her sweet voice comes again.

"Hey Logan?"

"Yeah?"

"One of these days . . . I'm going to save you back."

CHAPTER 7

Logan

Seven months later

I shift the SUV into park outside the address Ellie gave me—where her new flat is. *New semester, new apartment,* she'd said.

After the wedding, Prince Nicholas and Olivia's fame rubbed off on Ellie Hammond, in a big way. She's got a devoted group of fanboys all her own now and her breasts have gained their own Twitter handle: @Elliesweettits—not particularly creative. The bottom-feeding paparazzi have gone out of their way to zoom in on that particular asset whenever possible. It pisses me off—a lot. More than once I've had to restrain myself from shoving a long-range lens up a photographer's arse.

She's been living with her sister and her husband since the wedding—in the penthouse of an exclusive high-rise, which has made security simpler. Why Ellie wants to move is beyond me, and why she wants to move in November—when it's colder than Jack Frost's balls—is a complete fucking mystery.

It's as if Tommy reads my mind. "Prince Nicholas and your sister's place is as posh as it gets—tell me again why you want to leave?"

Ellie sighs. "Believe it or not, Nicholas and Olivia aren't that easy to live with. They're newlyweds—deeply, disgustingly in love. Their romance is like a fairytale, right up there with Snow White and the Prince. And I'm gonna die alone. It's depressing."

"Does that make us the dwarfs?" Tommy asks.

I raise my hand. "I got dibs on Cocky."

Ellie chuckles and opens her door without waiting for me to come around and do it for her. Hate it when she does that. I meet her on the pavement while Tommy climbs out and stands on her other side. The three of us look at the big, square building that will be Ellie's new home sweet home.

It's fucking grotesque. Hideous. A dump. If it hasn't been condemned yet, it damn well should be.

"You sure this is the place?" I ask.

Ellie squeals. "This is it! The perfect place to find myself."

"Looks more like the perfect place to hang yourself."

She waves a hand at me. "Oh, stop kidding around. Come on, get the boxes."

We grab the boxes from the SUV and walk inside. It's even worse there. The hallway smells like wet dog and the flat is a drab room with concrete walls and patches of missing paint. The floors are rotting in some spots, and most of the cabinets in the kitchen area are missing doors. The appliances are ancient and caked with grease, a flash fire just waiting to happen.

And Ellie's not exactly responsible with her candles.

I set my box down and say quietly to Tommy, "I'm gonna go speak to the prince."

He nods. "Took the words out of my mouth."

I point to Ellie. "Don't leave her alone."

Tommy chuckles. "In this neighborhood? Brother, I'm not even gonna blink."

A while later, I'm at the penthouse, sitting across from Nicholas in the library. "It's about Ellie's new flat. Have you seen it?"

He grins. "She was going on and on about it at dinner last

night. She seems very excited about having some independence, standing on her own feet."

"But you haven't actually seen the place yourself?" I push.

And his hands stop shuffling papers. "No. But judging from your tone, I'm guessing I should."

"The sooner the better."

He rises from his chair and I follow him out to the living room, where Olivia is reviewing paperwork for their new charitable venture. Since Lord Ellington acquired Ellie's mother's pie recipes and is selling them as fast as they can ship them, the diners are no longer serving them. Instead, they serve hot, nutritious meals instead, cold sandwiches and hot coffee—to anyone who enters. They're only asked to pay what they can.

Nicholas holds out his hand. "Road trip."

She stands, pecking his lips. "Where are we going?"

"Ellie moves into her new flat today—let's visit."

"She said she wanted us to wait until she got everything set up."

Nicholas meets my eyes over his wife's pretty, dark head.

"Let's surprise her. Your sister likes surprises."

When Olivia steps through the doorway of the flat, with her eyes as big as quarters, it's clear that Ellie isn't the only one surprised.

A booming sound comes from outside, a few blocks away.

"Hey guys!" Ellie greets her sister and brother-in-law. "I didn't want you to come by until I got everything ready. What do you think? Isn't it great?"

Nicholas, a man known for having a way with words, has trouble finding them. "It's . . . something."

And all Olivia can manage is, "Wow."

The boom sound comes again. Before I can comment, Nicholas asks, "Is that . . .?"

"Gunshots?" Tommy finishes. "Aye. They go off about every twenty minutes. Like a poor man's Big Ben."

A scraggly bearded vagrant, naked except for a dirty, worn trench coat, peeks into the window and waves.

I motion towards him. "The neighbors seem friendly."

Olivia marches to the window and pulls down the shade—and the whole bloody curtain rod falls down.

Did I say the place should be condemned? It should be bombed.

"Why is it so cold?" Nicholas asks.

Ellie's face scrunches a bit. "Yeah—there's a minor issue with the heat."

"What's the issue?"

"There isn't any."

She raises her finger. "But it's okay—I have a plan."

Nicholas scratches his brow. "Can't wait to hear it."

"I thought I'd get one of those outdoor fire pits and I'd put it by the window, of course, so the smoke can blow out."

"A fire pit?" Nicholas repeats.

"Yeah," Ellie goes on. "You know, the Native Americans used to have fires inside their tepees and the smoke would escape out the top," she explains.

"Tepees?" Tommy parrots.

"Right." Nicholas nods. "Okay. Ah, Tommy, can you take those boxes, please? Logan—get those on that side, and I'll carry these," he says, hoisting two large boxes near his feet.

"What are you doing?" Ellie asks.

"You're not staying here," Nicholas tells her.

"I know it's not perfect . . . but I love it," Ellie wails.

"We'll find you a new place to love. I'll even ask the owner to loosen the pipes so they leak if that'll make you happy, but you can't stay here. Absolutely not."

"But—"

"Holy shit!" Olivia screeches. And jumps. "There's a rat! A huge rat!"

"Don't hurt him!" Ellie yells. "I saw him before. I was going to try feeding him. I already named him Remy—from *Ratatouille*—he's cute."

"Remy's not gonna be so cute when he's eating your toes while you sleep," I tell her.

She points her finger at me, all cute and pissy. "You're not helping."

Olivia starts repacking boxes.

Ellie leaps towards her. "Wait, Liv! Back me up—sister code."

"You can't stay here, Ellie. There's no way."

"But it's got character written all over it," Ellie whines.

"I think you're mistaking character for the message the serial killer wrote on the wall in blood, after he dumped the bodies here."

Ellie scowls at her big sister, shaking her head, "Marrying a prince has made you soft, Liv."

Olivia laughs. "I was never hard enough for Remy. *Ever.*" The new princess snaps her fingers. "Let's go."

She then follows her husband and Tommy straight out the door.

While I close up a box at my feet and lift it, Ellie stands in the middle of the room, turning in a half circle. She's quiet and seems . . . tiny in the empty flat. Dejected.

I step up behind her. "There'll be other places, Elle."

Her purple tipped blond hair sways across her back as she shakes her head. "Not like this."

"No, they'll be better. Nicer, safer places. You deserve better."

She spins around then, with a burst of righteous energy. The tips of her small ears go pink and her cheeks are rosy with anger.

"You ratted me out to Nicholas," she hisses.

And there's a devil inside me that wants to tease her, toy with her—like a lad tugging on a girl's braids—just to see how she'll react when I do.

"Yeah, I did."

Ellie folds her arms, all adorable simmering fury—a pretty pussycat who just discovered her claws. "I didn't take you for a narc, Logan."

I shrug. "Now you know."

She jams her finger towards my chest. "You are on my permanent shit list, buddy. I'll never forgive you for this. Never."

I lean in close, dropping my voice. "Since now you'll actually be alive for all those years that you're busy not forgiving me, I'm gonna put this one down as a win."

She sticks her tongue out, then twirls around and stomps away.

And, Christ, even her tongue is cute.

Somebody fuckin' punch me.

CHAPTER 8

Logan

Six months later

For the next few months, Ellie stays put—at the well-secured penthouse with Prince Nicholas and Olivia. Their lives go on—there are social events and announcements and the occasional royal duty. The rest of their time is spent working on expanding the Amelia's charitable diners. Eric Hammond, almost two years sober now, has thrown himself into the venture and works every day at one of the three locations—cooking, washing dishes, interacting with employees and patrons—doing whatever needs to be done to keep the places running smoothly.

The press still swarms the royal couple like a nest of annoying nits, publishing articles that have no truth to them. But Nicholas settles in happily to married life and his mostly civilian American existence. While Lady Olivia, her father and Ellie adjust fully to their celebrity-by-association status.

And Ellie occasionally . . . dates.

It's a sore subject. Mostly because it irks the fuck out of me.

Her preference seems to be scrawny, self-important, worthless little twats. Ellie Hammond is a delicate prize, with so much to offer, and she's selling herself too bloody short.

My mood is black whenever a new one arrives on the scene,

and blacker during the few weeks they tend to hang around. Tommy always asks me if it's my time of the month—and I tell him to piss off.

He enjoys playing the jokester, but he's sharp; he notices things.

Then, one night, Ellie she comes home from an evening with her current tool, and I go from irked to furious in a red-hot minute.

"Motherfucker!"

And I'm not alone.

Nicholas, Tommy and I rush into the living room, where Olivia is calling for the butler, her voice electrified with rage.

"Where's my bat?" she yells before yanking open the closet door, and yelling into it, "Where is my goddamn baseball bat?"

"Olivia?" Nicholas steps towards her. "What in the—"

"Jesus, Mary and Joseph," Tommy hisses.

Because he's looking at Ellie's face. At the burgeoning bruise just starting to form on the smooth apple of her right cheek. I've been in enough fights to know what I'm looking at.

Someone fucking slapped her.

Ellie.

Someone put his hands on her, and now he's going to fucking lose them. I swear immediately and silently—to every saint I know.

"Olivia, please calm down," Ellie implores.

"David," Nicholas tells the butler, "bring a cold compress, please."

My eyes swing to Liam, standing just behind Ellie—he was her security for the night. "What happened?"

"I was in the hall, outside the flat—she came running out," Liam explains. "The guy was following her and I shoved him back, got her to the car and brought her here. I didn't see the mark until we were on the road."

Nicholas moves to Ellie, raising his hands slowly. "May I?"

Ellie nods and Nicholas gently inspects her injury, pressing with his thumbs along her cheek, feeling for broken bones.

"I'm okay," Ellie declares calmly. "Mitchell had a few beers, we were watching the game—he had money on the Mets. And I hate the Mets. When the Cardinals hit a grand slam, I laughed—I was just joking. And he . . . *pshhh* . . ." She swings her arm into a backhand, and my gut tightens.

"He slapped me."

Tears leak into her throat, choking her voice. "I was just . . . stunned, you know? But I only waited a second, then I grabbed my phone and got the hell out of there. I'm done with him. I think I'm done with all of them."

And then Olivia is there—pulling her baby sister into her arms, holding her close, smoothing down the back of her rainbow-tipped hair.

"Nothing seems broken," Nicholas says, anger making his tone like the sound of a tight guitar string. "But you should still see a doctor, Ellie."

She shakes her head in Olivia's arms. "No, I'm fine."

"I'll have a doctor come here," Nicholas offers.

"No. I just . . . I want to take a bath and forget this happened." She sniffles. "I'm fine, really."

"What about the police?" Olivia asks, hard and harsh. "This is assault, and that asshole should be in jail."

Ellie holds up her hands. "Please, Liv. If we file a police report, it'll be in the papers. All over the internet . . ."

"Screw the internet!" Olivia hisses.

But Ellie looks her in the eyes. "I want to let it go. And I'm asking you to let it go too. Please."

Olivia deflates a bit. She shakes her head, unhappy but resigned. "If that's what you want . . ."

"It is." She sighs deeply, pushing back her hair. "And now I'm going to bed, okay?"

Her sister's eyes crease with concern. "Okay. Do you want me to bring you a cup of tea?"

Ellie smiles ruefully. Because Olivia sounds more like her husband every day. "No. I don't want tea. I just want to sleep."

And then she walks out of the room and down the hall.

While Liam talks with Tommy, and Nicholas and Olivia speak with bent heads in soft tones, I slip down the hall behind Ellie. I catch up to her just outside her door.

"Are you all right?" I ask.

And there's a tortured note in my voice—anguished and sorry.

Her spine straightens and her hand stays on the knob while she turns around. Her blue eyes shine with unshed tears.

"You must think I'm so stupid," she whispers, making my chest squeeze painfully.

"I don't think that. I never would."

She blinks, and a tear slides over the mark on her face. "I make bad choices. I need to grow up. Because this is what happens . . ."

I'm already shaking my head again. "Listen to me, Ellie. Bastards like the one who hurt you tonight—they're like poisonous snakes that hide behind the colors of harmless ones. That's how they survive. It's not your fault. You couldn't have known."

"*You* would've known."

I tilt my chin. "I generally make it a rule to dislike everyone, so you can't go by me."

She laughs even while she's sniffling. And it tears at my fucking heart.

Because she's not just the kind of girl who'll leap off a

cliff without bothering to look—she'll take a running start and launch herself off it. Arms spread, head back. Free and alive.

No one is going to take that away from her—I won't let them.

"You see the good in people, Ellie. You trust. That's a good way to be, a brave way. I'll watch more closely from now on; I'll make sure this never happens again. You just be who you are. Leave the rest to me."

She wipes her eyes dry. "So it's like a . . . you jump, I jump, Jack and Rose kind of thing?"

"No." I take her hand in mine, brushing my thumb against her knuckles. "You jump . . . and I'll be there to catch you."

Slowly, I lean forward and press a gentle kiss to her forehead, like it's the most natural thing in the world. My lips linger on her petal-soft skin, inhaling the scent of orange blossom and a touch of jasmine.

Then I turn around, and walk back down the hall.

The next security shift arrives at eleven p.m., like always, to relieve Tommy and me. We take the elevator down, but rather than head out as usual, we circle around and wait in the alley by the back exit of the building. Tommy lights a cigarette and leans against the wall.

I check my watch and count, *four, three, two* . . .

The door opens—and Nicholas Pembrook appears. I cross my arms disapprovingly while Tommy plucks the smoke from his lips.

"No."

"Not happening, Your Highness."

His features go smooth and still. "I don't know what you two are talking about. I was just going for a walk."

"Yeah." Tommy laughs. "A walk all over the cunt's face who put his hands on Ellie."

The Prince clenches his jaw and I gesture between Tommy and me. "That's why you keep us around."

"To keep you out of trouble," Tommy adds. "No one's gonna sue us—we don't have a pot to piss in or a window to throw it out of."

I shrug. "We all look the same in these clothes anyway—no one can tell us apart."

Nicholas tries to argue, but I go on, "And besides, you've got bigger tasks to handle."

"What sort of tasks?"

The door opens at the top of the steps and a few seconds later, Lady Olivia steps outside.

And she's carrying her bat.

"Like making sure your Duchess stays put."

The Prince gives his wife an exasperated look. But she's unrepentant.

"Like you weren't thinking the exact same thing."

"Apparently, you're all thinking the same thing."

A voice drifts from the landing above. Ellie's voice. She comes marching down, arms crossed. She reaches towards her sister with a scowl.

"Let's go, Negan—hand Lucille over."

Olivia rolls her eyes and gives up the murder weapon.

"I told you I wanted to let it go. Now I want your promise, right now, that you'll leave it alone." She looks at her sister first. "Liv?"

She's unhappy, but she gives in. "Fine. I promise I'll leave it alone."

Then Ellie lays eyes on her brother-in-law. A man knows when he can't win. "You have my word, Ellie."

And she doesn't leave me or Tommy out.

"I promise, lass," Tommy says, making the sign of the cross and kissing his knuckle up to God.

I look Ellie straight in the face. "I'll let it go."

"Say you promise," Ellie pushes.

"I promise."

Sometimes, I lie.

Once we're sure Prince Nicholas, Lady Olivia and Ellie are safely under lock and key, Tommy falls in step beside me as we walk down the street. Both of us know exactly where we're going.

I knock on the door, then lean back against the wall so he can't see us through the peephole. And because Tommy's watched *Tommy Boy* one too many times, he says in a high-pitched, squeaky voice, "Housekeeping."

And the dumb wanker opens the door, just a crack, but it's enough. As soon as he spots me, his eyes go wide and he tries to slam it in my face. But I shove my way in and push him up against the wall by his neck. His pulse judders against my palm like the heart of a jackrabbit about to be torn apart by a wolf.

"You picked the wrong girl to lay your hands on."

He sputters. "Wait! I didn't mean . . . You can't do this. I'll report you. They'll fire you—take your job."

I squeeze his throat tighter, laughing, sounding maniacal even to my own ears. "You'll . . . you'll take my job?"

Then I stop laughing. "I'll take your cock off and shove it down your throat. Then I'll feed you, bit by bit, to the hogs, till all that's left of you is a steaming pile of pig shit."

He almost starts to cry.

Tommy locks the door and turns the television on, upping

the volume. Not loud enough to draw complaints, but enough to muffle the groans this cunt's about to emit.

Holding him by the throat, I toss him over to Tommy, who shoves him back to me, both of us circling, closing in. The twat's head turns, eyes darting back and forth between us. "Come on, guys, it was a mistake. This isn't fair—it's two against one. I don't even have a chance."

"'This isn't fair,'" Tommy whines. "You know why they picked us to guard the royal family? Two young nobodies from nowhere?"

"Why?"

Tommy shakes his head, almost pitying. "'Cause we're not nearly as civilized as we look."

And he might actually piss himself. Which would be messy, so I give him a small slice of hope. "I'll let you have the first shot."

His pupils are huge, prey's eyes. He doesn't lift his hands, doesn't take a swing.

And patience is not my strong suit. "The offer has an expiration point—about three seconds from now. Three . . . two . . ."

Panicked, he throws out his fist, hitting me in the chin, barely moving my head.

I laugh. "Bloody hell, no wonder you like to smack little girls. You hit like a pussy." I look to Tommy. "Your sister punches harder."

Tommy scoffs. "That's not really fair. Janey's especially badass."

I turn back to the sack of shit.

"You're doing it all wrong. You want to turn your hips and your shoulders into the punch. Use the force of your whole body. Don't push with your knuckles."

I demonstrate on his face. Quick. Hard. Pitiless.

And a tooth goes bouncing across the floor.

"Like that. See what I did there?"

He folds over, holding his mouth with both hands, blood seeping through his fingers. But all I see in my mind is Ellie's pretty face, marred with a nasty bruise from this bastard's hand.

"I don't think he gets it, Lo," Tommy says. "You better show him again."

Couldn't agree more.

Fifteen minutes later, he's nothing but a groaning pile of bloody clothes, bruises and splintered bones.

"Fucking hell," Tommy curses, fingering a spot of blood on the front of his light gray shirt. "You got club soda?" he asks the heap.

When there's no response, Tommy nudges him with his foot. "Hey! You got any club soda?"

The heap moans in the negative and Tommy shakes his head, disgusted.

"Useless bastard." Then he spits on him.

"Really?" I ask Tommy.

"What? It's my favorite shirt."

Tommy may have a touch of sociopath in him.

I crouch down and lift the shitbag up by his collar, my tone soft and serious, "You come near Ellie Hammond again, if she glimpses you on the street . . . I'll kill you with my bare hands."

Then Tommy and I stroll through the door.

Out on the pavement, heading for home, Tommy pulls his eyes from the tragedy of his stained shirt and glances at me. "You laid it on pretty thick at the end."

"What do you mean?"

We take the stairs down to the subway.

"I mean, if he's stupid enough to come sniffin' around Ellie again, we'd bust him up, sure—but we'd leave him breathing, wouldn't we?"

I take a moment to think about my answer before I respond.

"Yeah. Sure we would. I was just making a point."

Like I said . . . sometimes, I lie.

CHAPTER 9

Ellie

Logan is watching me.

He's been doing that a lot lately. Even when I don't catch him doing it, I feel it—like the brush of a hand on my skin. It makes me warm . . . tingly. And the spot on my forehead, where he kissed me that night . . . I can still feel that too.

I've talked with Olivia about moments that change our lives. How it's important but difficult to recognize them when they happen. Things that change us, forever. Logan was worried that Mitchell did would change who I am. It didn't.

But, he changed who I think other people are. I can't help that. It seemed like it came out of nowhere, without any warning or sign. But maybe there were signs, and I missed them.

Now I know to look beneath the surface, to be smarter— to question that what's on the outside, the words people say and the things they do, might be totally and completely different from what's really going on, on the inside.

I talked to Logan about it too, a few days later. About people who lie, misrepresent for all kinds of reasons.

He held up two fingers on his right hand and told me in that strong, steady voice: "Two guaranteed signs of lying—they fidget or freeze. They either move too much or work too hard to not move at all. You'll sense it if you pay attention; something about their look will seem unnatural . . . off. Anytime someone has to put effort into their words, you can bet what they're saying is a steaming crock of shit."

"Fade Into You" by Mazzy Star plays from my phone as I dip my brush into the bucket of paint and drag it up the wall. It's a good song to paint to. Slow and rhythmic.

I'm at the newest Amelia's location. Olivia and Nicholas have grown the coffee shop into a chain of "pay what you can" restaurants across the city. This'll be the third one, and the grand opening is in a few weeks, so I'm helping out. Nicholas and Livvy are in the kitchen setting things up—and making goo-goo eyes at each other like they so often do.

Logan leans against the wall behind me, his arms folded, his eyes alert—watching me. When the wall is covered in its first coat of paint, I lay the brush on a cloth on the floor and turn around to face him.

"What?"

He shifts his eyes from the front window, where he wasn't looking a second ago, to me.

"What 'what'?"

"Do I have paint in my hair?" I twist my body and look at my butt. "Did I sit in something?"

Logan scoffs. "No."

"Then what's with the deep-thoughted glares? I can hear you thinking from here."

He tilts his head and rubs his chin. "You should learn how to fight."

"Like Ronda Rousey? If God wanted me to be an MMA fighter, don't you think he would've made me bigger?"

"Not like Ronda Rousey." Logan shakes his head. "Like self-defense. You should know how to protect yourself."

"I thought it was your job to protect me."

"It is. And this is part of how I'll do that."

Logan crosses his arms, his biceps bulging against the sleeves of his dress shirt, and waits for me to answer.

"Okay."

"Good." He walks up to me, close enough that I can smell him. Logan always smells so good . . . like crisp, cold air, fresh wood and fall leaves.

He holds up his palm. "Punch my hand. Let's see what we're working with."

I step back, brace my feet and raise my fists—bouncing like a boxer. Then I give all I've got—landing my fist as hard as I can in Logan's open palm with a smack.

It was pretty badass, if I do say so myself.

"That was pathetic," Logan says.

Everyone's a critic.

I make a face at him.

"Have you ever gotten into it with someone before?"

"I pulled Liv's hair when I was seven. She was going to rat me out for breaking our mom's decorative cake plate and when she tried to retaliate, I locked myself in the bathroom until our dad came home."

"Wow." Logan lifts an eyebrow. "Okay." He claps his big hands together and rubs. Then he takes a step back, spreading his feet, and looks me in the face.

"Eyes and balls."

"Excuse me?"

"The most vulnerable spots on a man are his eyeballs and his cock."

By the power of suggestion, my eyes immediately drop to Logan's . . . latter.

And in his perfectly snug dress pants, the latter is . . . fucking amazing. Significant. I've covertly checked it out before and though I've never seen a bull in person, I can safely say that Logan could give one an inferiority complex.

He catches where I'm looking and a quick, deep chuckle rumbles in his chest.

"Let's stick with eyes for now," Logan says—almost teasingly. "We'll work on the cock in a bit."

Work on the cock . . . is it getting hot in here?

Over the next half hour, Logan shows me how to turn my thumbs into dangerous, eye-gouging weapons. How to duck and block and use my body weight to propel me away from an attacker. How to use my legs—the strongest part of my body— to stun and escape. He demonstrates how to squeeze my fists into rocks—thumbs on the outside, people—and punch a guy's nads up into his throat.

When we're finished, his shoulders are looser, less tense, his face is less scowly and there's the sound of pride in his voice.

"That's good, Ellie," he says quietly, after I throw my arm up in a block meant to protect my face. "Well done."

"Thanks." I nod.

But then the mood shifts, as if the air becomes thicker, weighted, more . . . sultry.

Because slowly, Logan sinks down to one knee in front of me—looking in my eyes the whole time. In this position, I could touch his shoulders, comb my fingers through his thick hair. He's the perfect height for me to bend down and kiss his mouth—the perfect height for him to kiss me back . . . in a lot of places.

My breath hitches. And I wonder he feels it too.

There's a sound of tearing Velcro, and Logan takes something off his ankle—a holster, with a small silver knife, about three inches long. Still on his knee, he takes the knife out and sunlight glints off the blade.

"Keep this on you all the time," he says seriously. "Just in case. If you wear a skirt, the strap will fit around your thigh."

And I almost laugh. Most girls get a ring from a guy on his knees. I get a murder weapon. But still, it makes me feel safe . . .

watched over. Like I'm something precious that deserves to be protected.

I take the knife from him, testing the surprisingly solid, heavy weight of it in my hand. I press my index finger to the tip.

Logan grabs my wrist tightly. "Careful. It's sharp."

There's a small, painless nick, a tiny bead of blood, so I put my finger in my mouth, sucking.

And Logan's watching me again.

Watching my mouth.

His chest seems to rise just a little faster, and his throat ripples when he swallows. He bends his head, curves his strong back, and then I feel his hands on my ankle, securing the strap. His touch is warm and self-assured. It's the way he always moves—confident and experienced. Logan knows his body and he knows how to use it, in every way possible.

I almost moan. The sound is in the back of my throat, but I keep it trapped. I never knew the ankle was an erogenous zone, but it sure as hell is now. A hot pulse of pleasure streaks from Logan's fingers on my bare skin, up my thigh, between my legs.

And I throb there, growing swollen and heavy as he keeps his hands on me.

Can he tell? Does he know? He's so aware of everything, always so attuned, I wonder if he can sense my arousal . . . smell it in the air that clings between us.

Logan pulls my pant leg down, pressing the hem over the knife it now hides. And when he stands, the spell is broken. The air loses its density, its depth . . . and goes back to normal.

We go back to normal too—the loyal guard and princess's sister.

Although it's my twentieth birthday and I'm officially-officially an adult—no more teen years for me—Livvy insists on baking me a cake. And having our dad and all the security guys who are practically family over to the penthouse to celebrate in the fancy formal dining room. She knows that no matter how old I get, I love this kind of stuff.

Streamers and balloons and flowers, twenty candles and one extra for good luck that I have to blow out in a single breath—but only after I make a wish. And only after they all sing "Happy Birthday" to me. Tommy sings loudest, 'cause that's just how he is.

Then, while David the butler clears away the plates, my dad wants to give me my present. But there's a catch.

"You have to close your eyes," he says. "No peeking."

And there's this lightness to his face, a contentment and excitement that I haven't seen in him in years. A decade. I can't imagine what his gift is—his three years of sobriety is already the most wonderful gift he could give me.

But . . . if he wants to add to the awesome, who am I to say no?

The whole gang comes along as he leads me out of the apartment, with his hands over my eyes because—yeah, I'm a peeker. Without looking, I know we're getting in the elevator and when we get off, the air feels cooler and sounds echo-y.

We come to a stop and then he takes his hands away. And I open my eyes. And I'm staring at a beautiful, buttercup-yellow BMW convertible with tan interior and a giant red bow on the hood. I don't know the model or the horsepower or anything like that—I just know it's so fucking pretty.

I scream.

So loud it hurts my own ears. But—nope—don't care.

I fling my arms around my dad's neck. "Thank you! Thank you so much!"

"Dad . . ." Olivia questions with a hint of worry in her tone that tells me she didn't know about this present. And she worries about me. Always.

My dad kisses my cheek and sets me back down. "The royalties from my deal with Simon have been good. She's twenty years old now, Liv. She's doing great in school—she deserves it." Then he looks back to me, his dark blue eyes—just like my sister's—sparkling.

"The car's from me, but the private parking is courtesy of Nicholas."

I skip over to my brother-in-law and hug him too. Hugs for everyone!

"Is your license still valid, Ellie?" Olivia asks.

"Bet your sweet bippy it is, Liv." And I dance like I have to pee. "So, can I, like, drive it? Now?"

"Of course you can," my dad says, smiling, holding out the shiny key. "It's yours, sweetheart." He kisses my cheek. "I love you, Ellie."

I hug him again. "I love you too, Dad."

When I walk around to climb in, my brother-in-law suggests, "Ah, maybe take one of the lads with you? Just in case there's trouble. Logan—would you mind?"

Logan nods. "Sure."

And I bounce in front of him. "This is going to be so awesome!"

He looks sort of ill.

"Yeah. Great." He holds up his fist and gives a pathetic "Woo."

I roll my eyes and slide into the driver's seat. It fits like a glove.

Then Tommy makes the sign of the cross in front of Logan. Blessing him.

In Latin.

Logan shoves him playfully. "Tosser."

He gets into the passenger seat and with a honk and a thumbs-up, we're off.

I pull out of the garage and onto the tight, one-way street. And I make my way across Midtown.

Slowly.

Because traffic doesn't give a crap if it's your birthday.

Once we're through the tunnel and onto the highway, traffic opens up. I dig through my purse for a quarter and hand it to Logan.

"What's this?" he asks.

The wind blows my hair wild and I tilt my chin up, enjoying the feel of the breeze and warmth on my face, smelling the sund-drenched air while "Fast Car" by Tracy Chapman drifts up through the speakers. Without active memorization techniques, human beings forget about 70 percent of their lives. It's a brain capacity thing—only so much can make it into the storage banks of long-term memory.

But this day—this moment, right here—I want to remember it.

"That's our GPS. Flip it. Heads we go left, tails right."

He shakes his head. "You're such an odd bird."

"No, I'm a free bird. You were there when I got my tattoo—I'm gonna suck the lemon of life, seeds and all. Now flip—quick."

He rolls his eyes and then flips the coin. It's tails.

I screech across three lanes of highway—with the sounds of angry horns blaring behind me—to make the exit ramp coming up quick on the right.

We end up at an outdoor paintball course in Jersey. A woodsy, rural kind of place that's probably brimming with mosquitos and Lyme disease. When I find out Logan has never played paintball before, I sign us both up.

There's really no other option.

And our timing is perfect—they're just about to start a new battle. The worker gathers all the players in a field and divides us into two teams, handing out thin blue and yellow vests to distinguish friend from foe.

Since Logan and I are the oldest players, we both become the team captains. The wide-eyed little faces of Logan's squad follow him as he marches back and forth in front of them, lecturing like a hot, modern-day Winston Churchill.

"We'll fight them from the hills, we'll fight them in the trees. We'll hunker down in the river and take them out, sniper-style. Save your ammo—fire only when you see the whites of their eyes. Use your heads."

I turn to my own ragtag crew.

"Use your hearts. We'll give them everything we've got— leave it all on the field. You know what wins battles? Desire! Guts! Today, we'll all be frigging Rudy!"

A blond boy whispers to his friend, "Who's Rudy?"

The kid shrugs.

And another raises his hand. "Can we start now? It's my birthday and I really want to have cake."

"It's my birthday too." I give him a high-five. "Twinning!"

I raise my gun. "And yes, birthday cake will be our spoils of war! Here's how it's gonna go." I point to the giant on the other side of the field. "You see him, the big guy? We converge on him first. Work together to take him down. Cut off the head," I slice my finger across my neck like I'm beheading myself, "and the old dog dies."

A skinny kid in glasses makes a grossed-out face. "Why would you kill a dog? Why would you cut its head off?"

And a little girl in braids squeaks, "Mommy! Mommy, I don't want to play anymore."

"No," I try, "that's not what I—"

But she's already running into her mom's arms. The woman picks her up—glaring at me like I'm a demon—and carries her away.

"Darn."

Then a soft voice whispers right against my ear.

"They're already going AWOL on you, lass? You're fucked."

I turn to face the bold, tough Wessconian . . . and he's so close, I can feel the heat from his hard body, see the small sprigs of stubble on that perfect, gorgeous jaw. My brain stutters, but I find the resolve to tease him.

"Dear God, Logan, are you smiling? Careful—you might pull a muscle in your face."

And then Logan does something that melts my insides and turns my knees to quivery goo.

He laughs.

And it's beautiful.

It's a crime he doesn't do it more often. Or maybe a blessing. Because Logan St. James is a sexy, stunning man on any given day. But when he laughs?

He's heart-stopping.

He swaggers confidently back to his side and I sneer at his retreating form. The uniformed paintball worker blows a whistle and explains the rules. We get seven minutes to hide first. I cock my paintball shotgun with one hand—like Charlize Theron in *Fury* fucking *Road*—and lead my team into the wilderness.

"Come on, children. Let's go be heroes."

It was a massacre.

We never stood a chance.

In the end, we tried to rush them—overpower them—but we just ended up running into a hail of balls, getting our hearts and guts splattered with blue paint.

But we tried—I think Rudy and Charlize would be proud.

One of the birthday moms gave me and Logan a leftover pizza, so we sat at a picnic table to eat together.

"I think you cheated," I tell him, chewing grumpily.

"Didn't have to." He smiles again, looking younger, boyish, and I wouldn't be surprised if cartoon hearts are floating above my head. "Though I'm not above playing dirty if it's needed."

Hearing Logan say "dirty" in his accent, with that full, strong mouth, makes my stomach flip-flop like a fish. I put the rest of my pizza down on the paper plate, pushing it away.

"You like to win."

He nods. "I do. But you surprised me, Ellie. You did well. You're a fighter—that's a good thing to be."

I pick at the chipping green paint on the picnic table, feeling weirdly shy.

"Thank you."

And Logan's voice turns quiet, husky. Almost . . . intimate.

"Did you have fun, Ellie-girl? Was it a good birthday?"

I look up, meeting his gaze. "It was perfect. I'll never forget it."

And I sense his dark eyes on me, reading me.

"I'm glad."

After a moment, he points to his cheek. "You've got mud on your face."

I brush my hand over my cheek. "Did I get it?"

"No."

I try a second time but must still miss, because Logan reaches out slowly and runs his fingers over the apple of my cheek, up to my temple and gently down to my jaw. My eyes slide closed at the sensation. It feels like a caress.

And I could totally be imagining it, but—screw it, it's my birthday, so I'm allowed to dream—it feels like his touch lingers just a little longer than needed.

When I open my eyes he's looking at me with a kind of thoughtfulness, an intensity—a heat—in his dark brown eyes that I know I'm *not* imagining.

Best. Birthday. *Ever.*

CHAPTER 10

Logan

Two years later

I am fucked. So fucked.

I've suspected as much for a while . . . but now I'm certain of it.

"Five inches! Stupid impulse decision—what was I thinking?"

Ellie isn't Ellie anymore. Not the girl I knew—with a spark in her eye and a ring to her laugh. The one I had to watch closely so she didn't walk into traffic, because she was so distracted telling a story.

"What do you think, Liv?"

Or maybe she was never really that girl at all. Maybe that's what I told myself, focused on, so I'd keep away.

Olivia smiles. "I think you look beautiful."

These days, I can't help focusing on other things: like the lovely curve to her hips, the sweet swell of her breasts, that beautiful bubble-arse that I can almost feel against me and a scent that drives me mad with distraction.

Ellie scoffs. "You said I looked beautiful when I was twelve with a mouthful of braces that had bread stuck in them every day after lunch."

"You were beautiful then too—the bread notwithstanding."

Ellie rolls her eyes. "You have no street cred."

I see her in my dreams now. Sometimes we're in my room, on my bed with me above her, moving deep inside her. Other times we're at the seashore, in the waves, with her wrapped all around me. And once we were in the fucking throne room at the palace. But most often, I dream of that picnic table, on her twentieth birthday. And in the dream, I kiss her like I wanted to. Like I know she wanted me to. And then I pick her up, plant her on top of that picnic table, slowly rid her of every piece of clothing she has and do a hell of a lot more than kiss her.

"Nicholas, what do you think?"

But that can't happen. It would change everything. Everything I've built for myself. My mates, my job, my whole life. I've always wanted to be a part of something bigger—something noble and lasting—and now I am. Messing with Ellie would obliterate that.

And the lass is fickle. Still young. She flits from boy to boy, interest to interest, like a frog hopping from one lily pad to the next.

"You look smashing. Very cute."

If something ever did happen between us, it wouldn't last—but the chaos it would bring, that would be forever.

"Cute? Oh God!" Ellie covers her face with her hands.

My gut tells me it's not worth the risk.

Nicholas whispers to his wife, "Cute is bad?"

So I determined I would shut down this mounting attraction to a woman who's out of my league. One I've got no fucking business looking at twice—let alone a dozen times a day.

"Of course cute is bad!" Ellie yells. "Mice are cute." She gestures to the small dog sitting on Olivia's lap. "Bosco is cute!"

Because I always go with my gut—and it's never wrong.

Nicholas glances at the temperamental pooch. "No. No, he isn't."

EMMA CHASE

Olivia covers the dog's ears and gives her husband a harsh look. He winks back.

And that plan had gone smoothly—until today. This moment. When Ellie came charging through the door, muttering to herself like a madwoman yelling at pigeons in the park.

Olivia mentions giving Bosco a bath, and she and her husband both leave the room.

Ellie looks at Tommy. "Well? What do you think?"

She's talking about her hair. She went to get it done for her big day—a college graduation makeover, she'd said.

Tommy winks. "I'd do ya."

I may have to smother him in his sleep tonight.

The bright colors that used to streak Ellie's blond hair are gone now. Leaving behind shades of deep honey and shiny gold—thick and soft. The kind of hair that begs to be touched and twirled . . . fisted and tugged on.

Ellie clicks her tongue. "That's not saying much—you'd do a corpse."

It falls just below her shoulders—exposing her face, making it look more angular, womanly—stunning. Her skin seems tanner, her shoulders more delicate, her tits fuller, her eyes a sweeter blue.

Tommy wags his finger. "Only if she were a pretty corpse. I have standards."

And then, at last, she settles on me, her delicate features hopeful but hesitant. Her pink tongue peeks out and rubs the fullness of her bottom lip. And I feel it in my cock, the rub of that tongue—the nip and pull of her wet lips—ghosting up and down on my aching, hard flesh.

In my dreams we do that on the picnic table too—*often*.

"Logan?"

I'm so distracted by my musings, I miss her speaking my name, and for a bit, I don't say anything at all.

"Oh well, it'll grow back," she says, embarrassment flushing beneath her cheeks. "Wearing a hat for the next six months won't be so bad."

I force the gravel from my throat.

"Beautiful."

Ellie's eyes flick back to mine.

"What?"

I hold her gaze, my tone deliberate and sure.

"You look beautiful, Ellie."

Her smile is small and seeking. "Really?"

I don't take my eyes off her. I wouldn't—even if I could.

"Prettiest lass I've ever seen."

So, so, so fucked.

They hold the graduation party on the garden rooftop of the penthouse—with waiters and Champagne and a trio of string musicians playing in the corner. I stand straight along a far wall, sunglasses on, watching, taking in the whole group. It's fairly small—good friends, Ellie's fellow students, her father and a couple family friends, as well as a few business associates from Nicholas and Olivia's charity whom Ellie has gotten to know over the years.

Marlow, her still-wild friend from high school, walks up to me, a straw held tight in her cherry lips as she drinks an orange cocktail. Her eyes slide across the way to Ellie, then back to me.

She wags her finger. "You're good, Costner. Very good. But I see you."

The back of my neck gets hot, but my face remains impassive.

"Go away, Marlow."

She's not a bad lot, but she's a shit-stirrer—she and Prince Henry would get on well if he were still single.

She smiles slowly, like a cat with a juicy mouse under its paw, and slinks up close to me. "It must drive you crazy."

And, as if I'm hypnotized or cursed, my gaze follows hers . . . straight to Ellie.

Her head's tipped back in a laugh at something someone just said, her eyes as bright as the sky above. The sunlight kisses her hair, giving it a golden glow. A halo.

"Not that you can't have her," Marlow whispers softly, right in my ear.

Ellie's wearing a tiny white skirt over those smooth legs—with a teasing hint of arse peeking out if she moves just the right away and someone, such as myself, is looking hard enough. Her lovely tits tease from beneath a flowy black top—the ones I dream of wrapping my lips around, running my tongue up and over, sucking on until her nipples are two tight, aching little buds and she loses her voice from moaning my name.

"But that after all this time, all these years," Marlow says, "finally, you can."

My throat feels coated with sand, making my voice scratchy. "Don't tell her."

It's an order, not a request.

The girl laughs, low and sultry. "Tell her? Oh, Costner, she wouldn't believe me if I tried."

It's towards the end of the party, when the sun is dipping below the New York skyline, that Olivia lets the big news slip. When her father hands her a glass of Champagne for a toast and she says, "I can't, Dad."

They've known for two months. Because it's part of the job to know these things and because I'm the one who drove them to their first doctor's appointment, I've known too. Ellie doesn't yet, but I'm looking forward to seeing her reaction. I'm sure it'll be something.

They'd planned to keep it as quiet as they could, for as long as they could. Because once it wasn't, it would be heard around the world. Loudly.

"Of course you can." Ellie smiles. "It's a Champagne kind of day—celebrate good times, come on!"

Olivia's shining eyes meets Nicholas's and she's smiling so brightly she's almost bursting. If revenge is a dish best served cold, happy news is a meal best shared. The Prince nods gently.

Olivia looks at her little sister, then up into her dad's dark blue eyes and rests her hand on her stomach. "No . . . I mean I *can't*."

Realization dawns. And then joy. Tears of it well in the older man's eyes as he embraces his daughter. And Ellie doesn't let me down—she squeaks and bounces and whoops so much I can't not chuckle. Then she's stretching her arms and trying to hug her sister and brother-in-law at the same time.

It's a beautiful scene. A family scene.

Three months later, it's a fucking mess.

Chaos all around. Outside the penthouse building, surrounding every Amelia's location—anywhere Nicholas and Olivia have been or might go—journalists, paparazzi and rabid fans follow. Americans don't have royalty, but they're more than happy to play foster family to ours. They've been bitten by the royal baby bug—and it's driving them all bloody mad.

We double security.

After the news gets out that Olivia is carrying twins, we triple it. And still, it feels unmanageable. Out of control. Fucking dangerous.

Because when one or two people want to shake your hand, it's a nice gesture. When tens of thousands want to shake your hand—it's a mob. And right now, the whole damn world is determined to shake Olivia and Nicholas's hands—even if they end up crushed in the process.

Which is why, late one night, I knock on the library door when I know Nicholas is there.

"Come in."

I sit down across from him and for a moment, we just sort of look at each other. Because he knows what I'm going to say—he doesn't want to hear it, but he knows.

"I can't keep her safe here. Not the way I want to. Not the way she needs. It's too public, too open. I can stop people from riding the lift with her, but I can't keep them out of the lobby. There's no perimeter; they won't let us block off the street. And the bigger her midsection gets, the worse it'll be."

The Prince leans back in his chair and sighs. "What do you suggest?"

"Relocate to an estate outside the city. A property we can secure. Lady Olivia stays put—no one goes in or out unless we know. The journalists, photographers and crazies won't be able to get within a mile of her."

Nicholas taps a pen on his desk, thinking out loud. "She'll be isolated."

"She'll be safe," I counter.

"And utterly miserable."

"She can put her feet up for a few months. Netflix and chill—you both can."

Nicholas laughs. "Which would actually be wonderful, for a few days . . . and then we'd slowly lose our minds. Give me another option."

I shrug. "Well . . . there's the obvious. I mean, the palace wasn't built just to look fancy; it's a fortress. It's your home—where royals are supposed to live and breed. Before you went and knocked that tradition on its arse. The guards are trained; the people in town are used to the royal family being about. They'll welcome you and Lady Olivia and your spawn, with open arms."

"The palace isn't Olivia's favorite place. The "spawn' has made her more emotional than usual. I don't want her to be upset."

And I get that. The palace is filled with some of the nastiest, snobbiest fuckers on the planet and Olivia once called its gates a golden cage.

"It doesn't have to be forever," I tell him, "but it needs to be for now."

Nicholas nods slowly. "I'll take it under consideration. Thank you, Logan."

I bow. "Night, Sir."

It takes him two weeks to consider, two weeks for him to convince his pretty, pregnant wife of what's in her and their future children's best interest.

And then we're packing our things . . . and heading home to Wessco.

CHAPTER 11

Logan

Being back in the capital of Wessco, at the palace with Prince Nicholas, is like slipping into an old, worn pair of boots. It feels good—familiar, comfortable—the same procedures, people and streets.

"Do you want to build a snowman…"

With one addition. There's a blond, *singing* pebble that gives me unattainable thoughts and filthy fantasies, in the boot—and its name is Ellie Hammond.

When Nicholas decided to come home for the duration of Olivia's pregnancy, Mr. Hammond chose to stay behind, to continue running the Amelia's charity. I didn't know what Ellie would do. But the idea of leaving without her was . . . upsetting.

I won't make a move on her—but I feel a hell of a lot better keeping her where I can see her. Keeping her close. For her own safety, of course.

Olivia, brilliant woman that she is, suggested it would be the perfect time for a gap year for Ellie, before she begins her graduate school program in psychology. So, she came along and will be spending the next year here in Wessco.

"Do you want to build a snowman . . ."

And now, we're in the dining room of Prince Nicholas's private palace apartments, where he, Olivia and Prince Henry are having breakfast the day after we arrive. I stand by the door and the sound of Ellie's energetic singing voice floats into the room, making me suppress a persistent grin.

"She watched *Frozen* last night," Olivia explains, nibbling on a slice of dry toast. "She's always identified with Anna, which I guess makes me Elsa." Her brow furrows. "I don't really know if that's a good thing or not."

That's when "Anna" bursts through the door. My eyes scan the length of her—her blond hair pulled up into a ponytail, a shine to her lips, her tight, sweet body encased in a simple dark blue dress that wraps around her waist and ties at the side.

It'll be in my dreams tonight. Because with just one firm tug on the knot, the whole thing will unravel and slip off her. Leaving her completely bare beneath. No knickers allowed in my Ellie dreams.

"Good morning, everyone!" She kisses Olivia on the cheek, then sits at the table, and a server pours her tea. "How did we sleep last night? It was the best night of sleep I've ever had in my life!"

I bet it was. She must've been exhausted, after walking miles around the palace halls and grounds last night. Ellie hasn't been back here since the wedding, and they were so busy with preparations, she didn't have time to explore. Now she wants to go everywhere, see everything all at once. "Suck the Wessco lemon" is how she described it.

"These old mattresses are amazing," Ellie comments, while taking a bite out of her croissant. "They don't make them like that anymore."

There's a reckless, immature twinkle in Henry's eyes. No good can come of it.

"Do you want to try something really amazing?"

"Henry . . ." Nicholas warns.

"Sure!" Ellie agrees.

This is bad. I have a bad feeling about this.

The feeling grows when Nicholas seems to know what his brother is suggesting. "It wasn't safe when we were ten; it's probably more dangerous now. She could break her neck."

Henry shrugs. "Only if she falls." He holds his hand out to Ellie. "Come on, this way!"

They scramble from the room. And while every muscle in my body strains to follow, I have to wait for Nicholas.

"What's going on?" Olivia asks.

He puts his hand over his wife's. "It will be better if you don't watch."

Ellie's sharp but happy scream—from the main hallway—blasts into the room.

Fuck waiting. I sprint out of the room with Olivia and the Prince close behind.

We stop, horrified, at the bottom of the long, tall, curving double staircase. Ellie straddles the thick, dark wood railing at the top, facing forward, ready to launch.

"Oh my God!" Olivia yells.

Nicholas shakes his head. "I told you not to watch."

Ellie gives herself a push and faster than I can get to her—like she's coursing down a hill of ice—she's sliding. It's a fifteen-foot fall to the marble floor if she loses her balance. If her weight shifts just a tad to the right, she'll go over.

This is what a heart attack feels like.

Ellie flies off the bottom, landing solidly on her feet, like a feline. I put my hands on her arms and help her stand upright.

She's laughing. "That was . . . awesome!"

"I told you!" Henry grins proudly.

"What was awesome?" Lady Sarah Von Titebottum, Prince Henry's fiancée, asks as she walks into the foyer, up to Henry's side.

Henry puts his arm around her shoulders and kisses her quickly. "I was just showing Ellie the best ride in the palace."

"You should try it, Sarah," Ellie says.

"No." Henry frowns, petting Sarah's long, dark hair possessively. "No, she can't try it. Absolutely not."

Sarah peers up at him through her black-rimmed, round glasses. "Why can't I?"

"You could break your bloody n—"

He stops mid-sentence, understanding blooming. He snaps his fingers and points at Nicholas, then to his own head. "Ohhh . . . I get it now. You were right."

"I always am," Nicholas replies.

With a lifted chin and a lecturer's voice, Henry looks at Ellie. "I shouldn't have shown you that. And you shouldn't ever, ever do it again."

"But—" Ellie begins to argue.

"No, no, once is enough. You tempted death and came out the other side . . . Only fools push their luck. Don't be a fool." He tugs Sarah by the hand. "We have the balcony appearance soon; let's get up there. If we're late, Granny will give us all hell."

"I can't do it."

We wait in the large red and cream ballroom, adjacent to the main balcony on the palace's north side. Since all the key members of the royal family—the Queen, Prince Henry, Prince Nicholas and Princess Olivia—are now in residence, the PR office thought a photo op was in order. They're all to appear on the balcony, together, and wave to the enormous crowd that's gathered outside.

And it's the crowd that has Lady Sarah white as alabaster. Some might say she's a bit . . . shy.

Henry sits in a cushioned antique chair, reading the paper. "All right." He turns the page and the subject. "Do you want to go to the new Vin Diesel film at the cinema? The premiere's this evening and I was invited. It doesn't look half bad."

Lady Sarah folds her arms. "*All right?* That's all you have to say? This is one of your duties, Henry." Lady Sarah points to herself. "It will be one of my duties when we're married."

Henry folds his paper and stands. "We won't be married for four long months. And, today, you're not ready, and that's *all right.*"

Lady Sarah worries her lip. "What if I'm never ready?"

"Let's just take each day as it comes." Henry places his hands on her shoulders. "You've done so well with the engagement announcement, the interviews . . ."

"*One* interview at a time. Because I didn't know if I could face a group of journalists without hyperventilating or passing out."

The more panicked Sarah becomes, the calmer Henry gets—she has that effect on him.

"But you got through it. Every interview—and you were charming and perfect. So today, Granny, Nicholas, Olivia and I will be the ones paraded out like zoo animals. While you stay here . . . and keep Ellie company." When Henry glances at her, Ellie hops over.

"I'd appreciate that, Sarah. I'd hate to be here all alone. It'd be awkward."

Liar. She's comfortable in her lovely skin whether it's on her own or standing in front of a stadium's worth of people—it's just how she is. But it's good of her to try and help.

Lady Sarah gazes at Henry's shiny shoes, her face heartbroken. "Do you ever think . . . that perhaps you should be with—"

"Do *not* even think of finishing that fucking sentence," Henry warns.

"Why not?" She lifts her chin. "It's the truth."

"The truth?" Henry mocks. "The truth is I wouldn't even

be here if it weren't for you. I don't know where I'd be or what I'd be doing, but I know it wouldn't be pretty."

"He's right, you know, Sarah." Prince Nicholas steps over to them. "Before you, Henry was an unmitigated disaster. Reckless, spoiled, self-destructive—"

"Thank you, Nicholas," Henry says. "I think she gets the picture."

Nicholas smacks his brother on the back and grins cheekily. "Happy to help."

Henry slips his hands into his pockets, rocking on his heels, telling Sarah, "I could say the same thing, you know. You don't think I know you'd be better off with someone whose everyday life doesn't send you reeling into a panic attack?"

Sarah shakes her head. "No, that's not true. I could never be better off with anyone else. I would never want to be. You're mine, Henry, and I'm keeping you."

They'd be disgusting to watch if they weren't so damn sincere.

Sarah fidgets with the diamond engagement ring on her finger. "I'm just afraid that I'll humiliate myself. That I'll embarrass all of you."

And Prince Nicholas is back. "You still don't get it. There's nothing you could do—literally nothing—that Henry hasn't already done to embarrass us." He shrugs. "We're immortal; we're immune."

Henry looks at his brother. "You're enjoying this too much."

Nicholas's green eyes practically dance. "I am, I know. I should try and stop, but I just can't."

"Okay, look," Ellie says, moving aside the heavy crimson curtain and pointing out the window towards the balcony. "Do you see that potted plant in the corner, there? If you have to hurl, Sarah, do it there. Then, Liv will block you with her amazing, ever-expanding stomach—and no one will notice."

"Or, most likely," Olivia lifts the hem of her long, flowy

polka-dotted skirt and moves closer to Ellie and Sarah, "I'll be throwing up right along with you. Whoever called it morning sickness didn't know their ass from their elbow because it ravages me all day long. They'll probably call us the Puking Princesses in the press . . . but it's got a catchy ring to it, so it could be worse."

Sarah laughs along with them, looking less like the color of a dead oyster.

The Queen breezes into the room, wearing a beige skirt and matching jacket with a large ruby broach on the lapel. Her tall, blond personal secretary, Christopher, is behind her, clipboard in hand. And everything stops. The men in the room, myself included, bow and the ladies curtsy, as is required on the first occasion of the day when one encounters Her Majesty.

Ellie bends her knees and sinks down gracefully, lowering her head. *Good girl.* It upset her that she'd mucked up her first impression with Her Majesty at Nicholas and Olivia's wedding. Some of the staff still talk about it—the legend of the tiny blonde who tackled the Queen.

"Are we ready?" the Queen asks no one in particular.

Henry steps forward. "Your Majesty, Sarah is—"

"Going to try her best," Sarah finishes for him.

Henry gives her a questioning look, but Lady Sarah nods reassuringly. "I want to try. It will be all right."

"Of course it will be all right," the Queen agrees, as if by declaring it, circumstances wouldn't dare to contradict her. "There's no need to worry—no one will be looking at you. It will be as if the rest of us aren't even there. They'll all be examining Olivia's bump."

"The public interest is ferocious," Christopher explains. "There are office pools around the city, wagering how much weight Duchess Olivia has put on each week."

Olivia looks down at her growing belly. "Great."

"Pay no attention to that, my dear." The Queen moves in front of her, smiling with approval. "You look wonderful. Very healthy. I'm thrilled for you." She smiles at Nicholas too. "Both of you."

"Thank you, Queen Lenora." Olivia takes her husband's hand. "We couldn't be happier."

"Although," the Queen goes on, "your due date is terribly close to Henry and Sarah's wedding day. It's important to spread these events out, you know. To maximize the positive coverage."

Olivia rubs her stomach. "I'll do my best."

The Queen pats her forearm. "I know you will."

"And in the future," Nicholas adds, "we'll be sure to keep the marital relations on a schedule more to Your Majesty's liking."

He's being sarcastic. But either Queen Lenora doesn't pick up on it or she's giving it right back to him. Peas in a fucking pod, those two.

"That would be appreciated." She nods. "Now, shall we?"

The Queen takes a few steps towards the balcony, stops and turns around—noticing Ellie for the first time. One thin eyebrow rises as Her Majesty walks a circle around the lass, checking her out from all angles.

Ellie lifts her head. "I'm Ellie Hammond, Your Majesty. It's an honor to meet you again."

"Yes, I remember you. You're all grown up, aren't you? Very lovely."

"Thank you. Yes, I just graduated college—with my BA in psychology."

"How nice." Queen Lenora thinks for a moment before looking towards the balcony, then back to Ellie. "You may stand on the balcony beside your sister to greet the crowd with us. You are a relation by marriage, which endows you with certain privileges. We should remind everyone of that."

Nicholas's brow furrows.

And Ellie's eyes go wide. "Holy sh—"

But she catches herself.

"I mean . . . yes, Your Majesty." She curtsies again.

Once the Queen turns her back, Ellie's eyes flare and her jaw drops. She looks at me, giving me an excited two-thumbs-up, bouncing in her shoes.

I give her a smile and nod.

And then, they walk out onto the balcony. While I stay inside—watching—as Ellie takes her place alongside the royal family. Where she belongs.

The next day, Prince Nicholas and the Queen are in the drawing room, playing chess. I stand in the hallway, hands behind my back. The door is open just enough for me to hear their conversation, and while I don't tend to pay attention to chatter, the mention of one particular girl has me acting like a gossipy old biddy—hanging on every word.

"What are your plans for Eleanor?" the Queen asks.

"Eleanor who?" Prince Nicholas asks absently.

"Olivia's sister, of course."

There's a pause, and I picture him looking up from the board—with curious eyes.

"Her name's not Eleanor."

"No?" Her Majesty wonders. "Eloise? Elizabeth?"

"No. And no. Ellie is her full name. *Just* Ellie."

As far as I'm concerned it's perfect for her. A sweet, happy-sounding word. Made for whispering and worshiping.

The Queen does not agree.

"Hmm. How unfortunate."

There's a click of marble against wood, as one of them moves a piece on the board.

"In any case," Queen Lenora says, "what are your plans for *Ellie*?"

Nicholas sighs. "I don't have any. She's taking a gap year; she'll help Olivia when the babies arrive."

"Two nurses have already been employed and the Palace is interviewing nannies as we speak. How much help does Olivia think she'll need?"

It sounds like Nicholas takes a sip of something—the glass makes a chiming sound when it's set back on the table.

"Olivia doesn't want to hire any nannies."

There's a brief pause, and then one word comes from the Queen that says it all.

"*Nicholas.*"

"I know."

"The nanny is a child's first educator. The first level of instruction on who they are, their responsibilities, how they must conduct themselves."

"I'm keenly aware of that fact."

"Your children will be expected to attend public events at a young age. Running around like little heathens may be acceptable in America, but it certainly won't do here."

Nicholas laughs. "Let's get them born first—and we can worry about their heathenism later."

But the Queen is not amused. "You must speak with her, Nicholas."

"Olivia and I will work it out," the Prince replies firmly. "In our own time. You should focus more on the game in front of you. Check."

There's a weighted pause, accompanied by a quick sniff. "Back to . . . Ellie. There is a new mayor of Averdeen."

Averdeen is in the south, the second-largest city in Wessco.

"George Fulton. He's young, handsome, a mesmerizing speaker from what I'm told. He has a very bright future ahead of him. It would be helpful to have his support, to have him on our side in the years ahead. I was thinking of inviting him to the palace, for tea. And introducing him to Ellie."

There's a burning clench in my gut—tight and uncomfortable.

"It's not the sixteenth century, Grandmother," Nicholas replies dryly. "We don't form political alliances through marriage anymore. Check."

"Yes, thank you, Nicholas—I am aware of what year it is. You and your brother haven't robbed me of all my wits. *Yet.*"

"However, he's a fine young man from what I understand," the Queen continues. "Good family. Respectful. Successful. It wouldn't hurt to introduce them."

The mayor's mansion in Averdeen is practically a palace—beautiful and regal. The kind of place Ellie belongs, with servants to wait on her, a veritable army to protect her and a well-spoken man who would adore her. How could any man not?

Nicholas sighs. "Fine."

"Excellent."

There's the sound of more shuffling chess pieces, and several quick moves later the Queen declares triumphantly, "Checkmate."

There's a silent, shocked pause, and then Nicholas stutters, "How . . . did you do that?"

"You become too aggressive when victory is at hand—you lose sight of anything else. It makes you vulnerable." There's a rustling of fabric as the Queen rises to her feet. "Work on your long game, my boy."

CHAPTER 12

Ellie

One month later

There's a lot that's awesome about living in a palace. The rooms—one huge, historical, beautifully glamorous room after another, are better than any museum exhibit. The flowers—miles of blooming gardens in colors I didn't even know existed, and giant vases filled with fresh-cut blossoms of every kind, set in hallways and on table centerpieces. The servants—a tray of tea is waiting in my sitting room every morning when I wake up, my bed is made for me, my laundry cleaned and folded without my asking and my room is straightened twice a day.

This is definitely the life.

But, there's a downside too—not to living in the palace, but to being among the elite who *do* live in a palace:

"A stalker? What do you mean I have a stalker?" Livvy asks.

We're in Winston's office. He's the head of palace security, and from what I can gather, he's like Cher, he only has the one name.

We were called here—me, Olivia, Nicholas, Henry and Sarah, for a security briefing. Logan is here too, standing close to the wall, behind Winston's desk. And my heart does a flaily, off-beat pitter-pat. Because I haven't seen much of Logan lately. If I were the paranoid type, I'd think he was avoiding me.

"Stalker isn't exactly the term I'd use," Logan says. "More like . . . an obsessive, who doesn't like you very much."

Nicholas sits in the chair next to Olivia, holding her hand.

"But why me?" she asks.

"Royal pregnancies tend to get the mad ones all worked up," Winston, a gray-haired but solid looking man, replies.

"How many notes have been sent?" Nicholas asks.

"This is the third," Winston tells him.

"What post are they coming from?" my brother-in-law asks.

"Different every time—West Rothshire, Averdeen, Bailey Glen. No fingerprints, no DNA. Each note is threatening and focuses on Lady Olivia and the children."

"What do the notes say exactly?" I ask, feeling sick.

Logan answers before Winston can.

"The specifics don't matter. We're monitoring the situation. We notified you so you'll all be aware, but . . . don't worry. Nothing is going to come of this."

"Don't worry?" I parrot. "This is like some Game of Thrones bullshit right here—how the hell are we supposed to not worry?"

Henry explains.

"It's not as if we don't ever get hate mail. Or online threats—it happens all the time. I had five stalkers by the time I was sixteen."

Henry shrugs at my sister. "You're not really a royal until you have a stalker—welcome to the club, Olive."

Nope. That doesn't make me feel even a little bit better.

Despite the news about the psycho stalking Olivia and Nicholas, apparently, the show goes on. This is what it means to be a public figure, a royal. With Henry and Sarah's Big Fat Royal Wedding just a few months away, there have been a ton of brunches and lunches and other events all geared toward celebrating the upcoming event. Which is why, the next night, I'm in a limo feeling like a movie star wearing a gorgeous, shiny, silver cocktail dress, with Nicholas and Olivia looking every inch the fairytale royal couple. We're on our way to Starlight Hall, where Henry and Sarah's friends are throwing a party in their honor.

There are photographers and fans waiting outside, in roped off areas behind a wall of security. I shiver when I think the man obsessed with my sister could be in the crowd. But then the door opens, and Logan is holding out his hand to me.

When I touch him, when I slide my hand into his and feel his fingers wrap around mine, a mixture of thrilling electricity and warm comfort races through me. Touching him is my drug, my addiction—though I try not to be a freak out about it. And knowing he's here, watching over us like a powerful, invincible guardian angel, settles my nerves and, like always, makes me feel safe and cared for. Because Logan would never let anything bad happen to any of us.

And I believe with all my heart that there's nothing he can't do.

The Starlight Hall is aptly named. It's a beautiful room with murals of lush rolling landscapes on the walls and a domed ceiling of thousands of small white iron-framed panes of glass. The guests are similar to the ones at other events I've attended with Olivia—a mix of young, sophisticated blue-bloods and older aristocratic lords and ladies wearing clunky jewels and big intricate hats.

Olivia and I sit at a table, chatting with Simon Barrister and his wife, Franny. I've met the couple a few times over the years—through Simon's business with my father and because he's Nicholas's closest friend. Liv met Franny on her first trip to Wessco and she was a good friend to her, fierce and honest, when my sister really needed a friend. Franny is the most beautiful woman I've ever seen in my life, with perfect, porcelain skin, glittering onyx eyes and mahogany hair.

She's also one of the funniest. Because she's so direct. Practically brutal.

"Death." Franny tells my sister emphatically. "Childbirth is like death. You'll think that you're dying and the pain is so bloody awful, you'll wish you were already dead."

Simon and Franny have a three-year-old little boy, Jack, with sparkling blue eyes and red hair just like his dad.

"So you're saying it's . . . not so bad?" Liv jokes.

Franny laughs and Simon gazes at her like it's the most magical sound he's ever heard.

"I'm just trying to prepare you." Franny insists. "I wish someone had prepared me."

Then she looks over at her husband adoringly and strokes her hand down his arm.

"But, afterwards, when you haven't died and they place that little bundle in your arms, you feel reborn. Like you've just accomplished the most perfect, important, wondrous thing you'll ever do. And you want to do it again and again."

Later, the topic turns to nannies.

Liv holds Nicholas's hand in hers, toying with the wedding ring on his finger.

"I don't know about nannies—I don't think I want one."

"One?" Franny exclaims. "You're having twins, you need an army of them."

My sister tilts her head from side to side, unconvinced.

"Don't be an American Bitch, Olivia. Nannies are a part

of our culture—especially for you and Nicholas. I can't imagine how I would have turned out if I was left to be raised by my mother. It would have been a disaster."

Simon nods to Nicholas. "Hopefully, you'll have better luck at keeping them employed. Ours quit, often—dropped like flies."

Franny smirks, looking devilish and beautiful. "I can't imagine why."

And Simon grins, delighted by her. "It's because you threaten them, darling." He turns toward us. "When they take Jack to the park, Franny reminds them if anything should happen to him, she'll slit their throats when they return."

Franny shrugs adorably. "I'm just being honest. They should be forewarned."

Later, I'm on my own, sipping a vodka and cranberry, while my sister and Nicholas are on the dance floor, gazing into each other's eyes. Simon and Franny are there too, clasped together, rocking in time to the music. I see Henry at the other end of the room, talking animatedly, surrounded by a group of people who are listening and laughing in response to his every word. Sarah is a few feet away, chatting with her blond sister, Penelope. She an actress in LA, only visiting for a few days, and then she'll return for the wedding.

A new song comes from the band—an instrumental version of "Play That Song" by Train. I watch Henry leave his group and go over to Sarah—swooping her up, holding her around her hips, above him—both of them laughing and loving. I can't help but smile when he moves them onto the dance floor and slowly slides Sarah down his body until her feet touch the floor.

If I can find someone who looks at me half as adoringly as

Henry Pembrook looks at Sarah Von Titebottum, I'll be happy for the rest of my life.

I sigh. Because love is all around me. And I'm Ms. Lonely.

And then my gaze is moving . . . I don't have to scan the room to find Logan, I know just where he is—it's as if my brain has a 24/7 GPS on him.

But the crazy, awesome, amazing thing that gets my heart pounding so loud it drowns out the sound of the music? When I look at Logan St. James across the room, he's not searching the crowd for threats. He's not looking in front of him, so he's ready for whatever may come.

Instead, when I indulge in my daily Logan stare-fest . . . he's staring right back at me.

An hour later, I sip my second drink, and am on my way to an awesome buzz, while chatting with Sarah about her Wessco Blue Coats charity work. She started a reading program a few years ago, and though she won't travel with them, now that she and Henry are engaged, she still organizes book drives and fundraisers. It's surreal to think that she'll be a queen one day. Crazy. Because she's so . . . normal. But she's also gracious, intelligent and genuine, all the qualities a country would want in a queen.

She giggles, telling me a story about her friend Willard and his wife, Laura, when all of a sudden she stops mid-sentence. And the color drains from her face—even her lips turn to chalk.

I put my hand on her arm. "Sarah? Are you all right?"

She doesn't reply.

I'm not sure what to do. I know Sarah's painfully shy and I don't want to embarrass her. So I turn around and motion

Logan over. He comes immediately and focuses on Sarah as soon as he makes it to my side.

"Lady Sarah? What is it?" Logan follows her gaze to where it's frozen on the tall, gray-haired man across the room. "Him? The man by the door?"

Logan takes one step and Sarah grabs his arm in a panic. "Don't! Don't go near him. He's . . . dangerous."

I take Sarah's other hand in mine—it's ice cold. "It's all right. He can't hurt us. Logan would never let that happen. We're here with you. You're okay."

She doesn't blink, doesn't take her eyes off the man, and I'm not sure if she heard me.

"Get Henry," Logan tells me. "Now."

I give Sarah's hand a quick squeeze and leave her with Logan. Then I weave between guests until I find the blond prince talking with a small group of friends by the bar. I thread my arm through his, smile broadly and use an over-the-top Cockney accent when I say, "Beggin' yer pardon, gents. Have to steal the Guvnah, here, for a minute."

As I lead him away, Henry asks softly, "What's wrong?"

"It's Sarah. Come on."

We cross the room smooth and steady, so as not to draw too much attention to us. Henry smiles and nods along the way, but there's a tension to his features—until he reaches Sarah's side.

"The lord by the door," Logan tells him. "Do you know who he is?"

Henry turns to look and his whole body goes stiff. "St. James, take Lady Sarah in the back room."

"He's smaller than I remember," Sarah says, in a whispery, airy tone.

"Sarah . . ." Henry tries again.

"Do you think it's because the last time I saw him, I was a child?" she asks. "Or perhaps I've built him up in my mind to be a monster, when really, he's just a man. A terrible man."

Sarah covers her mouth with her hand. "My mother is here . . . Penny . . . they can't see him, they'll—"

Henry slides his hand into her hair and brings her face to his. "Go in the back with Logan and Ellie. I will take care of this."

Sarah blinks, breathing deeply. Then she shakes her head. "No. No, I can do it. I need to, I think. Just . . . stay with me?"

Henry brushes her hair back. "Always."

With a nod from Sarah, the future king and queen walk hand in hand toward the man by the door, with Logan and me following behind. They stop a few feet away. He bows to Henry and looks Sarah over in a detached, indifferent sort of way.

"Sarah. You're looking well."

Sarah squeezes Henry's hand so tight, her knuckles turn white.

"You were not invited here," she says, with slightly more strength in her voice.

The man adjusts his cuffs. "I'm the father of the bride. I need no invitation. I still have acquaintances in the city, how would it look if I didn't attend?"

Sarah's laugh is harsh. "Father? No." She shakes her head. "No, you lost that privilege the moment you put your hands on my mother. And on me."

My head whips around at the confession. *Oh, Sarah.* Logan's face is immobile and his attention on Sarah's father remains unflinching.

"You are nothing to me now," she tells him. "You are not even a shadow in the farthest corner of my mind. I have put you behind me. We all have. And that is where you will stay. I'd like you to leave now. You need to go."

The lord hesitates. "Now you see here—"

Henry steps forward, leaning in, his voice menacing and sharp—like a blade.

"Don't go—*run*. While you can. If you speak to the press or to anyone—if you fucking whisper her name—I will know. And I swear, on my mother, I will bury you alive beneath the palace so Sarah can walk on your grave every day of her life."

He stares back at Henry for a few tense beats. And then—without even glancing Sarah's way—he turns around and walks out.

"I think . . ." Sarah almost wheezes, her voice soft and gasping. "I think I'd like to go in the back now."

Henry nods and guides her away. Logan walks in front of them, clearing a path through the guests, and I follow. The room is small—a little sitting area with just one table and a pitcher of water, and a chaise lounge. A "fainting couch," they used to call it, and I wonder if this is the room they used to bring the ladies for smelling salts, when their corsets were too tight.

As soon as Logan closes the door behind us, Sarah covers her face with her hands and sobs into them. Henry sits on the lounge and pulls her down onto his lap, holding her close, rocking her in his arms. I pour a glass of water from a pitcher and set it within his reach.

"I don't even know why I'm crying," she stutters. "It's just . . . overwhelming."

Henry strokes her jaw and kisses her forehead, whispering, "You did so well, my love. So brave. I'm so proud of you."

"This is the last time, Henry." Sarah looks into his eyes. "This is the last time I will ever cry because of him."

Henry nods and tucks Sarah against him.

Logan and I discreetly slip out the door, and close it softly. I stay with him while he guards the door to make sure Henry and Sarah aren't disturbed. Because even though the party hasn't stopped, standing beside Logan is the only place I want to be.

CHAPTER 13

Ellie

Over the next two weeks, Queen Lenora takes me "under her wing." She says I have "potential" and she wants to see me reach it. I'm not going to lie, it's exciting to have her attention, to be in her presence, and I've started taking notes on my phone on the little gems of advice she gives out. She's so elegant, powerful—I've never met a woman with such a commanding attitude and self-possession. And she can compartmentalize like a boss. Queen, Grandmother, Diplomat, female version of General George fucking Patton.

I don't know what her idea of my potential is, but if she's thinking of me as the future in-palace psychologist, count me in. I could really sink my teeth into the issues of the royal family—relationship conflicts, political conflicts, passive-aggressive internal resentments galore. It'd be a dream job—better than Dr. Melfi analyzing mob boss Tony Soprano.

Nothing exemplifies this more than the recent afternoon we were having tea in the east garden—me, Queen Lenora, Livvy and a friend of the Queen's, Mayor George Fulton. We're surrounded by tulips and bluebells, at a white wicker table with butterflies flapping past, like a page straight out of the beginning of *Alice in Wonderland*.

"Tell us about the new transportation initiative you're working on, George," the Queen says.

George Fulton seems young to be a mayor—maybe twenty-seven or twenty-eight. He's cute in a tall, blond, lanky JFK sort of way. His accent is nice and he smiles easily.

He explains the cutting-edge technology they're installing on the Tube that would propel the trains with magnetic power instead of electricity.

"That's brilliant," the Queen comments. "Isn't that brilliant, Eleanor?"

I don't correct her about the name. I'm not an expert on etiquette, but I get the feeling if it's rude to correct your host, correcting the Queen of Wessco is a major freaking no-no.

So I nod and smile. "It's really interesting."

"We're planning on renaming the first renovated station the Margaret-Ana, after your mother, Your Majesty."

"That would be lovely," Queen Lenora says. "Mother was a forward thinker—ahead of her time." Then she turns to my sister, motioning to her big baby belly. "And speaking of names, Olivia, I've been meaning to discuss the children's names with you."

Liv sets her teacup down. "Their names?"

"Yes. Although we don't know if it will be two boys, two girls or one of each, it's crucial that they are well thought out. Symbolic and representative. Nicholas's grandfather's side of the family has been neglected in recent years, so you and he will be expected to make up for that now."

"Oh. Uh . . . well, what were you thinking?"

"Ernstwhile."

There's a pause in the air—even the bees stop buzzing—and the word just sort of hangs there, like a bad smell.

My sister's not sure if she heard right.

"Ersntwhile?"

She heard right.

"Yes. A fine, strong name, with history behind it. And for the boy—"

"Ernstwhile is the *girl's* name?" Liv asks, wide-eyed and horrified.

"Yes, of course. Nicholas's great-great-aunt Ernstwhile; she was a very resilient woman."

With a name like that, I think she'd have to be.

"And for the boy—Damien," the Queen declares.

Cue *The Omen* music.

Olivia's one, true fear. She watched the movie secretly when she was nine, after our parents went to bed one night, and it scarred her for life. I still remember her combing through my four-year-old hair, searching for a 6-6-6 tattoo—just to be safe.

"Nicholas and I were thinking of more . . . common names."

The Queen shakes her head. "If you had wanted to name your children Bob or Tina, you should have married a plumber. You married a prince. The grandson of a queen. That comes with obligations."

My sister is usually spirited, lively—the spunk is strong in our family. But the pregnancy, the move, the pressure of carrying the new generation of Pembrooks, the relentlessly dickish press who still haven't gotten over her bagging Wessco's favorite son—it's been hard on her. Sapped some of her toughness. So now, Olivia . . . wilts, before my eyes.

"I think I'm going to lie down for a little while."

"Do you want me to come with you?" I ask.

"No." Her voice is quivery. "I'm fine on my own."

Without another word, she waddles up the path to the palace.

And it takes only about ten minutes before my brother-in-law comes charging back down, his eyes bright green and shooting sparks.

George bows. "Your Highness."

"Fulton." Nicholas nods, while looking hard at his grandmother. "Ellie, George, would you excuse us, please?"

We start to get up, but the Queen lifts her hand.

"No. We're in the middle of tea. I'm sure anything you need to say can be said in front of them."

"All right, then—stop it."

The Queen looks taken aback.

"Stop what?"

"You know *what*. We're not chess pieces; stop trying to control the board."

Queen Lenora folds her hands. "Is this about Olivia?"

Nicholas raises his arm toward the palace. "She's in our room, crying her eyes out right now."

The Queen huffs. "Well, that's ridiculous. She's being entirely too sensitive."

Nicholas throws up his hands. "Of course she's sensitive—she's seven and a half months pregnant with twins! She's uncomfortable all the time. She can't sleep—she can barely breathe! The paparazzi are climbing the palace walls, the press is tearing her to pieces and there's not a damn thing I can do to stop it, and a psychopath is leaving sadistic notes addressed to her on our doorstep. And now *you*—"

The Queen's words crack the air like a whip. "Watch. Your. Tone."

My brother-in-law stops and takes a deep breath. He rubs his hand down his face and looks off toward the horizon. When his gaze turns back toward his grandmother he's calmer, but cold.

"I brought her here so she could rest in safety. So she could relax. If you make that impossible, I will take her someplace else. And if you wish to have a relationship with your great-grandchildren, then I'm telling you now, Grandmother—stop it." He pauses to let the words sink in, then adds, "We won't be having this conversation again. I hope that's clear to you."

The Queen doesn't respond with words, she just sort of breathes—like a dragon who wants to smoke a prince's ass. Nicholas waits for her to nod, and when she does, he bows to her and walks away.

"Never have children, Eleanor," she tells me stiffly. "Ungrateful to the core, the whole lot of them. Write that down."

Dutifully, I tap on my phone.

Then, George, Queen Lenora and I sit silently. And it's so *awkward*.

I try to fix it. "I think Ernstwhile's kind of cute. Maybe we can call her . . . Ernie."

Her Majesty doesn't crack a smile.

Then George makes a sound. "Ballsack."

My face scrunches and I turn to him. "Uh…gesundheit?"

He grins, gesturing to the Queen. "I was just agreeing with you, Your Majesty, names should be carefully considered. I have family on my father's side—the Ballsacks—who made the unfortunate decision to name their oldest Harry. They didn't think that one through at'all." He shakes his head. "Or say it out aloud."

I hear the name in my head and snort.

Then I add my two cents. "I went to school with a girl named Alotta. Alotta Bush. She was captain of the cheerleading squad. Strange but true."

George chuckles and while the Queen doesn't join our discussion, I see her lips twitch.

"The first girl my brother loved was named Constance Uma Natasha Theresa," George says. "Turned out to be a fitting acronym."

And I full-out laugh, "Oh my God."

The Queen sips her tea and resumes our regularly scheduled "non-cheeky" conversation.

"The National Museum has a new Monet exhibit opening

this evening, George. Will you be attending while you're in the city?"

George grins. "I had planned on it, Your Majesty, yes."

"You should bring Eleanor with you." She looks at me. "You haven't been to the museum, have you?"

"No, not yet."

Queen Lenora nods. "Then it's settled. You'll go together and have a wonderful evening."

George meets my eyes over his teacup and his cheeks turn pink.

Because he senses the same thing I do—we've just been royally set up.

Not cool, Lenora . . . not cool at all.

A little while later, I'm walking down the hall to Nicholas and Olivia's room, to check on my sister. And I see Logan at the opposite end of the hall. I didn't think he was working; I hadn't seen him yet today—and my body reacts the way it always does when he's close. My pulse picks up, my breath quickens, hope and attraction swirl in my stomach, making me feel slightly nauseous, but not in a bad way.

His strides seem purposeful, and they're aimed directly at me. We meet up outside Olivia's bedroom door. His eyes are dark, almost black with intensity, and I wonder what he's going to say.

"Are you going out with that guy tonight?"

Not exactly what I was hoping for.

But he's leaning down so close, my brain still short-circuits. "'That guy'?"

"George Fulton. The mayor."

"Uh . . . yeah. I met him today at tea. The Queen suggested we go . . . you know . . . as friends."

I don't know why I added the last part. It's not as if Logan cares. Only when he clenches his jaw and drags his gaze off to the side, it kind of feels like he might.

"There's no reason I shouldn't go, is there?" The hope in my voice is pathetically loud.

"No," he says softly. "No good reason at all."

For a moment, neither of us moves or blinks.

"Hey, Lo!" another security guard calls from down the hall. "Katy's tonight, yeah?"

Logan nods to him and my stomach withers.

"Katy's?" I ask.

"It's a pub. The upper-class tend to hang around at The Goat; me and the lads hang around Katy's."

"Oh. Well, I guess we both have plans tonight, then."

"So it seems." He touches my arm, squeezing just slightly, and that familiar, exhilarating zing races through me. He moves closer as he passes, almost whispering in my ear, "Have fun, Ellie."

Then I'm watching him walk away, his strides long, his back straight—and his ass . . . mouthwatering.

And just like that, the appeal of going to the museum tonight, of going anywhere where Logan isn't, fizzles like an Alka-Seltzer tablet.

The opening of the Monet exhibit at the Wessco National Museum is a big deal—think Met Gala, minus the space-age outfits. The stylist dressed me in a gorgeous royal-blue strapless cocktail dress, with silver platform heels. The short, snug cut hugs my small frame sexily, while the flare of the skirt makes it flirty, not trashy. With my blond hair down and wavy, I feel confident, beautiful—grown-up. A woman going to a sophisticated social event, not a girl going to a prom. That's new for me.

There's press at the entrance, photographers—they shout questions and jostle for prime positions, all of them wanting the scoop on the promising politician and the princess's sister. It'll make quite a headline. Ever since the wedding they've been interested in me—and my boobs—even though neither is really very substantial. It's been fun, a trip, a wild ride—sharing a little slice of Nicholas and Olivia's spotlight.

But in the bright, snapping flash of the cameras, I have an epiphany: this could be my life too.

I have connections now, to wealthy, known people—the kind who run cities, and make laws, and rule countries. That's what the Queen meant all this time about my potential—I have the potential to have my sister's life.

If I want it.

And that's always the question, isn't it? Where do you see yourself in five years? Who will you be? What do you want?

George Fulton is a dream date—he's fun, charming, smart and attentive. We discuss the artwork and Monet's life as we slowly wander from one painting to the next. I like George. He's easy to like. I like him the way I like Tommy Sullivan or Marty or Henry.

A friend-like.

But the intensity in his eyes doesn't make my insides melt. The sound of his voice doesn't make my knees go shaky. The smell of his skin doesn't make me think filthy, dirty, secret things.

There's only one guy who does that.

Only one who ever has.

So like every other date I've been on since that early

morning over five years ago, when I hopped down the steps into the coffee shop and came face to face with a breath-stealingly handsome bodyguard, wearing a killer tie—my thoughts drift away from my date . . . and straight back to Logan.

The painting in front of me is of a woman embroidering, with a little girl at her feet. On the wall beside it, there's a quote—I think it's from the Bible: *"When I was a child, I spoke and thought and reasoned as a child. But when I grew up, I put away childish things . . ."*

I glance down at my ankle, where my little lemon tattoo is etched. And I feel the hug of the knife holster that's wrapped around my thigh—that I wear like an engagement ring, religiously, every day.

It's almost fucking poetic.

I'm a fraud. I haven't been sucking the lemon of life—I've been hiding behind the rind. Playing it safe. Refusing to take the biggest chance of all.

I need to put away childish things. Like high school crushes and bodyguard dreams. I have to put them behind me.

But the only way I'll ever do that is by confronting them—*him*. By laying it on the line, putting my bare, beating heart on the table for him to see. And if he smashes it with a sledgehammer, well . . . this analogy took a dark turn…but the point is: Logan either wants me like I want him or he doesn't.

And it's time to find out. To hear it straight from the hung-like-a-horse's mouth. Then I can move forward. Move on, with or without him. But I really, really hope it's with him. That I'm not the only one feeling this.

George and I have wandered over to a small alcove in the corner, and I put my hand on his arm. "I have something to tell you."

He smiles. "I was just thinking the same thing."

And then we speak at the same time.

"I can't wait to see you again."

"I have to go."

When my words penetrate, he slides his hands into his pockets and his forehead crinkles. "Well ... this is uncomfortable."

"I'm sorry. You're a great guy—an amazing guy . . . but . . . there's someone else. There's been someone else for a long time and I have no idea how he feels about me, but I need to find out. I have to give it a chance."

George looks at me for a few moments. Then he leans over and kisses my cheek.

"Whoever he is, he's a lucky man."

I smile a thank-you.

"I'll have the car drop you wherever you want to go."

"No, that's okay. I've got it covered." I put my hand over his. "Good night, George."

George's two bodyguards, who shadowed us here tonight, stay with him while I walk out of the back door of the museum and hail a taxi. It's time to seize my destiny, take the bull by the horns, grab the lemon with both hands and suck until my cheeks hollow out . . . and maybe, if things go well, I'll get to swallow.

CHAPTER 14

Ellie

I've seen enough eighties movies—*Pretty in Pink, An Officer and a Gentleman, Sixteen Candles*—to know how this should go. I'm supposed to step out of the cab, walk through the double doors of the bar with the breeze blowing my hair back, search the room until our eyes meet, then—boom—the romantic background music surges. I raise my hand and beckon him close, then Logan kisses the hell out of me and/or swings me up and carries me away. Roll the credits.

Reality is . . . not an eighties movie.

So, when I get out of the cab, my dress snags on the door, tearing a little. I step in a puddle on my way across the street, soaking my foot and creating my very own squishy, farty background music.

Jesus Christ on a candy cane.

I keep my head down and avoid eye contact with a loud group of guys smoking outside the tavern next door—and then I cup my hands around my face and peek in the window of Katy's Pub.

There's a small front room with a wooden bar and a few round tables and chairs. I see a hallway in the back that a man in a flannel shirt walks in from, carrying a pool stick. Logan sits at the bar, his brown hair falling over his forehead, a tall glass of dark beer in front of him. A pretty bartender with shoulder-length auburn hair leans his way on her elbow. And then Logan chuckles at something she says—flashing straight, white teeth, his eyes crinkling with laughter.

Jealousy—green and ugly—steams from my ears. And though I recoil at the sight, it's as if my feet are cemented to the ground and my hands are super-glued to the glass.

And then it gets worse.

A little girl, with swinging blond pigtails and a pacifier in her mouth, comes rushing out from behind the bar. The female bartender chases after her, but Logan beats her to it, scooping the toddler up into his strong arms. He tilts his head, talking to the child and wagging his finger playfully, making her smile around her pacifier. And the woman comes around the bar and stands close to Logan, gazing up at them both.

They look like they're very well acquainted—wholesome and happy. They look like a family, and it feels like I'm bleeding inside.

Someone walks past me and into the bar, turning Logan's attention to the door.

To me.

His eyes widen when he spots me, then narrow. He mouths my name like he can't believe what he's seeing.

Shit.

I flee. Bolt. Haul ass.

Cowardly? Yes, but also instinctual. I scurry down the street like I'm seven-fucking-teen all over again. And thirty seconds later, his voice booms behind me.

"Ellie! Hey—hold up!"

I stop, 'cause there's no point in running. I take a breath and prepare to lie. Because I'm not ready to tell him yet. Not like this, out on the street, next to a Dumpster that smells like it's got a dead body rotting away inside. I spin around and plaster a big smile on my face.

"Logan! Hey! Fancy meeting you here—it's a small world after all."

He's staring at my dress, looking . . . flustered. Logan is never flustered. "What are you wearing?"

"A dress."

"You look . . . bloody fantastic."

Just as I'm about to smile, he snaps out of it. And Special Agent Pissed-Off is back in charge. "What the hell are you doing here, Ellie? You're supposed to be out with Fulton."

"My night with George ended early. I wasn't feeling it. So, I decided to go . . . sightseeing." I lift my hands to the . . . row of crumbling small houses with overgrown gardens and sinking roofs. I should've thought that one out better. "And I got lost. You know me . . . silly, flighty Ellie."

He braces his hands on his hips, frowning down at me in that sexy way of his. "You can't wander around—especially not here. Come on, I've got my car—I'll take you home."

A drunk on the corner slurs, "I'll take ye home, luv. Grab my cock tight and I'll show ye the way."

Logan and I yell at the same time.

"Piss off!"

"Screw you!"

Then we walk silently for a few moments, side by side, him gazing forward, me gazing at him, trying to work up the nerve to say all that I'd planned to a few minutes ago.

Instead, other words tear out of me. "Is she yours?"

Logan's brows draw together.

"The little girl," I clarify, feeling an ownership over him I know I have no right to. "Is she yours?"

"No."

And everything inside me loosens with relief.

"No, she's Kathleen's girl—the bartender. It's her husband's family's pub. Connor—I went through training with him—he's still enlisted; he's deployed right now. I check in on them when I'm around."

Oh. A friend's wife and little girl. That's better. It's *great*.

"That's nice of you."

We reach the parking lot behind the bar and Logan guides me to a clean gray Nissan Altima. He opens the door for me. Then he walks around, starts the car and pulls out of the parking lot.

"Do you live near here?" I ask, because I only just realized I don't know the answer.

"No. My place is outside the city—about twenty minutes away."

"Oh."

We're quiet for a few moments.

Until Logan asks, "Do you want to see where I live?"

For a second, I have no words. He may as well have asked me if I wanted to see heaven. Or Disneyland, or a really sexy Mars.

"Yeah! I'd love to. Let's do it."

We pull up to the curb of a large fenced lot at the end of a quiet street. The moonlight shines down on a two-story brick house, with a wide wraparound porch and a white, three-person porch swing. A single light is on above it. And on one side there's a round room with a pointed roof, like a tower on a castle. There's a short driveway, just dirt, with construction materials, ladder and buckets stacked neatly beside it.

I stand outside the car, staring. Amazed.

"Whoa."

And Logan's watching me. Watching my face, my every reaction.

"When did you buy this?" I ask.

"A few years back. My dad left me some money when he passed—turned out to be legally earned, which was surprising."

"Your father died in prison?" Logan had told me some things about his father when we chatted during my study breaks, while I was pulling an all-nighter at the NYU library and he was on duty. "I'm sorry."

"Don't be. Wasn't much of a loss. Most helpful thing the bastard ever did for me was die." He shrugs. "Anyway, remember when I went to Wessco for that one week?"

I do. I remember it felt like a month.

"Took care of the paperwork then, his burial. And one afternoon it was sunny and I was just driving around, clearing my head, nowhere to go . . . so I took out a coin and started flipping it for directions."

I laugh. "My GPS! You got that from me."

His eyes drift over my face. "Yeah, I did."

Hot little bursts go off inside me—excitement, pride—a thrilling sense that Logan was thinking about me even when he was so far away.

"And it led me here. It was for sale as-is, not even half finished when I first came across it—just the foundation and the ground floor. But it was a good foundation—solid. Something I could build on. Something that would last."

He gazes up at the house, and I examine his profile. That strong, straight jaw, the full, lush curve of his mouth as he speaks in that accent I adore.

"I hired a builder to finish the job, put a roof on her, used the original plans—they came with the house. And I had a groundskeeper maintaining the property while we were in New York, making sure the squatters stayed out and the vermin didn't move in. But since we've been home, I've been working on the inside. Finishing it—making it livable."

I look up at the house—it's sturdy, secure, and the land around it is quiet and serene. When it's done, it'll be a warm place . . . a safe, happy, wonderful place to come back to at the end of every day.

A home.

And it's like a sinkhole opens beneath my feet and I'm falling.

"Are you staying in Wessco? When we all go home to New York, after the babies are born, are you . . . not coming with us?"

He squints for a moment, like he doesn't understand the question. Then shakes his head, "Of course I'm coming back with you. You're . . . I mean, my job with the prince," he looks into my eyes, "it means everything to me."

Logan lifts his hand toward his home. "This'll be for later, a place to eventually settle. Or maybe it'll be an investment."

And my feet are back on solid ground again.

"Do you want to see the inside?"

I nod so hard I bounce. "Yes, I'd love to."

We walk up the path together, side by side. Logan puts his large hand on my lower back, and my skin tingles, burns. "Careful, there's some debris—don't want you to fall."

But he'd catch me if I did.

The inside of Logan's house looks Victorian in style—a large staircase with a thick square railing in the foyer, an open layout with big rooms, high ceilings, wood floors that have been sanded but not yet lacquered. Logan reaches up and tugs on a cord, lighting the bare bulb that hangs from a long wire where, one day, a chandelier will be. The walls are unfinished, open, exposing the solid wood beams, brick, and electrical wires.

With hushed footsteps, because it feels strangely like walking somewhere sacred, I follow Logan from room to room. In what will be the living room, there's only a mattress on the floor, covered by a clean sheet and folded blanket. That's where Logan sleeps—where he lays his head and body every night. Maybe his *bare* body.

It calls to me—makes me want to lie down on it, press

my naked skin against the same fabric his has touched and roll around, bathing my body in his scent.

And I don't care how crazy it sounds.

Despite the lack of appliances—there are just empty spaces and protruding wires where the stove and refrigerator will be—the kitchen is inviting. Muted, gray marble countertops, cherry cabinets, a tiled backsplash of one-inch white and clear glass squares. There's a window above the stainless-steel sink, with a view of the backyard that would make even doing the dishes something to look forward to.

"You need curtains," I say.

"I don't have walls."

I laugh. "Curtains make a house a home, Logan. They're the eyebrows of a house. Have you ever seen how freaky someone looks with no eyebrows? You don't want to do that to this place—all the other houses will make fun of it."

And he laughs—a deep, rich rumble in his chest that I want to feel against my cheek.

His fingertips slide up my arm. "Come on, the best part's upstairs. I want to show you."

Logan takes a flashlight from the counter to light our way up the stairs, down the hall into the rounded tower room. It's what will one day be the master bedroom. It's enormous, as big as our whole apartment above the coffee shop in New York.

But that's not the best part.

The best part is the ceiling. It's a skylight—all of it—displaying the dark expanse of night and hundreds of twinkling stars, like the heavens are the ceiling.

"There are shades built into the glass," Logan explains. "They'll close with the push of a button, so I don't end up sunburned in my sleep."

"Logan . . ." I gasp. "It's *magical.*"

He's standing close to me, his arm just a breath's away from mine. His grin is easy and relaxed. "I'm glad you like it, Ellie."

My voice becomes breathless, words slipping from my lips without a worry or thought. "Just when I think you can't amaze me more, you show me this."

He turns to face me, his chin dipping. "I amaze you?"

"All the time. You always have."

And here in this dim room, with the light aimed downward, it feels secret and safe. Charming and perfect. Another world—another dimension, where nothing and no one else exists. Just Logan and me, together, in this moment, beneath the stars.

"Logan?"

"Yeah."

"Do you . . . do you ever think of me?"

He doesn't blink or turn away. His dark eyes shine in the shadows, holding my gaze.

"Do I . . .?"

The shrill sound of his phone ringing stops his words. Logan slips the phone from his pocket and puts it to his ear.

"Yeah?" His forehead creases and he covers his other ear with his hand, trying to hear. "What? Where are you? All right, all right—I'm coming now."

He punches the disconnect button.

"We have to go."

We drive in silence, Logan's whole demeanor changed with that call. He looks at the road with a do-not-fuck-with-me expression and a death grip on the steering wheel. His shoulders are tense and his forearms are corded. As we drive, I notice that the scenery around us changes. The suburban homes fade into run-down buildings with graffiti, barbed-wire gated lots, abandoned houses and storefronts with black iron bars on every window.

We pull down a dark street and park at the curb in front

of a ramshackle house. Logan reaches under his seat and takes out a small, black handgun. It's mini, kind of cute, as far as guns go—if you can look past the whole capable-of-blowing-brains-out thing. He lifts my hand and wraps it around the butt of the gun.

"Tell me the rules," he says.

Immediately, I know what he's referring to. A few weeks after Logan showed me how to throw a punch and strapped a knife to my ankle, he took me to a gun range. So I'd know how to use a weapon if I ever needed to, without shooting myself in the process. There were rules he made me repeat back to him more than once:

"Don't put my finger on the trigger unless I'm going to pull it. Don't point at anyone unless I plan to shoot them. Don't shoot anyone unless I want to kill them."

"Good." He nods.

"You stay in the car with the doors locked. If someone tries to break the window to get in, don't wait, don't warn, you point and you pull the trigger—and you keep pulling until it stops firing. Do you hear me, Ellie?"

I nod, looking across the street and out the window. Then I whisper, "Logan, are we in the taint?"

The corners of his mouth quirk. "Yeah we are. If I'd had a choice I wouldn't have brought you here, but I couldn't leave you alone at the house."

A crash and yells come from inside the house.

"I have to go in." He looks me in the eyes. "Stay in the fucking car, Ellie. Yeah?"

"Yeah, I will."

And he's gone. Charging up the steps, through the front door.

Silence closes in tight around me. It's eerie—no cars are honking, no one out walking and talking, there's not even a dog barking. Those are the sounds of a city, the sounds of life. The absence of those sounds means life has moved away or is too afraid to come out. In either case, it's not a place you want to be.

The screen door of the house bursts open—snapping back with a bang and falling off its hinges. Logan stands on the front steps and literally throws a guy down onto the pavement. He lands hard but gets to his feet quickly, gripping a long butcher knife in his hand. Logan shakes his head and goes after him. My heart crawls into my throat when the guy swings the knife at Logan's stomach, but he jumps back, grabs the guy's arm and twists his hand back at an unnatural angle. The guy drops the knife and falls to his knees, screaming.

Logan drags him up and slams him face first on the hood of the car.

"That's enough, Logan. That's enough." A woman comes out of the house—older, short, with more gray than black in her long, dark hair. Behind her a few more people spill out, but there's one girl in particular who catches my attention.

She's thin, maybe in her thirties, with the same dark hair, but her face . . . she looks strikingly like Logan.

And that's when I know—these people are Logan's family. The one he never talks about. The guy still pinned to the hood of the car looks like Logan too—probably a cousin, maybe a brother.

Logan kicks away the knife on the ground, then takes his phone out of his back pocket.

"What are you doing?" the younger woman asks. They all stand around him, just outside the car.

"I'm callin' the cops to come get him."

"You can't do that," the older woman says. "He's already out on bail—they'll lock him up for good."

"Who gives a fuck?"

The woman jabs her finger at her chest. "*I* give a fuck! He's my son."

Logan points at the house. "He went after his cousin with a knife~"

The younger woman moves in then. "You've been gone too long, Logan. Ian's the best earner we have."

There are rumbles of agreement from the crowd.

"What the hell are me and Mum supposed to do if he's locked up?"

"Get a job, for Christ's sake! An honest one. Go to school, make a life for yourself!"

"This is our life!"

Logan shakes his head, looking disgusted.

And his sister sneers.

"You think you're so high and mighty? Saint fucking Logan, rubbing arses with the royals. Well fuck you—you're no better than the rest of us."

"Oh yeah, I am," Logan swears.

And she slaps him, hard and loud and right across the face. I see his head snap to the side. My mind goes blank. White, with righteous fucking rage.

When the bitch goes to slap Logan again, I climb out of the car, point the gun to the sky and pull the motherfucking trigger.

BOOM!

For a little gun, it's got one hell of a blast.

I have their attention now. And the rules go right out the window.

I point the gun at Logan's sister. "You call him for help, he drops everything and comes here, then you fucking slap him? I. Don't. Think. So."

They don't get to treat him like this. Not while I'm here.

"Ellie . . ." Logan says sharply.

"You will not hit him again. *Ever* again! Got that?"

"Ellie," Logan says, softer—because I'm screaming now. And my hand is shaking just a little.

"I want you to apologize to him—right fucking now."

She clenches her jaw shut and murders me with her eyes.

I lower my arm, aiming at her foot. And I'll do it, I swear—it won't kill her but I bet it'll hurt like a bitch.

"And make me believe you really mean it or you lose a motherfucking toe."

"Ellie!" Logan barks.

But I ignore him.

The douchebag brother laughs and the mother seems interested in personally ripping my head off just as soon as she possibly can. But my gaze stays pinned to the sister.

Slowly, she turns to Logan, her voice id a little less hateful. "I'm sorry, Logan."

With that, my anger dissipates. Leaving me drained . . . and sad. Because it shouldn't have been like this for him—he should've been loved and supported and admired. Not this—not these awful people.

I shake my head at them.

"You don't deserve him. Not any of you."

And I lower the gun.

"Can we please go home now, Logan?"

He backs off from where he still has his brother pinned to the car, and his brother slinks into the house, cradling his hand. Then Logan turns toward his mother, quiet and firm. "Don't call me again, Mum. I won't come."

When we're both in the car, I hand him the gun, barrel down. He takes it without comment, clicks the safety and puts it back under the seat.

"Are you okay?" I ask.

"I'm good."

Logan pulls away from the curb, down the street and onto the highway. Away from this sad place.

I breathe out a long breath. "So that's your family."

"That's them."

I watch him as he drives. Because I can; because I like being this close to him. "You should be so proud."

"Proud?" he scoffs, disbelieving.

"Proud that you are who you are. Of what you've made of yourself . . . if that's where you started out."

"Thanks, Ellie," he says a minute later. "And, I'm grateful for what you said back there. You, sticking up for me like that . . . it was cute."

"Cute?" I say it like it's a dirty word.

"Very cute?" Logan tries.

"I was hardcore. I was scary—threatening. *Grrrr.*"

And the bastard laughs at me. If he didn't look so gorgeous doing it, I'd be pissed. Except not really.

"You promised you'd stay in the car," he reminds me.

"Yeah, well since me getting out of the car prevented you from getting slapped again," I put an accent on my words, imitating Logan. "I'm gonna put this one down as a win."

He laughs again.

After flashing his ID at the security checkpoint, Logan drives through the rear gate of the palace. He pulls around to the west-side courtyard, to the exterior entrance of Nicholas and Olivia's apartments. There's a uniformed guard outside the door, but we're parked far enough away, under a tree, that it feels private. Intimate. The air in the car is close and I inhale his scent—wood, and crisp air and man. I watch the pulse in his neck thrum, slow and steady, and I want to lean over and kiss him softly right in that spot.

"I have to tell you something, Logan."

"It's late, Elle. You should—"

"But—"

"You should go in, now."

The words come easier than I thought they would. Simpler. Because they're just the truth.

"I like you, Logan."

His eyes slide closed, but he's not shocked. "Ellie—"

"I always have. It's always been you. *Always*."

"You don't want to—"

"And more than that . . ."

"Don't—"

"I want you. I want you so much, some nights it feels like my skin is on fire. My bones burn with it."

"Fucking hell—"

"I can't think, I can't eat . . . When I sleep, you're all I see." I rub my neck, and everything inside is needy and tight. "When I touch myself . . ."

"Christ, Ellie—" He sounds like he's drowning.

" . . . you're all I feel. You, Logan."

And then he stops talking. But I know he hears me.

"Do you feel it too? Do you want me, Logan?"

His throat ripples when he swallows and I want to lick him there. Suck on him with my lips—right in the center of his throat, that thick, manly Adam's apple.

When he speaks, his teeth are gritted.

"No, I don't want that. That's . . . not what this is for me."

His words are crushing. My ribs squeeze and my chest tightens too hard to take a breath. And it hurts . . . it hurts so much. I'd hoped and I wanted . . . and I thought I sensed something from Logan tonight, something I felt, that he felt for me . . .

But then, I don't just draw a breath—I gasp.

Because I'm looking at him—really looking at him—maybe for the very first time. With new, open eyes. I'm looking into the face of the man who showed me how to spot a liar.

His expression is blank and rigid. His brown eyes are flat. Dull.

"Their look will seem unnatural . . . off," he'd said. *"Any time someone has to put effort into their words, you can bet what they're saying is a steaming crock of shit,"* he'd told me.

And slowly, I smile.

"You're lying."

CHAPTER 15

Logan

She's trying to kill me.

With her words, her looks, her innocent touches—brushes of her arm and hip as she passes me—and with the tiny, tempting outfit she's wearing today. Bloody Christ—my head's a mess. Has been a mess since she smiled at me in the car last night, a smile that was confident and sure, and then she called me a liar. Even when I denied it, Ellie wasn't having it.

"You are so lying right now—holy shit!"

My voice is cold, harsh—for both our sakes.

"Ellie, I don't feel—"

"Do you like me, Logan?"

I swallow hard. "No."

"That's a lie too!" she squeaks, completely delighted. "It's like a superpower! Is this how it feels to be you?"

She goes to touch my chest and I jump back in the small confines of the vehicle as if her hand is on fire. Bad move.

"Are you scared, Logan?"

Fucking terrified. Of a girl. A small, seductive, beautiful girl who owns me. Who could wreck me.

"I don't get scared."

"I scare you. This thing between us—"

"There's nothing between us."

She waves her hand dismissively. "Now you're really fucking lying. Of course there's something between us." She changes tactics, leaning closer and lowering her voice. "Do you want to kiss me, Logan?"

And just the words, the mere suggestion, brings such scorching images to my brain—of the magnificence of what kissing sweet Ellie could be— sucking lips, nipping teeth and wet, searching tongues.

I sound like a man being tortured, because I am—in the truest sense of the word.

"No."

Ellie wets her lips and her chest heaves, bringing her breasts nearer—I would just have to lower my head just an inch to taste her.

"Liar," she whispers.

And I growl. "Ellie . . . fuck."

"Yeah, we'll get to that." She smiles, so damn cute I want to kiss the hell out of her, then turn her over my knee, lift her dress and kiss her there too.

I press my fists into my eyes, trying to force the thoughts out. Trying to regain control of the situation. Then I point towards the palace.

"Ellie . . . go to your room."

She laughs in my face.

"Do you want to come with me?"

Christ help me. "No."

By some miracle, she steps out of the car, but before closing the door she leaves me with one giddy parting reply.

"That's a lie too."

After Ellie was safely inside the palace, I went back to my house—and found no peace.

Because she was there—I could smell her, as if she'd infused the walls with her orange-blossom scent—I could see her in every room, as if she'd left her spirit behind. I heard her words in my head—the most perfect words she'd ever spoken to me.

I want you so much . . .

When I touch myself . . .

And then I did the same. Fisted my cock and imagined it was her delicate hand on my hot flesh. I thrashed on that mattress, jerked myself off hard and fast, and when I came, my back arched and it was her name that tore from me, echoed off my empty walls.

Still, I couldn't sleep. I jerked off again, slower the second time, drawing it out, picturing her lithe body skimming down my torso—all the things she'd do to me if I let her. All the things she'd let me do to her. Eagerly. Filthy, dark, offensive things— the places I'd fuck her, all the spots she'd let me come—in her mouth, on her tits, in her hair, on her arse, buried deep in her tight, hot pussy.

It's as though the floodgates have opened and all the desire I've had for her, all the thoughts I've kept at bay, are now raging free and out of control. It would be so easy to give in. So bloody fantastic—I ache with how good it would be.

But then I ache for a different reason.

Because I would lose everything. All that I've built through the years—my duty, my noble calling. It's all I have. The lads on the team, the royals—they're the only family I've got. And if I cross that line with Ellie, set one toe over it, it's gone. Up in smoke. No going back, not after that.

Fuck me.

I thought about calling in sick for my shift, just to avoid the unholy temptation. But it seemed cowardly.

So now I'm here, in the late afternoon, at The Horny Goat, watching Ellie sing and dance onstage—doing everything she can to break my resistance. To tempt me, tease me, bloody mesmerize me.

And it's working.

I should have been a fucking coward.

"Ellie's really belting them out, huh?" Tommy says.

That she is. She's been through a whole playlist of

meaningful songs at the karaoke machine: "What About Love," "Angel of the Morning," "Silver Springs."

I'm not an idiot. I know what she's saying. Saying to me.

And now she starts a new song—"Piece of My Heart". I watch her—can't watch anything else. She really gets into it—closing her eyes and crooning like Janis fucking Joplin. Tugging her hair, shaking her arse.

And I'm hard. As stone.

All for Ellie.

She circles her pelvis, and I imagine gripping those slim hips and holding on while she rides me. Grinds her pussy right on my cock.

"Almost like she's singing to someone." Tommy nudges me.

I grunt.

And the tosser's eyes practically twinkle. "Something you want to share with the class, Lo?"

"Nope."

Take it . . ." Ellie sings, like a needy plea.

And fuck me, the thought of her begging sweetly, on her back looking up at me with those big blue eyes, drives me straight to the edge. I actually take a step towards the bloody stage—I want to grab her, toss her over my shoulder and carry her cute arse out of there like a caveman. Like she belongs to me.

Instead I turn my back on the stage, eyeing the shiny bottles behind the bar. I've never been much of a drinker—but I could use about a dozen shots right now.

"I'm gonna take off. Check on things at that palace, then punch out early," I tell Tommy.

And I don't even feel bad about doing it. Because self-preservations kicks cowardice right in the nuts.

Tommy nods, slow and knowing. "You do that. I'm on Ellie detail for the rest of the night. Run, Forrest, run."

I flip him off.

And walk out the door, Ellie's voice chasing after me as I go.

I leave the car with Tommy at the pub and hoof it back to the palace. To take my mind off Ellie, I check on the progress of the investigation into Lady Olivia and Prince Nicholas's stalker. We still haven't caught the fucker. It's like he's a ghost, dropping his nasty notes here and there, then evaporating into the ether. And it's escalating. The last one came with photographs. Shots of Olivia in the palace gardens, picnicking with her friend, Simon Barrister's wife, Lady Francis, and their three-year-old boy, Jack.

The photos weren't taken with a long-range lens—which means the bastard was on the palace grounds. And that's why he sent them: because he wanted us to know he'd slipped inside. That he's getting closer. We pumped up security around the perimeter, but it still eats at me. A niggling worry. As Winston said, obsessed nutters come with the territory. They're common for people as well known and powerful as the royal family—for every thousand subjects who adore them, there's one who wants to see them burn like witches.

But this one's uncomfortably persistent. And bold. Gives me a bad vibe, and I make a note to follow up directly with Winston tomorrow.

Around dinnertime, I drive away from the palace, but I don't go home. I can't—too many temptations there. The priests always said masturbation could turn us blind—and I like my eyesight the way it is.

Instead, I go to Katy's Pub. I'm greeted when I enter, loosen my tie, grab a pint at the bar and head into the back room to shoot some pool. The room is windowless and dim. A top-notch place to block things from the outside, to pass the time so fast you don't realize it's passing. A space to forget . . . and hide.

I play a few rounds with the regulars. Then shoot on my own, focusing on the simple act of knocking a billiard ball into the cup. It's relaxing, centering—sort of like my idea of yoga. A bit later, after I land the eight ball in the corner pocket, I straighten up and stretch my neck. I head back out to the bar for another pint.

But when I step into the outer room, I see the other patrons and Kathleen holding her daughter in her arms, gathered around the bar. Silent and serious—they're all focusing on the small television screen mounted to the wall in the corner.

The cue in my hand drops to the floor with a crack.

For a moment I can't move, can't think—can't even fucking breathe.

Because of the image on that screen.

The image of black smoke pouring out the windows of The Horny Goat. Of red-hot flames licking the wind and climbing up the walls. Encompassing it—devouring it—obliterating it from the world. Like it had never been there at all.

"Poor Macalister," someone whispers. "Hope he's all right."

And it's as if my soul turns to dust, like I'm a statue of sand disintegrating in the breeze. Because I know—I know it in my *bones*—Ellie is in there.

In a heartbeat, I'm out the door. Running, muscles stretching and screaming—sprinting faster than I ever have. It's like I'm running for my life . . . because I am.

I pump my arms and turn the corner, my shoes slapping the pavement. But it feels like I'm moving through liquid. Through gelatin. Like that nightmare everyone has—I push and lean and strain and reach but I can't go fast enough.

Move, move, fucking move!

Her face flashes in my mind. Smiling. Laughing. Her dancing eyes and flittering gait.

I promised her. I swore I would keep her safe. Be her guard, her wall, so she could fly free. And I will not fucking fail her.

I can smell the smoke now. If I look up I'll see the gray mist and the ash in the air, but I won't look. My eyes are on the ground, one foot in front of the next. Bringing me closer. To her.

I'm coming. Almost there.

There's no space for sorrow or recriminations. Not yet.

I see it in my mind—how it'll go. How I'll get to her, find her, wrap her in my arms—shield her from the heat. Carry her away from the flames. I'll be there for her.

I'll save her.

Because that's who I am. That's what I do. Why I'm here— the only reason I'm here.

And she belongs to me.

Ellie is mine to have and to hold. To save and keep. Forever and always.

At last, I see The Goat ahead of me. My eyes find the door, engulfed in flames. I push and leap and shove my way through the crowd. The heat is on my face, blistering against my skin— suffocating and scorching. My lungs strangle on the acrid smoke that coats the air. But it doesn't matter—she's in there, so that's where I need to be.

I clear the crush of people and am just a few steps from the door . . . when I'm hit, tackled from behind and knocked to the ground.

My heart roars, even if my throat can't. I push and fight, ready to destroy whatever's stopping me.

But another weight piles on, and another, pinning me down.

Later, I learn it's the firefighters, gripping me, holding on. They're shouting in my ear, but I don't hear them. I only see the door.

And then I'm shouting. Screaming my lungs raw.

For her. Calling her name.

But I can't hear my own voice.

It's drowned out, overwhelmed by the inferno and the deafening sound of cracking, splintering wood. As the roof of The Horny Goat caves in, sending an eruption of deep-red sparks into the air like a volcano.

And anything or anyone—is consumed by flames.

CHAPTER 16

Logan

"Where were you?"

Olivia, the Duchess of Fairstone, my Lady and so much more, looks down at me with an ashen face, her eyes like two sapphires left out in the rain—hard and wet.

I don't know if she means to sound accusatory but I hear the blame in her voice.

Where were you? Why weren't you there? What were you doing, you worthless cunt?

Or maybe . . . maybe it's just my own guilt, burning me alive.

I open my mouth to answer, but the words are lodged behind the lump in my throat. I have to clear it to speak.

"She was with Tommy. I left off early."

We're in the front parlor of Guthrie House. Where we've gathered—me, Olivia, Nicholas, Henry and Sarah—to wait for news while the fire marshals investigate and Winston and his army of Dark Suits chase down leads. Evan Macalister, the owner of The Goat, is in the hospital being treated for smoke inhalation. Tommy's one floor below him, unconscious with a concussion from a falling beam. Both of them were dragged from the burning building; the other patrons all made it out on their own.

Except Ellie.

"Why?" Olivia asks.

I rub my eyes. "I don't . . ." *Hold it together. Don't you fucking break, now.* "I can't remember . . ."

When I was seventeen, in the military, I watched a man die next to me. Sniper shot came in, got him right in the heart. I remember seeing the hole in his jacket, the fabric singed around the edges. He didn't bleed, not right away. And he didn't fall at first; he stayed standing.

A dead man standing—looking down at the wound in his chest. Waiting to bleed out.

That's what I am now.

The pain's there—an exquisite, intense agony, the likes of which I have never known. But I don't feel it. I can sense it, like it's shored up on the other side of a wall, a rising tide.

And I have to hold it off, just a little while longer.

I can't think of her. Can't picture her face in my mind. Those haunting blue eyes—the most beautiful I've ever seen. The sound of her voice . . . her laugh. One wrong word, one thought, and the anguish will surge over the wall. It'll send me to my knees and I don't think . . . I don't see how I'll ever get up again.

Prince Nicholas walks into the room, his expression drawn and hesitant. Olivia sees it too.

"What is it?" She glances past his shoulder, waiting to see if anyone follows behind him. "They told you something—I can see it in your face. What is it, Nicholas?" Olivia's voice sharpens, bordering on hysterical, and the sound echoes in my veins. "You have to tell me!"

He clasps her arm, pets her hair, then rests his palm on her round stomach. "Easy, love. Be easy."

Then Nicholas looks down at the ground. "They found something—a phone—that they think may be Ellie's. They want to see if you can identify it."

Olivia nods, and her husband gestures to the man just

outside the door. He steps in and presents a clear plastic bag. Inside is a charred, mangled heap. When he turns it over, I see traces of the pale pink phone case—and remnants of what used to be an *E* etched in rhinestones.

She bought it on a Sunday, at one of the craft tables at the spring market, just a few days after we'd arrived in Wessco. It had seemed like a common, trinkety thing to me—but to Ellie it was a treasure. Handmade—not another exactly like it in the world, she'd said. And she'd smiled so brightly. So happy.

Olivia stares at it for a few moments, and then her face just crumples. She covers her mouth with her hands and this sound comes from her throat—an awful, wheezing, keening sound, the kind a mother dog makes when her pups are taken away.

Nicholas pulls her into his arms but she struggles, grasping and twisting at the front of his shirt with her fingers, tears streaming down her face. "I would know, Nicholas. Listen to me. I would feel it. I would know if she was . . ."

Olivia squeezes her eyes closed and shakes her head.

And my wall weakens and cracks.

"I don't believe it." She whispers, like a prayer or a wish. "I don't believe it."

"Shhh . . ." Nicholas holds her face, wipes her tears with his thumb and swears, "Then I won't believe it either."

They stare into each other's eyes for a moment, then Olivia takes a deep sniffling breath and tries to pull herself together. She rubs at her damp cheeks with one hand and cradles her stomach with the other. "My dad . . . I have to call him. I don't want him to hear about it on the news . . ."

Henry rises, but keeps hold of Lady Sarah's hand where she's seated near the fireplace. "Granny has already spoken to your father. The jet's on its way to New York. To bring him here."

The reality of what that means presses down on me—that the Queen herself doesn't believe this will eventually end with a phone call from Ellie, explaining a silly misunderstanding or mishap.

She thinks it will end some other way. A way that requires Eric Hammond be here with his one remaining daughter, because she'll need him. They'll need each other.

And the tide inches higher.

I stand up, quick and stiff, a good tin soldier.

"I have to go."

I have to get out of here.

"I'll head to the hospital, see if Tommy's awake yet. I'll report in if he says anything."

As soon as Prince Nicholas gives me the nod, I'm out the door. Almost running.

But in the hall, a voice stops me.

"Logan."

It's Lady Sarah. Slowly, I turn to face her, and her big brown eyes swim with compassion.

"I just . . . I just want you to know, whatever happens, this isn't your fault. I know it can feel like it," she shakes her head, "but it isn't."

She's a kind lass. Gentle. It radiates from her and wraps around anyone nearby like a comforting blanket. It's why Henry is so protective of her—why he guards her so carefully.

But at this moment, that comfort could shatter me.

So, without a word, I nod, my face tight, hard—probably angry. Then I bow quickly and leave as fast as I can.

It's in the sterile, cold hospital, outside Tommy's room, that I realize I look like day-old dog shit. My cheek and hands are scraped bloody from the firefighters pressing me to the gravel. I'm covered in black soot and smell like a fire pit from hell. Strangers pass, raking their gazes over me with varying expressions of shock, concern and wariness.

And I don't fucking care. I feel nothing.

Somewhere a television's on—a news update on the fire, but I block it out.

My eyes meet the kelly-green orbs of Janey Sullivan, Tommy's fiery redheaded older sister, through the window into his hospital room. Without hesitating, Janey comes out and hugs me with long, strong arms.

"Hey, Lo."

I lift my chin at the view of Tommy, closed-eyed and unnaturally still in the hospital bed.

"How's he doin'?"

Janey cocks her head. "My brother's always been hard-headed—this time it came in handy. The doctor says he'll be fine . . ."

Beside Tommy's bed Mr. and Mrs. Sullivan chat away, having a whole conversation with their son without him saying a word.

". . . as long as my mum and da don't talk him to death."

I snort, but just can't muster a smile. Then Janey's face sobers and her voice goes softer. "They're sayin' Duchess Olivia's sister is missin'."

Heat rises in my throat, sealing it up.

I nod.

"Tommy said you two were close?"

A thousand memories rush me at once and I shut my eyes to focus on pushing them back.

"Oh, Logan. I'm so sorry."

I shake my head, rub my stinging eyes. "They're still looking. Nothing's official."

Janey puts her hand on my shoulder, squeezing. "If you need anything, we're here. You're family too. Most times we like you even better than Tommy."

That gets a tug from my lips—not quite a grin, but a bit better than a frown. It's like Tommy said—Janey's badass.

I point towards the door to his room. "Can I see him?"

"Yeah, sure. Come on—I'll drag my parents downstairs to get something to eat so you can sit with him a bit. It'll give his ears a rest."

After the Sullivans leave the room, I sit in the chair next to Tommy, taking note of his terrible coloring—he's almost as white as the sheets. There's a bandage on the back of his head, covering a couple dozen staples and stitches they said he needed to close the gash.

I look at him hard, willing my best friend to open his eyes.

"I'm losin' my fuckin' mind, here, Tommy. I need you to wake up, mate." I lean forward, bracing my elbows on my knees. "I need you to tell me you know where she is. You dropped her off somewhere . . . or she left with some bloke—I don't even care. As long as she's safe. As long as she's all right."

There's a pressure on the back of my eyes that blurs my vision. And my voice cracks. "I really fuckin' need you to do that. You're the only hope I've got left."

Regret is the sharpest blade. It stabs, slices off pieces of my insides as I drive home. It's dark now and raining. A cold, steady downpour that saturates your clothes and numbs your skin.

But I'm not numb.

Because my wall has crumbled. Collapsed in great, heaving chunks. I don't fight the pain when it rushes me, consumes me. Sitting in the car in the driveway outside my house, I sink down into it, letting it swallow me whole, a thousand blades cutting at once.

When I step out, the rain soaks me. I brace my hand on the roof of the car, groaning from the grief. The agony.

I like your tie.

She was here. She was beautiful and precious and so very alive.

One of these days . . . I'm going to save you back.

And I had all those years, all those moments when I knew—I *knew* what I felt for her, but I was just too fucking cautious to do something about it.

I like you, Logan.

Men aren't supposed to be hesitant. Not men like me. And not about women like her. But she wasn't just some girl. She never was. Not from the very first moment.

Do you ever think of me?

Her words drift through my mind, repeating in whispers like a taunting song, as I walk up the path to the front steps of my house.

It's always been you. Always.

So many mistakes and missed chances.

Do you feel it too?

And I'm sorry. I'm so fucking sorry.

I sink down to my knees, because my legs refuse to hold me up anymore. My back bows and I lift my face to the sky, letting the rain mix with the regret and sorrow leaking from my eyes.

Because I should have told her. I should have given her those words. And I would give anything . . . I would die for the chance to go back and tell her now. Tell her the truth.

I feel it too, Ellie. I always have.

CHAPTER 17

Ellie

A white light.

That's the first thing I see when I open my eyes. I squint, then blink against its brightness. And the sound of rushing water fills my ears. No . . . rain. Raindrops on rooftops. Where are the whiskers on kittens?

If I'm quoting *The Sound of Music*, I must really be out of it—one too many glasses of liquid courage at The Goat. It takes me a minute to wake up and realize where I am. Whose rooftop the rain is pounding on and how the heck I got here.

And then I remember. I cover my eyes with my hand, to shield them from the porch light.

At Logan's house.

I wanted to see him, talk to him, and I knew I couldn't do that under Tommy's watchful gaze. So, a few hours after Logan ghosted me I shimmied out the bathroom window—and thank God, God made me like I am, because it was a tight freaking fit. Then I skipped down the alley, caught a cab and came here.

But, of course—no Logan. And like an idiot, I'd left my phone on the bar, and I couldn't even call him. His porch swing was looking mighty comfy and I can now confirm it's amazeballs.

I sit up, rubbing my eyes and patting down my hair, in case I've got swing head. And then a noise comes from over by the steps. It's a whimper—like the sound a wounded animal would make. Slowly, I walk over, and that's when I see him.

Logan, out in the rain, kneeling on the walkway, bent over and pressing his forehead to the last step, groaning words I can't understand. And I know something awful has happened.

"Logan?"

He rears up, leaning back on his calves, his eyes wide and wilder than I've ever seen them. Out of control. There's a cut on his cheek and black streaks on his clothes. His mouth opens, then closes. He stares at me, breathing hard.

"Are you . . . are you real?"

He reaches out his hand toward me. And it's trembling.

I come down the steps, into the rain. "Of course I'm real, Logan."

I feel tears rise in my eyes. Because he looks so devastated. "Are you all right? Are you hurt? What happened?"

I kneel down on the sopping path, take his hand and press it against my cheek. As soon as he touches me, he inhales a deep, scraping breath and yanks me forward. Clasping me to him. He engulfs me in his arms. Wholly. Fully. Like he's trying to absorb me. Squeezing so tight, it's hard to breathe.

And it's not just his hand that's trembling—he's shaking everywhere.

So I stroke his back and whisper, "It's okay—it's okay, Logan. I'm here. *Shhh* . . . I've got you."

A shudder tears through him. "You weren't there." He moans against my neck. "You weren't there and no one knew . . . I couldn't find you."

He pulls back, his face heartbroken and furious at the same time. He holds me by the arms, shaking me a little. "Don't do that again. Ever!"

"Okay," I soothe, stroking his face, feeling his rain-soaked cheeks. "I won't ever do it again. You'll always be able to find me—I promise."

"Always," he insists, dragging me against him, pressing our bodies together.

"Yes. Always."

I barely get the words out before Logan's mouth is on mine. Covering me, possessing me. His hands slide into my hair, gripping almost desperately, holding me immobile as he presses his lips hard against mine, moving and tasting, groaning roughly.

It's not a gentle, joyful kiss—it's urgent and demanding. Frantic. Whatever happened, it's shaken him badly, and I know deep down, he needs this—to just feel me. Logan's lips move to the corner of my mouth, across my cheek and my closed eyes, trailing harsh kisses up to my forehead. He lingers there, his lips shuddering against my skin.

And the rain comes down on us, weighting our clothes, dripping from the ends of our hair, running in rivulets over our hands. Logan presses his forehead against mine but keeps his eyes closed tight.

His words sound lifeless. Vacant. "There was a fire at The Goat. It's gone." He flinches then. "I thought you were gone too. I thought I'd lost you."

My hands are on his neck, his jaw, pulling him closer. And the horror of what he's saying seeps into my mind and swells in my throat. "Oh no! I'm so sorry, Logan. I came here, for you—I didn't know. You didn't lose me. I'm here—I'm right here."

And I'm crying now, tears streaming down my face with the rain.

Logan opens his beautiful brown eyes and sparkling drops of water cling to his heavy, dark lashes. And his voice is clear and deliberate.

"I think of you."

My breath catches. "Really?"

He brushes my wet hair back, his forehead still pressed to mine.

"All the time."

Logan strokes my cheek. "I like you."

And then I'm crying and smiling at the same time. "I was hoping you'd say that."

He sweeps his thumb across my lower lip and looks into my eyes.

"I feel it too, lovely Ellie."

"You do?"

He nods against me. "I always have. From the very first."

My fingers skim the stubble on his jaw, his chin, his neck—I just want to touch him.

And then, so gently, Logan takes my face in his hands and kisses me. It's a whisper of a touch, at first, a soft stroke of his lips. I reach up and press against him, kissing him back, feeling his soft, full lips, taking as much as giving, savoring every sensation. I sigh when I feel the stroke of his tongue. Slow and exploring but firm against mine. It slides and flicks and my lower stomach clenches in the most desperate, amazing way. Logan covers my upper lip with his, sucking just a bit; then, with a breath that feels regretful, he pulls away.

His hands move down my hair to my shoulders, over my arms, like he can't stop touching me.

"We have to go to the palace. Your sister . . ."

"Oh God—Liv—she must be a mess."

I'm the worst sister ever. Someone needs to get me a plaque.

"I have to call her."

Logan stands us up, keeping hold of my hand, and walks me through the rain to his car in the muddy driveway. "I have my phone—call her on the way."

Logan

There are tears and hugs when I get Ellie back to the palace. We go to the yellow drawing room, because the Queen herself would like to see that Ellie is alive and well. Henry and Sarah are there too, as are Prince Nicholas and Olivia. She tackles Ellie the moment we walk in, sobbing, and then Ellie is sobbing too. And apologizing. The way she tells the story, she left The Goat to get some air, wandered off and got lost. Then, hours later, she just happened to pass me on the street as I was walking home from the hospital.

It's the biggest crock of shit I've ever heard. It doesn't even make sense . . . but they're all just so happy, so relieved that she's safe, that no one questions it.

I don't confirm what she says; I remain straight-faced, neutral. I won't lie to Nicholas—ever. But there are conversations he and I need to have—and I have no intention of having them tonight.

I have other plans—important plans—and I'm eager to get started.

Those plans are delayed when the Queen calls for wine. Albert, the butler, hands me a glass and I take it, join in the toast and drink—but it's completely bizarre. To be drinking with this group of important people, like I'm one of them. Like I belong inside this room instead of outside, watching the door.

I push the thought aside when Ellie uses Olivia's phone to call their father in New York. And there are more tears. Eric Hammond will be coming to visit in a few days' time, but now that Ellie has been found, the mad, grieving rush to get to Olivia can be delayed.

After Ellie hangs up and the wineglasses are cleared, it seems like it's time to disperse. Call it a night. Put my plans into motion.

But they're delayed again.

And this, I'm not expecting. I don't think anyone is.

"We want to get married," Henry tells the Queen, holding Sarah's hand.

Her Majesty nods. "Yes, of course you do. But the time will go by quickly and there is still much to be done."

"No." The light-haired prince shakes his head. "We want to get married tonight. Here. Now."

I don't think I've ever seen the Queen look confused. I don't think anyone has ever seen the Queen look confused—or surprised. But at the moment she's both.

"What?"

"Ellie could have died," Henry tells her in a clear, calm voice. He's thought this out; he knows what he wants and he's determined to have it. "Mum and Dad died young, and the only consolation was that they had all those years together. Life is so short, Granny. It goes by so quick." Henry pulls Sarah closer against his side. "I don't want to spend another minute longer than I have to, not being Sarah's husband."

"No one else has to know; it'll just be for us. We'll keep it a secret," Lady Sarah offers. "We'll still have the service and the reception as planned, of course."

"That day will be difficult for her," Henry explains. "She'll do it because we both understand it's expected, but there will be worry and anxiety. But here, now, there will only be joy."

Sarah leans forward, eyes begging. "Please understand, Your Majesty."

And Henry adds, "Please say yes."

She could easily say no. Members of the royal family need the Queen's permission to marry—it's a law. An outdated one, but still a law.

But I've long suspected something about the Queen that no one else has: despite her steely exterior, Her Majesty, Queen

Lenora of Wessco has a soft spot. It may be small and rarely used . . . but the bugger's there.

Her eyes shift between Henry and Sarah, then she puts her hand on each of their shoulders. "It's a fine idea. Very romantic."

She folds her hands in front of her. "Christopher, tell the Archbishop his services are needed now. Do not tell him why."

Christopher bows and scurries off to fulfill the command. The Queen returns her gaze to Lady Sarah. "You will need a dress."

"I have one," she assures the Queen excitedly. "It's white and perfect, and I've never worn it."

"Good." Queen Lenora nods. "Then all you need is a tiara. Thankfully, I have a few to spare."

And that is how the future King and Queen of Wessco end up getting married in a garden, beneath a clear sky after a rainstorm, at midnight.

Old Fergus, the cantankerous butler who first served Nicholas and now Henry at Guthrie House, plays the violin as Lady Sarah walks herself down the lantern-lit aisle. She's holding a bouquet of wildflowers, her hair long and straight, her dress sleeveless and snug at the waist, with a short, puffy skirt.

She looks like a fairy princess who wandered out of a storybook.

And when the Archbishop asks her if she takes Henry as her husband, the answer sounds as if it bursts straight from her heart.

"I do . . . I do!"

Later, when Henry is told he may kiss his bride, and he takes her in his arms . . . I've never seen such a look on a man's face. Like he's holding a star, a cherished, sacred piece of heaven, in his very hands.

It's in that moment that I realize and accept—when Ellie walks down the aisle to me, and we say our vows and trade our rings . . . I'll be looking at her in exactly the same way.

I look at her that way now.

And I can't remember what I was thinking—why I've been fighting so hard against it—why I thought any of it mattered. But that stops now. Tonight.

Ellie stands across the garden, watching the ceremony. I drift over to position myself behind her, close enough to breathe her in, but not so close that it seems out of place.

"I'm coming to your room tonight." I whisper against her hair. "If you don't want that to happen, tell me now. I can't stop myself, Ellie."

"I don't want you to stop, Logan. Not ever." She turns around, her blue eyes shining in the moonlight. "Come to my room . . . I'll be waiting."

CHAPTER 18

Ellie

light the candles in my room, the long ivory sticks on the fireplace mantel, the subtly scented votives on the nightstands beside the bed. I dim the overhead lights and brush my teeth, running my hands through my hair, tucking one side behind my ear. I'd already switched my damp blue dress for a short nude pleated chiffon gown when we got back to the palace, and I strip that off, leaving me in only a champagne silk slip, bare and braless beneath it.

Then I stare at my reflection in the mirror. My eyes are bright and my cheeks are flushed pink. Every nerve ending is awake and alive.

I tremble.

Not with nervousness—I could never be nervous with Logan; he's too careful, too caring with me. No, I quake with *anticipation*. Desire. It floats through me like smoke, swirling inside, making my blood rush and my heart gallop.

I've wanted this so much, wished for it for so long.

And now it's happening.

Please, God, please let him hurry.

After Henry and Sarah's beautiful ceremony, we toasted with Champagne. Unlike when we first came back to the palace, Logan didn't join in. He stood by the door, waiting and watching.

Olivia stuck to my side like glue, touching my arm and holding my hand, as though she needed to reassure herself I was really there. I don't blame her; I feel awful about scaring her and my dad—everyone—so terribly.

But at the same time, the urgent need to break away from the group and go to my room to await Logan wound up inside me like an overtightened spring, until it was ready to pop. Finally, *finally,* we said our good-nights. Logan was gone then, not by the door, as if he'd faded into the shadows—no one but me noticed. I walked with Nicholas and Olivia back to their apartments, and I hugged my tired sister and relieved brother-in-law one more time before making it up to the refuge of my room.

And now I wait. I've already waited so long, you'd think I'd be used to it. But this need inside me is stronger than it's ever been—sharper, more acute, feverish. Every muscle in my body is strung tight and my skin is tender, overly sensitive. My teeth grind and the blood rushes in my ears, echoing *soon. Soon, soon, he'll be here soon.*

There's a knock on my door.

And my soul comes alive.

I fly to the door and pull it open.

Before I can take a breath or see him clearly, Logan steps into the room, grabs me, pulls me against his chest, kicks the door closed with a bang—then spins us around and presses me up against the wall. And he's kissing me, we're kissing each other, desperate and grasping and wild.

He tastes like red wine—like oak and blackberries—and the drag of his mouth across mine makes me drunk. Logan lifts me like I'm weightless and his fingers curl around my thighs, palms sliding. He moves his hips between my legs, pinning me against the wall with his pelvis, rubbing against me, making me wet and throbbing.

Somebody once told me a slow-burning fire is the hottest—and it must be true. Because Logan and I are a fucking inferno.

He yanks at the strap of my slip and it snaps. He pulls the fabric down, exposing my breast, and his mouth devours me. He suckles and licks urgently, opening his mouth wider to envelop nearly my whole breast. It's as if he wants to taste every inch of my skin all at once.

Then he's back to my mouth, kissing me long and deep and wet, until I'm shaking in his arms.

"I'll give it to you sweet, Ellie." He breathes hard. "I swear I'll make it so fucking sweet you'll ache . . . but now I just . . . I need . . ."

My hips rotate and I'm rubbing myself up and down on the rock-hard length of his cock beneath his pants. My head thrashes.

"I know. I know, Logan. Just take . . . please."

I need him inside, now. Pressing into me—surging deep.

I squeeze his shoulders, grasping at the starched cotton of his shirt. It feels manly under my palms. His scent, his rough groans, the tight hold of his large hands, the stab of his hot tongue—everything about Logan is strong and hard, domineering, and so deliciously male.

He moves one hand from my leg and I feel him tearing at his pants, the scratch of his belt against my thigh as he frees himself.

Yes, yes . . .

My desires clash—because I want to see him, see everything. I want to hold him in my hand, stroke and hear him moan. But that yearning evaporates when I feel the touch of hot, silken flesh against my pussy. I feel the girth of his cock against my soft opening. I'm slick, slippery for him, but he's so big he has to push through my tight muscles. I lift my knees, stretching my joints to open for him.

He moves forward slowly, steady and unyielding. And then Logan is sliding inside me. More, more, impossibly long. There's a dull pinch as I stretch around him, until all of him is buried within me—deep and full—and the wisps of his pubic hair tickle the sensitive skin of my inner thigh.

I feel so full. Complete. I squeeze my muscles, clench my pussy hard, just to feel more of him deep inside.

His arms are contracted tight under my hands, his breath brushes against my lips, his forehead rests against mine. "Ellie," he whispers, and no word has ever sounded sweeter. "Ellie . . . Ellie . . ."

We kiss roughly, my tongue invades his mouth, caressing his, licking, searching inside. Logan's hips pull back and his cock retreats just a little, then he slides back and we moan together, greedy for the friction. He pulls back again, farther, withholding more—then thrusts back in, harder. Needier.

And the rhythm starts. Over and over—it's the wet slide of his cock, my clasping squeeze, and the deep, harsh push back in.

This. Always this. It's more than I dreamed, better than I fantasized. It's hard and full and perfect, and I want to live the rest of my life with Logan's hard cock buried deep inside me.

Pounding against me. Ramming inside me.

Fucking me, needing me, loving me.

His hips circle between my legs, twisting as he thrusts, dragging his pelvis across my clit. And the pressure, the tension, builds between my legs.

"Don't stop! Oh God, more . . . more . . . fuck . . ."

I bite his neck, his earlobe—for real, not gently. Because it's so good. Because if I don't, I'll scream the goddamn house down.

I feel his big hand covers my breast, squeezing greedily and the snap of his hips between my legs. It's wild and untamed and raw. We move, grinding against each other without thought. It looks like fucking, sounds like rutting . . . and feels like making love.

I hold his face in my hands, kiss his open mouth and inhale the air he expels.

"Come inside me, Logan."

My plea tears a moan out of him, low and long against my shoulder. And he thrusts so hard, my head jerks back.

"Come inside me." I slide my hands through his hair, down his spine, under his shirt, caressing his skin, clinging to him. "I want to feel it, feel you." And then I'm chanting, "Please . . . please . . . please . . . please."

I'm right there, right on the edge—I tilt my hips, reaching for it, pleasure coiling inside me, waiting to explode.

"Please . . . please . . . *Logan* . . ."

I sob his name and my head tilts back against the wall as stars burst behind my eyelids. My legs lock around him and I squeeze everywhere, coming and coming . . .

Logan thrusts one last time and groans against my skin. I feel the pulse of his cock, the hot rush of his fluid and, fuck, it makes me come even harder.

What seems like minutes later, after the grip of our orgasm settles into loose-limbed intoxication, Logan lifts his head and guides my lips to his. And his kiss is tender and soft. His knuckles brush my cheeks, caressing like I'm fragile. Made of glass. Gently, he slips out of me and lowers my legs to the floor.

I lean against Logan, on knees of Jell-O. Without a word, I unbutton his shirt and tug it from his shoulders, because I want to see him. I want to enjoy every inch of this beautiful body. And he wants me to. It's there in the smile that plays at his lips and his heavy-lidded, amused expression.

Once I free him from his clothes, he lowers to his knees. Then kisses between my breasts, his lips trailing down my stomach, he slides the ruined slip to the floor.

Flashing a sexy grin, he stands, scoops me up and carries me to the bed.

And there, like he promised . . . Logan gives it to me sweet.

Logan

After our exertions against the wall, and the bed, Ellie and I enjoy a shower together.

She's very pretty when she's wet.

I wash her hair, rubbing her scalp, tilting her head back when I rinse the shampoo out, making her lovely little tits rise for my waiting mouth. And those beauties taste every bit as good as they look.

Then I wash Ellie everywhere else, massaging her legs and back to keep her from aching tomorrow. I kiss her forehead and she smiles up at me like I'm the king of the fucking world. Her world.

After wanting her so much, for so long, the feeling of her tight, slick and hot around me made me lose my mind for a bit. But in the soothing calm of the shower, I ask her what I should've asked her about before—birth control. It's my job to keep her safe in every way, and I feel like a tool for being so reckless.

Ellie tells me she's been on the pill for years. *Girl issues*, she says with unusual shyness.

And I'm glad for it—I like feeling her bare, nothing between us, flesh to flesh.

But if there was a baby, I would take care of her, give her whatever she needed, *be* all she needs.

There are abilities I'm skilled at—familiar with—fighting and fucking, battles and weapons, sensing danger, and knowing how to keep those in my care safe from harm.

But love . . . I'm ignorant of it. The word has never passed my lips, and the feeling is as alien to me as the sentiment.

What I do know, what I'm sure of, is that I would die for Ellie. Kill for her, live for her. The vow echoes through me with every beat of my heart. She is the most important person in my life. She has been from the beginning, and she always will be. There will never be another.

I don't know if I'll be any fucking good at love. I'm not quite sure how it's done. But, for her, I'll learn.

And I'll do my damnedest to get it right.

We lie on our sides, resting but not spent, stroking each other, looking and smiling at one another. I used to think the phrase "gazing into each other's eyes" was stupid. Fake. I mean, really, what man does shit like that?

Now, apparently . . . I fucking do.

And it's not dumb or artificial at all. Because Ellie is mesmerizing. Her face is an ever-changing landscape of expressions—each one cuter, sexier, more enchanting than the next. Her lips have a thousand different smiles and her eyes sparkle and swirl with infinite shades of blue.

If I manage to die gazing at Ellie Hammond's face, I'll go out a happy man.

"When did you know? The very first time?" she asks.

I play with a strand of her hair, brushing its softness against my fingertip, thinking way back.

"It was at the museum, I think. When you flirted with me . . . and I thought, if this girl were a bit older, I'd be all over her."

Her eyebrows reach for the sky. "That long? I never knew."

"I didn't want you to know. I thought if I pushed it away, ignored it for long enough, it'd go away." I kiss her nose and whisper like a conspirator. "It didn't."

"Did you know that I liked you?"

I chuckle. "Aye. Your poker face is . . . well, you don't have one."

Ellie sticks out her tongue—that cute fucking tongue that's teased me for years. I chase after her mouth and I suck on her tongue. Then, laughing, I tell her, "I figured it was just a crush. A girlish fancy that would fade when you grew up."

Ellie leans over me and pecks my nose, whispering in the same secret tone, "It didn't."

"No." I run my hand through the damp strands of her hair. Relieved—relieved and . . . wonderfully content.

"So what happens now?" she asks.

I open my mouth to answer, but there's a knock at the door.

"Ellie? It's me—are you up?"

It's Olivia. The doorknob jiggles and thank fuck it's locked, or this would've been an eye-opening visit for the Duchess. I tilt my head towards the toilet and Ellie nods.

A minute later, I hear their conversation through the door.

"Is everything okay?" Ellie asks.

"Yeah, I just . . . wanted to see you. I had a bad dream. Nicholas is still sleeping; I didn't want to wake him—I had to make sure you're okay."

I hear Ellie move out into the hall, probably to embrace her sister. "I'm okay, Livvy. I'm so, so sorry. I won't scare you like that again, I swear."

"I love you, Ellie."

"I love you too."

Then her tone turns teasing. "And I love both of you . . . even if you turn out to be little Ernie and an Omen demon baby."

Together, the sisters laugh.

When I hear Ellie close her bedroom door, I step back into the room.

"Coast is clear." She grins, turning the lock.

I fall onto the bed, moving to the center, pushing a hand through my hair and watching her walk towards me.

"I have to tell Prince Nicholas," I say on an exhale.

Ellie slips her robe off and joins me on the bed.

Pouting.

"You don't want me to tell him?" I ask her.

She crawls over to me, her lovely arse in the air. "No, I understand the situation."

The thing is, I don't think she does. She doesn't realize the complications—or the changes that will have to be made.

But I'm at peace with it—I'll do what has to be done, as long as I get to keep her.

Ellie trails feather-light kisses along my ribs. "Maybe you could wait on thinking about Nicholas . . . until your semen isn't still trickling out of my body?"

I choke out a laugh. "Fuck . . . the things that come out of your mouth."

She smiles slyly and kisses lower—down my abdomen, around my navel—and lower still.

"At this moment, I want you to focus more on the things going *in* my mouth."

And my breath whistles out of me.

"Oh yeah?" I ask, sliding my hand into her hair, gripping a bit, just tight enough for her to feel it.

"Yeah." Ellie licks her lips. "Big, hard things."

I scrape my teeth on my lower lip, the way I want to scratch them across her soft, pale breast—the way I will, very soon.

"That so?"

She nods. And then my girl grins—cheekily.

My lips drag up into the smile I know she loves.

"Do you ever think about this?" she asks. "Me doing this to you?"

"It's my very favorite thing to think on."

I grasp my stiffening flesh and trace her lips with the head of my cock. "This, love? Is this what you want?"

And she fucking moans. I feel it against me. "Yeah, I want that, so much." She keeps her eyes on mine, slipping her little tongue out—licking, just the tip. I stroke my cock back and forth against her tongue, grazing it with every pass, wet and warm.

It feels incredible and looks fantastic.

Then fantastic gets even better.

Ellie opens that pink, pouty mouth—but holds back. She lines us up and waits . . . waits for me to lead. And I'm all about indulging her. So I push the wide crown past the ring of her lips and thrust up into the wet sucking heat of her mouth.

And her eyes roll closed, like it's the most blissful thing she's ever tasted.

Christ, she's trying to kill me.

When the tip of my cock nudges the narrow back of her throat, I stop. And Ellie eagerly takes over. Wrapping her hand around the thick shaft, working her mouth up and down, taking as much of my length into the heaven of her mouth as she can.

It's wet and sloppy and beautiful.

She worships my cock. Devours it. Hums around it, kisses and adores it with every suck and slide of her perfect lips.

Ellie licks my cock like a lollipop and palms my balls like they're her new favorite toy. My heart races and my breath pounds.

"Ellie . . ." I warn, because I feel the tightening, the liquid heat racing and ready to surge. "Ellie . . ."

She moves faster, pumps harder, sucks tighter, wringing the pleasure from me. My hips circle and lift, pushing up into her mouth as she moans around me. And I'm utterly wrecked.

" . . . fuck . . . *fuck* . . ."

With a broken groan I come in her mouth, down her throat, pumping again and again. It feels like I'm flying and sounds like I'm dying.

When it's over, after the haze of pleasure clears from my vision, I grab my beautiful girl and hoist her up my body. With one thought in my mind—the same thought, coincidentally, that I also had that day, long ago, in the museum: I like to give as good as I get.

EMMA CHASE

Sunlight peeks over the horizon, cutting a golden swath across the floor, creeping until it finds Ellie's face. With my chest pressed to her back, I lean up, over her, watching her eyes scrunch, her nose wrinkle, as she awakens slowly, blinking at the brightening sky streaming through. Then my face is buried against her hair and the soft crook of her neck. She smells like sex and sweat and me.

Then Ellie rolls over, pushing me on my back, blocking the window with her tempting little body and raining kisses down on my cheeks, my eyelids—eager and soft.

"It's a dream. Go back to sleep. It's not morning yet." She presses her cheek against my chest—holding, hugging, clinging. "Don't leave me."

And the way she says it tugs at my gut—because it doesn't feel at all like teasing.

I tilt her face up to me so I can see her eyes. "What's that about, now?"

"Tell me we're going to be together. Like this," she pleads.

And I don't hesitate. "We're going to be together. Every day and every night, just like this." I reach up and kiss her, sealing the words.

Then I add, "But I need to speak with Prince Nicholas, before anyone else knows. Even before you tell your sister."

"But—"

"He's like an older brother to me, Elle—his opinion matters. I don't want him to think I disrespected you or took advantage. I want to be clear about my intentions and I want him to hear it from me, first. He trusts me—I won't have him believing I'm like all the other arseholes who've let him down or betrayed him."

178

She thinks about it, her eyes warm and light—almost silver. "Do you think he'll be mad?"

"I don't think he, or any of them will be happy." My knuckle brushes the apple of her cheek—so pretty. "They had plans for you."

"Will you get in trouble?"

"Depends on your definition of trouble." I shrug, teasing. "They might throw me in the dungeon, for fucking above my class." My hands find her arse, squeezing. "But, oh, it was worth it."

Ellie bites my arm.

"Don't worry." I take her hand in mine, threading our fingers together. "Everything will be fine, I promise."

Turns out, sometimes I lie—and don't even know it.

CHAPTER 19

Logan

I plan on speaking to Nicholas about Ellie the very same day, but he's scheduled to give a speech for a children's charity that requires him to travel in the helicopter, and there's no chance for us to chat alone. The next day, Olivia's feeling poorly, and she and the Prince spend the whole day sequestered in their bedroom.

And that's how it goes, for the next day and one more after that—I try to take him aside, to find him alone for a moment, but, as it often does, shit keeps getting in the way.

But nothing gets in the way of me and Ellie. I would obliterate anything or anyone who tried. We keep our distance when we're around others, acting friendly—normal.

Then, I go to her room at night—or when I can't, she comes to me. She leaves word for her sister that she's going to the cinema and I volunteer to guard her. But instead, we go to my house, where we don't have to mind our groans and shouts and cursing gasps. We're mad for each other. Insatiable. And it's all so good . . . so easy.

On the fourth day, they're together at breakfast—Ellie, Olivia, Nicholas, Henry and Lady Sarah. Ellie sends a warm, secret smile my way, and I'm determined to tell the prince today.

I clear my throat. "Prince Nicholas—"

"A present arrived for you, Lady Olivia. Looks like it's for the little ones." Sylvie, the new kitchen maid, places a square box on the table in front of Olivia, wrapped in pink and blue paper with a white bow.

"Thank you, Sylvie."

Olivia gazes at the gift for a moment, then begins to tear the paper, revealing a worn, brown cardboard box underneath, with a folded note taped to the side. And something about it rubs me all kinds of wrong. It doesn't seem like something any acquaintance of the royal family would send.

I move forward, putting my arm in front of Olivia to stop her from opening it.

"Has this been through security?" I ask the maid.

Her eyes are wide. "No, it was just delivered at the rear entrance. I thought I'd bring it right in."

I take the box from Olivia. It's a solid weight. I set it on the bureau, away from the table, then I take the knife from my side and use the blade to lift one edge, just slightly. Just enough to see what's inside.

And when I do—I curse.

"What is it?" Ellie asks, standing, her eyes wide and round—looking young, innocent—and something pulls inside me to protect her from this.

"What's in the box, Logan?" Olivia asks.

I shake my head "I'll take care of it—you needn't worry."

"Logan." Her voice is firmer, more of an order. "Tell me what's in there."

"Yeah, what is this, *Seven*?" Ellie whispers. "Come on, Morgan Freeman—what's in the box?"

Nicholas closes his eyes, troubled but resigned. Then he nods sharply at me.

"Puppies," I tell them. Hating that I have to say the words. "Two small ones."

Lady Sarah covers her mouth and Henry pulls her near.

Olivia cradles her heavy stomach, where her twins lay. "Are they dead?"

I nod, rigidly—my rage building.

"What does the note say?" Olivia asks. And there's fear in her voice.

Again, I look to Nicholas. He wraps his arms around his wife. "Read it, Logan."

With a cloth, so as not to disturb any fingerprints, I peel off the note and open it.

My eyes go straight to Ellie's, embracing her with my gaze, letting her know that it's all right, nothing will touch her—or her sister. Not while I'm alive.

And then I tell them: "It says . . . *soon*."

The chair explodes against the wall, sending wooden shrapnel into the air and scattering across the floor. Prince Nicholas is an expert at keeping a tight rein on his emotions, wearing a mask of indifference to hide his feelings. He doesn't lose his temper often. But when he does, it's quite a sight.

A side table is next, meeting the same fate as the chair, taking a china vase out with it.

"Son of a bitch!"

We're in Winston's office, having just reviewed the security footage from the rear entrance where the package was found. And there's nothing—nothing of substance.

One minute the back entrance is empty, then a stream of people exit during a shift change—and when the last of them passes, the box is outside the door. There's no shot of any of the workers placing it there, but every one of them have still been questioned.

Whoever's doing this is a fucking ghost—a ghost that

knows the palace well. He's on the inside, or used to be, and that makes it so much worse.

It's betrayal. Treachery—even treason.

Nicholas heads for the door, but his brother blocks his way.

"Where are you going?"

"I'm going to find the bastard."

"He's doing this to draw you out," I remind him. "To make you slip up, so he can get in closer."

"Then I'll make it easy for him!" Nicholas glares. "And when he comes at me, I'll rip out his fucking jugular."

Henry holds up his hands, speaking soothingly, as though talking to a man on a bridge, determined to jump. "I know, believe me—if it was Sarah I'd want to burn the world down too. But, Nicholas, if you go out half-cocked, it will only make it worse. It's infuriating . . . but you know that's the truth."

Nicholas's face twists with frustration. Then he advances so that he's nose-to-nose with Winston. "Find him!" his voice booms righteously. Like the king he was raised to be. "I don't care what you have to do—unleash your most vicious dogs, look in every closet, every corner, turn every house in the damn city upside down—but . . . Find. Him."

Winston bows. He's a retired killer, an assassin—the kind who could shoot a man in the face while sipping his tea and not spill a drop. And he's completely devoted to the Crown.

"It will be done, Your Highness."

Calmer, or maybe just drained, Nicholas nods. "I'm going to be with my wife."

And today is definitely not the day.

I spend the next day in Winston's office, analyzing plans for Prince Henry and Lady Sarah's official wedding, just five weeks away. We look at the measures from every angle, searching for weaknesses and finding ways to lock them down, in the face of the current threat.

I don't see Ellie once the whole long day and the absence gnaws at me, makes me needy, hungry. I want her near me, with me, in my sights, all the time. And because it's been hours and hours without a glimpse of her, I'm wound up tense like a hot fucking coil.

Then, just as my shift is ending, I get a text. Telling me to meet her.

The throne room isn't used for decrees these days. It's a public exhibit, part of the tour, but at this hour, half past ten, it's closed and empty. I step into the dim, echoing room, lit only by the electric candles burning on the walls. Ellie stands on the raised platform beside the jeweled throne, running her hand down the smooth golden arm.

When she spots me, she runs. And it's a joyous thing to see. I catch her when she jumps and wraps her arms and legs around me like a lovely vine.

She sighs against my mouth. "I've missed you."

She feels it too. The craving, the strain, the uncomfortable itch that's only satiated when we're together.

"Have you missed me?" she asks.

I groan against her lips. "I burn for you, sweet girl. I dream of you, even when I'm awake."

Her smile is warm, her blush pink, as she goes after my shirt—working the buttons and kissing my skin.

"What do you dream? Tell me."

I carry her towards the bearskin rug in front of the unlit fireplace. "An hour ago, I was picturing you in my kitchen, wearing nothing but tiny little knickers and a snug cotton shirt that showed off your perky, fantastic tits."

She giggles against my throat, leaning down to drag her tongue over the war falcon tattoo on my shoulder and arm.

"And you were dancing," I tell her, nipping at her plump earlobe. "Shaking your sweet, tight arse like you used to while baking your pies in the coffee shop."

Ellie tilts her head back, finding my eyes. "I didn't think you'd noticed."

I take her lower lip between my teeth, running the tip of my tongue across it.

"It was all I fucking noticed."

I uncurl her legs from my hips. But when her feet touch the rug, she doesn't move down to the floor like I thought she would. Instead, with a wicked gleam in her eyes, Ellie backs her way towards the golden throne, pulling me by the hand.

"I had a dream too. That's why I told you to meet me here."

She sits down in the royal chair, lifting one foot onto the seat, raising the skirt of her pretty pink dress and flashing me her bare, glistening pussy.

Wicked, clever girl.

Ellie drags one finger through her slit. My cock twitches, and my pulse pounds.

"I imagined you tasting me, like this, right here."

I lick my lips. "Is that so?"

"Aye." She smiles cheekily, imitating my voice. "And then you sat down and I rode you, fucked you, right here."

This is a hallowed space, the throne a sacred relic—like an altar in a church, or one of those creepy statues whose eyes follow you around, waiting for you to transgress. But at this moment, I don't care.

"I'm going to hell for this," I mutter.

Ellie grins. "Then you should make the most of it before you burn."

Good advice.

Like the sinner I am, I go down on my knees. I spread her legs with my hands, impatience making me rough, hooking her calf over my shoulder. And I kiss her, open-mouthed, between her legs. She feels so fucking soft against my lips, so hot and slippery against my tongue. And she's sweet—like thick, melted sugar.

"Holy . . ." Ellie begins, but doesn't finish. The words lost on a moan.

I suck on her, lap at her, eat her like a plump summer peach. I could do this forever; exist on her alone. Ellie slips down the throne, lifting her hips, offering herself up to my mouth. I thrust my tongue into her heat and she gasps, clenching around me. I grip her hips, slide her back and forth against me, fucking her with my mouth, scratching the tender skin of her thighs with the stubble on my jaw.

Then I drag my lips up to her clit—swollen and full. A hard, quivering, needy little bud. I open her with my fingers and kiss her there, love her there, rub my tongue against her in perfect, tight little circles, until her legs quiver and her hips jerk.

Ellie comes apart with a cry—wild and shameless—with her hand tugging on my hair as her hips gyrate against my mouth. I lick at her gently as the last spasms of pleasure float through her. I slide my sleeve across my mouth and place one soft, tender kiss on her smooth pelvis.

Then I stand and tear my shirt off. I yank her dainty red dress up, because I need to feel her—skin on bare skin. I push my trousers down, just low enough to free my demanding cock, then I pick her up and take her place on the throne. Her legs straddle my hips, and her pussy—so wet and hot—hovers above my dick.

In one move, I push her down and thrust up, burying myself in her beautiful, gripping tightness. We both groan.

Ellie strokes my face, meeting my eyes with her languid, heavy-lidded gaze.

I slap her thigh, just hard enough to sting.

"Come on, lass," I hiss. "Fucking ride me. Make your dream come true."

My filthy command wakes her right up. And her pelvis slides forward and back, stroking me from base to tip. Her breaths come hard, her chest heaving.

She rides me faster, finding her rhythm, taking her pleasure. And she's beautiful.

"I love your dick," Ellie pants. "It's so big, it fills me . . . so good . . . it's so good."

"My dick thinks you're pretty grand too."

We laugh together, in the secret, sultry way only lovers can.

But then there's no more teasing. I grasp her arse, fingers digging into her flesh—helping her move. She rocks over me, harder, wilder. And the heat gathers, builds; my heavy balls tighten with the need to explode, my cock thickens with the desire to come, flood her, fill her.

"You're coming with me, Ellie." I groan. "Come with me."

I latch on to her nipple, suckling relentlessly.

"Oh . . . oh . . . oh . . ." she moans.

And then she contracts around me, milking me, pulling my orgasm from deep inside my fucking soul.

Afterwards, we're a bit silly with the satisfaction. Not tired or spent, but almost giddy. We stand, kissing and tickling, all gentle, teasing touches and soft smiles.

Ellie bends down to get her dress, and I'm so captivated by the view of her arse, I don't realize the throne room door is opening until three people are walking through it.

Shirtless, with my trousers up but open, I spin around—holding Ellie behind me, blocking her from view.

"Logan?" Prince Nicholas asks, squinting like he's seeing a ghost.

Lady Olivia and Prince Henry wear the same expressions.

Before I can formulate a response, Ellie peeks out from behind me.

"Hey guys . . . what's up?"

"What were you *thinking*?"

I wasn't. That's the problem with letting your cock run things—he doesn't think. Or, if he does, it's only about just the one thing. Dumb bastard.

"Did you realize how reckless you were?"

Sure, I did. *Afterwards.*

After Olivia whisked Ellie away from the throne room for her own interrogation, I was brought here, to Nicholas's office.

I nod. "It was stupid."

So fucking stupid.

Behind Nicholas, Henry paces back and forth, with a large open book in his hands.

"Didn't we used to have a dungeon downstairs?" the blond prince asks his older brother.

"Could've sworn I found it when I was six or seven. Gave me nightmares for a week." He points at an image in the book and smiles manically. "That device looks like it hurts—we'll order two."

Huh. I thought I was just joking with Ellie about the dungeon.

Nicholas ignores his brother and pins me with damning eyes. "Anyone could have walked in on you, Logan. The staff, visitors . . . photographers."

My stomach churns at the thought of sweet Ellie's bare assets photographed without her consent—splashed across front pages for the whole world to consume. *Jesus.*

"Do we still hang people?" Henry asks, philosophically. When he doesn't get an answer, he adds, "If not, I'm bringing hanging back."

So that's what Justin Timberlake would sound like if he were a serial killer.

Nicholas sighs, rubbing his forehead. "How long has this been going on?"

I lift my chin. "Depends on what you mean by 'this,' Sir."

Henry snaps the books closed. "I didn't like the way you looked at her at the wedding." He braces his hands on the desk beside Nicholas—leaning over and glaring at me. "So, he means just how long have you been sticking it to the girl who's like a little sister to us?"

I hold his furious gaze for a few seconds, breathing slowly. "That's . . . a fairly recent development."

Then my voice grows stronger. Because I'm not ashamed.

"But I have loved her for a long, long time."

I didn't mean to say it, didn't mean to even think it . . . but it's the truth. Simple and straight.

And the indignant wind goes out of Henry's sails.

There's a knock at the door.

"Come in," Nicholas says.

Lady Sarah steps in, wearing her nightclothes under a fluffy ivory robe and a chastising expression. Behind her glasses, her eyes narrow on Henry.

"So this is how it's going to be? Married only a few days and I already have to search the palace to drag my husband to bed?"

Henry goes to Sarah, like an invisible rope is reeling him to her. "Dragging me to your bed is something you'll never have to do, love. You can even tie me there whenever you like, and I'll be happy to reciprocate."

He kisses her mouth, as she blushes deep and bright.

She leans back. "Then why are you down here instead of up there with me?"

"There was an emergency."

"What kind of an emergency?"

"You're not going to believe it."

"Try me."

"Logan and Ellie are fucking."

She automatically glances at me, and her cheeks deepen to a shade of crimson. "I'm sure there's a more delicate way to word that, Henry."

Henry nods, soberly. "You're right, I'm sorry. Let me try again: Logan and Ellie are humping, like insatiable randy bunnies, all over the palace."

Sarah shakes her head. "You're hopeless."

The Prince grins broadly. "It's part of my charm."

"What am I going to do with you?"

Henry kisses her again. "Take me to bed. Obviously."

He nods towards his brother. "You've got this?"

"Yes. Good night, Henry, Sarah."

And the happy newlyweds exit the room. Leaving Prince Nicholas and me alone.

He stares at me across the desk with a penetrating, unreadable expression. This man whom I respect and admire. Who's been more of a mentor, an older brother to me, than anyone related by blood.

"Prince Nicholas—"

"I'm not a fool, Logan."

I should have told him from the beginning. Found a moment, made the time. Before I ever laid a finger on her.

"No, you're not."

"I've suspected an . . . attraction . . . between you and Ellie for some time, possibly before you did."

"Yes. I realize—" I begin.

"You are everything I'd hoped for her. Everything I'd prayed she'd find."

My thoughts stop in their tracks. And my voice is faint with surprise.

"Really?"

"Of course." He nods, smiling with warmth in his eyes. "You're a good man—dedicated, hardworking, loyal. I know you'll put her happiness above all else, that you'll keep her safe. Olivia believes the same."

And it feels like a blessing. The best kind.

Then Nicholas's features sober, grow serious.

"But . . . Logan . . ."

I lift my hand, stopping him, because I already know.

"You don't have to say it. I understand. I'll speak with Winston in the morning, first thing."

CHAPTER 20

Ellie

"You stuck-up, arrogant son of a bitch!"

I yell the words as I charge into Nicholas and Olivia's private dining room—like Joan of fucking Arc on the French battlefield. I came straight here after I talked to Logan, right after he finished meeting with Winston, head of security. Right after he turned in his badge or sexy dark clothes or whatever the hell bodyguards have to turn in when they stop being bodyguards.

I love Nicholas, he's a great guy—which makes his current douchery all the more upsetting.

"Ellie!" My sister stands up.

"He fired Logan," I tell her. Then I only have condemning eyes for her hubby, who's still sitting. "How could you do this to him? This job is his life; it means everything to him."

"Not everything." Nicholas's eyes are cool green and unsurprised. He tosses his napkin on the table. "For the record, I didn't fire him. He resigned."

"But you would have fired him if he hadn't resigned."

"Yes, I would have."

Slowly, my sister turns. "Nicholas?"

"I would no sooner allow Logan to guard you or Ellie than I would ask a surgeon to operate on his wife. I've been in his shoes. I've had to choose between duty and love, and I know how it ends."

"That doesn't make any sense. Logan can still be a bodyguard, and be with me."

"Really?" my brother-in-law asks. "And how would that work, exactly? The upcoming ball that will kick off Henry and Sarah's wedding festivities—did you want Logan to come with you? By your side, as your date, a guest?"

I've imagined that. Being on Logan's arm, dancing with him, laughing with him—while he's clad in a sharp, perfectly fitted tuxedo like James fucking Bond.

Mama like.

"Well . . . yeah. I do want that."

Nicholas nods. "And how will he enjoy the party, attend to you . . . and guard the door at the same time?"

I stomp my foot, getting frustrated, because I see the sense Nicholas is making—and I don't want to.

"He wouldn't have to be on duty then."

"All right, then let's imagine how it will be when he *is* on duty. Picture it—we're all at an event together, shaking hands, accepting flowers. Then, suddenly a shot rings out. What does Logan do? Who does he cover first?"

"I don't know."

"Yes, you do. Don't think, just answer—who?"

I say the first answer that pops into my head—the only answer.

"Me. Logan would cover me first."

Nicholas leans forward, his features softening. "Of course he would. Just as he should—I would expect nothing less." His eyes dart to my sister. "But the fact remains that I have to think of Olivia, of our children. And for the men assigned to guard her, *she* must come first—she is the priority. I like Logan very much; I always have. I trust him and would willingly depend on him. I like the two of you together, Ellie. But his feelings for you have compromised him and he's unable to fulfill the duties of his position. It's as simple as that."

A weight sits on my chest, bending it in. Crushing guilt.

"It's not fair."

"Life often isn't," Nicholas says gently. "Logan had a clear choice to make. He understood what he was doing. He knew he could have you or his job—not both. And he chose you."

Logan

"I still think it sucks."

I'm on the mattress in the half-constructed living room of my house, on my side, listening as Ellie rails against the unfairness of life, watching her hang soft yellow drapes on the rods I installed this morning.

She's wearing one of my button-down shirts and nothing beneath. It's long on her—but when she stretches up high to make an adjustment, her scrumptious arse teases me with a glimpse.

Speaking of sucking . . .

She has such a lovely arse. I want to kiss her there, lick her there, hear the high-pitched whine in her voice as she comes while I fuck her there. My cock juts out, hard and ready, and my balls throb.

She needs to finish those bloody curtains. Quickly.

"It's the way it is, Ellie-girl. I knew that when I signed up for security detail and I was fully aware of it when I went to your room that night."

She looks back over her shoulder. Her blond hair shimmery

in the sunlight, the shirt inching up her creamy thighs as she twists.

"Is that why you stayed away all those years in New York? Even after you knew you . . . liked me? Because you knew you'd have to give up your job?"

"I stayed away because you were young. And I wasn't sure if you'd want to stick with a bloke like me."

Ellie she shakes her head. "Dummy."

Then she appraises her handiwork around the windows, tilting her head, stepping back . . . right into my waiting hands.

I grab her tiny waist, turning and rolling her under me on the mattress. Then I get right to work on getting her out of my shirt, baring her pretty tits that I can't stop sucking.

She combs her fingers through my hair. "But what are you going to do, Logan?"

"Right now? I'm going to fuck you senseless."

My Ellie likes that idea. She smiles.

"And then?"

I look to the ceiling, contemplating. "Then I'm gonna drag this mattress upstairs and fuck you slow and gentle, beneath the stars."

That gets her giggling.

"And tomorrow?"

I thrust my hips forward between her spread legs, sliding my hardness through her soft, lovely wet heat.

"I'll repeat the process." My breath picks up, because she feels so good. "But we'll use different positions. You're easy to pick up and spin around—I can get quite creative."

"Logan . . ." Ellie moans, lifting up, begging without words for me to thrust inside. To take her, ride her, make her writhe and moan.

Her hands reach down between us, spreading across my hips, her thumbs hooking and holding my lower pelvis. "I love it like this. You pressing into me, giving me your weight, feeling you rock against me right here."

A jolt of passion blazes up my spine, and I kiss her deep and quick—pressing my lips too hard against hers, but too far gone to stop.

"I can't get enough of you, Ellie . . . I'll never, ever get enough . . ."

Ellie

I wake to the feeling of Logan kissing the back of my neck.

He's always up before me, but one of these days I'll figure out a way to pry my eyes open first so I can enjoy the sight of his handsome face, relaxed and peaceful. I wonder if his mouth smiles while he dreams, or if it frowns in that serious way it sets when he's on duty. One day I'll know.

His breath tickles my neck and he kisses me again, his lips so warm against my skin. I open my eyes to the living room, lit from the daylight outside the window but not blindingly bright, thanks to my trusty curtains. We never made it upstairs last night—I wore the boy out—we wore out each other. The sheet is soft and warm beneath my naked body, the mattress a perfect cushion.

And my chest feels so full, like my heart has grown too big for it.

I turn onto my back, looking up into the deep brown eyes that I have adored from the first moment they met mine. Logan's smile falters and his forehead wrinkles as he gazes down at me. His hand cups the side of my face, wiping away a tear that trickles from the corner of my eye.

"What is it, Ellie-love?"

I didn't even realize I was crying. Maybe it's knowing that he chose me, while understanding exactly what that meant, what he'd be giving up. Maybe it's being in this house that smells like fresh-cut timber, warm stone . . . and home. Or maybe it's waking up in his arms, to his kiss—this man who has become everything to me.

Whom I would do anything for. I didn't understand those words before, not really, but now I know. I know what my father felt for my mother, what Liv feels for her husband.

I want to cherish Logan. Adore him. My heart, my body, my soul—they're already his.

The only thing left to give him is words.

"I love you, Logan." My heart swells. "I love you. I love you. I love you . . ."

The corners of his mouth curve up and he leans down close. "Ellie, I—"

There's a crash outside the front door. A horn honking, shouts and voices arguing.

Logan looks in that direction, cursing. "What in the fuck . . ."

He rises from our mattress and slips into a pair of jeans and walks shirtless toward the ruckus. "Stay here."

I don't listen. I button his shirt around me, slide into my black leggings, then catch up to him in the foyer. Through the curtainless front window, I see people—lots of them. There are also cars and vans.

What in the fuck is right.

Logan opens the front door and a hundred cameras click at once—like a machine gun firing. They're reporters, photographers . . . and they're in Logan's front yard.

There's a break in the crowd, a parting of the sea, and James pushes his way into the house, slamming the door behind him. James is a good friend of Logan's and a former member of Nicholas's personal security team. He went back with him and Olivia to Wessco that first summer and guards the royal family at the palace now.

"Morning, Lo." He nods. "Miss Ellie."

"What the hell's going on, James?" Logan asks.

James cocks his head apologetically. "You are." He glances between me and Logan, his blond hair falling over his forehead. "While they wait for the babies to be born and the wedding day to arrive, the press is looking to fill their pages with some kind of scandal. And you two are it."

Logan drapes his arm around me.

"Also," James continues, "I brought the car. The Queen wants to see you. Now."

That doesn't sound good.

Logan and I wait in the Queen's private drawing room—an amazing custard-yellow-and-dark-wood-accented room—wearing the wrinkled clothes we threw on from last night. Queen Lenora strides in like a pissed-off general—if the military uniform were a pink skirt and jacket, and pillbox hat.

Logan bows and I curtsy.

She smacks several newspapers on her desk—tabloids. All with screaming headlines about me—the bright-eyed royal relation getting down and dirty with the rough security guard from a shady family. *Great.*

"I am so disappointed in you, Eleanor." She shakes her head. "Poor George. The young mayor had such promise for you. I can't imagine what he will say."

I raise my hand. "He actually texted me this morning. He

said thanks. He's had a crush on the upstairs maid forever and now he's finally got the guts to ask her out."

The Queen lifts her nose. "You could have reached so much higher. For a man of importance, of significance."

She turns to Logan and lowers her nose at him. "And you— you had a duty to this family to protect her—"

I step forward, cutting her off—knowing it's improper and inappropriate but not giving a single shit.

"He *has* protected me. Since the day I met him—in every way he knows how. Don't you dare question his loyalty to your family."

"Ellie!" Logan hisses quietly. Because even now, he's trying to protect me.

Queen Lenora shakes her head. "You could have been Madam Eleanor, Lady Eleanor, Duchess Eleanor . . . and you've chosen to throw that opportunity away."

I stand taller, straighter. "My name isn't Eleanor. It's Ellie. And Logan St. James *is* a man of significance and importance, and if you can't see that, it's your loss. I don't need a title." I look at Logan. "I just need him."

The Queen scoffs, regally, of course. "Oh, good grief."

She turns to the painting behind her—the one of her husband, Edward—and shakes her head at it, like it's the only thing that understands her.

Then, with a breath, she focuses her attention back on Logan.

"Leave us."

Logan hesitates for just a second—looking to me, checking with me—and I nod. He bows low to the Queen and leaves, closing the door behind him.

Queen Lenora steps closer. "I was your age once. Though I'm sure my grandsons can't fathom it, it's true. You are young, and full of hope and beauty, and foolish faith. You believe love can fix everything. Cure any ill." She shakes her head, looking in my eyes. "It can't. And though I had different aspirations for you, you have made your choice. I wish you well, truly—I hope you and your guard find every happiness."

The Queen walks stiffly back behind her desk.

"But, Ellie, if you think things will be easy now, that the two of you will simply ride off into the sunset unaffected by the realities of your situation . . . you should prepare to be mistaken."

CHAPTER 21

Logan

I sit in the antique chair outside the Queen's office, waiting for Ellie. Across from me at his desk is Christopher, Her Majesty's personal secretary. He's solid—a big fucker—long reach. It gets me thinking.

"Hey Christopher, you ever do any fighting? Boxing? That sort of thing."

He adjusts his glasses. "I fence."

Fencing. I could work with that.

The phone on his desk rings.

"Yes? Yes, right away." He looks to me. "Winston would like a word."

I hook my thumb at the door. "Tell Ellie I'll see her back in her rooms when she's done here." Then, as I pass his desk, I add, "We should chat—about training. You're the Queen's secretary; you're with her all the time, her last line of defense. It'd be good for you to know how to handle yourself. I could show you a few things."

He thinks it over . . . and then he nods.

Down in Winston's office, I find him and a few of the lads going over the security detail for the wedding. Since I'm no longer privy to that information, they stop the discussion when I walk through the door.

"You wanted a word?"

Winston's flat eyes and blank expression turn my way. "I wanted to inform you, I've assigned a detail to your house as well as a car and a driver for you and Miss Hammond to make use of."

For a second, I think I've heard him wrong.

"Why?"

"In the short term, the guards will keep the press at bay. In the long term, they'll protect you and Miss Hammond. The car and the driver as well."

"I don't want a bloody detail around my house."

"I'm not concerned with what you want, St. James. It's protocol—you know that."

I almost laugh. Because protocol is for aristocrats—not for fucking me.

"I'll handle the press. And I can protect Ellie just fine."

The thing that's so eerie about Winston—he has almost no inflection in his voice. No emotion. He doesn't get upset or frustrated; he doesn't argue. He's like the Terminator—no matter what you do or say, he just keeps going, moving forward, doing things his way.

"No, you can't. That's the point."

One of the newer guys—a bulky, big-mouthed sod—speaks up from the couch across the room. "Leave the guarding to us, St. James. You just focus on keeping your pretty little golden ticket happy."

I narrow my eyes and take two steps towards him—and I spot Winston on my flank, positioning himself, just in case.

"Come again?"

Dumb-fuck shrugs. "You telling me you're not gonna put

on a tuxedo and sip Champagne at Prince Henry and Lady Sarah's ball, coming up? I mean, good for you, mate—we got to take the chance to move up when we can. And you hit the jackpot. I say enjoy it, for however long it lasts."

My first instinct is to punch him in the mouth—knock him out cold. But I see his face, and it's stupidly sincere. Congratulatory. He's not trying to be a dickhead . . . and somehow that makes it worse.

Ellie's door is open. I close it and lock it behind me. She's standing before the open balcony, watching the rain pour down. The sky is an angry gray, and the cool wind blows the curtains and lifts the honey-toned tendrils of Ellie's hair.

She seems unusually calm. Contemplative. And I wonder what she's thinking.

I come up behind her, slide my arms around her waist and pull her back against my chest. I kiss her temple and smell the rain on her skin—fresh and clean.

"What are you doing?" I ask.

"Watching the storm. Isn't it beautiful, Logan?"

I tilt my head, to gaze at her face. "Breathtaking."

She smiles prettily.

"Are you all right? After your chat with the Queen?"

Ellie turns her eyes back to the sky. "I'm fine. But I guess Nicholas doesn't call her a battle-axe for nothing, huh?"

"No." I chuckle. "It's a well-earned nickname."

I kiss her neck, her ear. There are things I should say, things we should talk about, but right now I crave her. I want to hold her, feel her, beneath me and all around.

"I'm mad for you, Ellie. Gone for you. I want you so much."

She turns in my arms, lifting hers around my neck. And

her sweet blue eyes are liquid with the same desire that flows through me.

"You have me, Logan. I'm right here," she says softly. "I'm yours."

I kiss her slow and deep. And I don't stop, my lips never leaving her skin as I bring her to the bed, lay her down and peel the sweater and leggings from her body.

Ellie watches me lift my shirt over my head. Her gaze follows my hands, caressing me, as I unbutton my trousers and push them to the floor. Holding her eyes, I come to her on the bed, bare in every way.

And with the wind and rain raging outside, Ellie and I make our own refuge, our own paradise. She moans my name when I slide in deep, and she clings to me. I hold her so close as I stroke slowly inside her, whispering tender words and sacred promises.

It's genuine and raw—more than our bodies joining, it feels like our souls have too.

When she told me she loved me this morning, it was the first time anyone had ever said those words to me. The only time. And it's so precious to me, *she* is so precious to me, I tremble with the depth of it.

We find our pleasure together, coming at the same time. It feels exquisite, it feels like love. What I have with Ellie, what we've made in this moment, is what I've been wanting my whole life—something noble and lasting. Pure and good and true.

The next few days are crazy, difficult. I used to think I was accustomed to the press, to the bullshit stories they pull out of thin air. But this is another level of messed up. They camp outside Logan's house—on the sidewalk, waiting for one of us to show up. What used to be his private sanctuary has turned into a circus, a freak show.

They follow us everywhere. Logan almost gets into a fight at the flea market, when a paparazzo makes a nasty comment about my boobs. It's only the security detail trailing us that stopped him from shattering the asshole's jaw.

Logan throws himself into finishing the house, and it's turning out so beautifully. One time, I tell him he should pick construction or remodeling for his next career, only half teasing. But he didn't answer. I think he's struggling with leaving his position, that it's turned out to be harder than he thought. Whenever we're out in public, he's tense and quiet—not that he was Mr. Chatterbox before. But at night, at the palace where we've been sleeping, when we make love—then I feel him. He looks at me with the eyes I know, smiles and whispers and kisses me like the man I love.

In those moments, when it's just him and me, and the rest of the world doesn't exist, we're perfect. And happy. And I catch a glimpse of what our future will be, if we can just make it through this gauntlet.

A week later, the day of Henry and Sarah's celebration ball arrives. Amazingly, there hasn't been a single peep about their secret garden nuptials, and I'm glad. It still belongs just to them. They don't have to share it with the world.

The ball will be my and Logan's first official public appearance together. I can't wait to be on his arm. I can't wait to see his face when he sees my dress—a long slinky gown the color of sea-glass in the sun, that plumps my cleavage and shows off my ass. Move over @Elliesweettits—once Twitter sees photos of me in this number, @Elliesexyarse will be trending world-wide. Not that I actually care, the only place I want to be trending is in Logan St. James's naughty fantasies.

I spend the day with Livvy and Sarah getting beautified, a perk of living at the royal residence where the glamor squad makes palace calls. Our hair is washed and blown out, our nails are filed and painted, we're waxed and plucked within an inch of our lives. And then, at seven sharp, we meet at the grand palace staircase for pictures.

Sarah wears a red strapless ball gown, stunning, with her hair pinned up in countless shiny curls. Henry, looking strikingly handsome in a formal tuxedo with tails, can't take his eyes off her.

Olivia, with her big, round, beautiful belly, looks gorgeous in an emerald green, one shoulder chiffon gown paired with simple—and cushiony—nude flats. Nicholas insisted, because he didn't want her feet to hurt.

The palace has commissioned famed photographer, Jillian Sabal, to take posed and candid shots of the royal family. Logan's late, so I try to call, but the call goes to voicemail. I send him texts but he doesn't answer. My anxiety grows as pictures are taken at the staircase without him. My disappointment is devastating. While he wouldn't have been included in the portrait shots, I thought we'd get to take one or two pictures of just me and him—and they would've been so amazing.

Where is he?

Then it's time for the receiving line, and the ball is starting without him.

And I get this horrible, sick sinking feeling in my stomach. Because he's been so on edge lately, strained and unhappy. There's a tiny whisper of worry that maybe something happened to him, an accident or an injury—but deep down I know that's not true.

I text him again. I call five more times. I don't worry about looking desperate because this is Logan—we don't play games. At least, I didn't think we did.

I watch the ballroom entrance, hoping he'll appear, because I'm a hopeful person.

And it's only after an hour of dancing, when the white-gloved waiters serve the perfect, elegantly plated dinner, that my hope disintegrates and my disappointment starts to heat, boil—turn to anger.

Because Logan isn't coming.

When we pull up to the house, it seems deserted, quiet and dark, even though he has electricity now. There's a black SUV in the driveway that belongs to the security guards, and two guys I don't recognize sit inside the vehicle. They nod to James as he closes the car door behind me. When he moves to lead me up the path, I stop him, because I don't want an audience for this.

I find him in the kitchen, sitting in the dark, at the table we found at a flea market two days ago. His shirt is open, unbuttoned, and a black tuxedo tie hangs loose around his neck.

And I don't know what I feel, because it's like I feel everything at once. For the first time since I met him, my hero looks lost, my guardian angel has a broken wing. And I want to mend him, save him the way he's always saved me. I want to love him until he feels found.

But there are other emotions too—the stab of hurt, the sting of humiliation, the sharp slap of anger.

"What's going on, Logan?"

He doesn't look at me, but just continues to stare hard at the half-empty bottle of liquor in front of him.

"I'm a fool. I *look* like a fool."

I move closer, close enough to smell the aroma of whiskey floating around him. "That's not true. That could never be true."

He lifts his finger, correcting me. "I would've felt like a fool if I'd shown up to the fancy ball with you tonight."

"Why?"

He raises his hand toward the door. "It's in all the papers. I'm the fucking East Amboy bodyguard who's pounding the princess's sister to become a pampered royal. I have guards around my house because I'm incapable of protecting myself. Or you."

"I don't care what they say, and neither should you. They lie. They lie all the time about Nicholas and Olivia and Henry. They've lied about me too—you know that."

He shakes his head. "It feels different to be the person they're lying about. All I ever wanted was to be a part of something bigger than me—and I'm not a part of anything now."

I try not to flinch. Because he doesn't see that he's a part of me, a part of *us*.

"You said you were all right with it," I remind him.

"I know what I said!"

"You said you knew what you signed up for when you came to my room that night."

I hate how my voice sounds—whiney and immature.

"It's not just about that. It's also about you. The Queen was right, Ellie."

"Right about what?"

"About all you're giving up."

"Giving up?"

"Castles and carriages. The fairy tale your sister has. I'll never be able to give you that—you'll be settling for less. It's important that you understand that now, not five years down the road when you resent me for it."

I stare at the wall, because if I look at his face, I'll cry. And

I want to be strong. Angry. I've never been any good at angry, but I give it my best shot.

"Fuck *you*, Logan. Is that who you think I am? Is that what you think is important to me?"

"I'm just trying to look at it from all angles. Prepare. It's easier for you. Being related to the royal family is a good thing; no one looks down on you for it."

"It could be a good thing for both of us."

His face tightens, anger pierces the soulful eyes that I love so much.

"I make my own way. I look out for myself and everyone around me; I always have. To think people will look at me like some pussy gold digger, like some fucking twat who's using you, makes me sick. Makes me want to kill someone—I can't stand it."

The vehemence in his voice shocks me. Logan's only ever spoken to me carefully, kindly. To hear him talk with so much . . . disgust . . . well . . . it fucking hurts.

"Were you even going to show up tonight? Or call? Or were you planning to leave me hanging without a word?"

Unbearable silence follows my question. And answers it.

"That's a dick move, Logan."

He stares at the bottle on the table. "I'm sorry. I meant to go and then I was getting dressed and looked at myself in the mirror and just . . . couldn't." He exhales. "I need time to figure out what my life looks like now. Where I go from here."

"We can figure it out together," I try.

But he says nothing. And it feels like my chest is caving in.

Because he needs "time." And we all know what that means.

"Are you . . . are you breaking up with me?"

There's the slightest pause—and in that half-a-second my sorrow is so immense I can't breathe. It like I'm drowning.

Then Logan throws me a lifeline.

"No, Ellie." He gets up from the chair, swaying a bit, and moves closer to me. "No, I'm not. I just—"

I remember, from all those years with my dad, the stinging sensation of not being wanted. The echo of that rejection seeps into my bones and makes my insides curdle. I remember how it feels to love someone who wishes he didn't have to look at you, or talk to you.

And it feels just like this.

"Okay, Batman—you brood it out on your own in the Bat Cave. I'm gonna go."

"That's not—"

But I'm already rushing for the door.

When I pull it open, he's there behind me—his hand pushing it closed.

"That's not what this is." I feel his other hand on my shoulder, his warm, hard chest against my back, his voice in my ear—scraping and sorry. "You are everything a man could want, Ellie—everything *I* want. This is on me. I just . . . I have to work it out in my head."

I nod sharply. "Yeah, so you said. You let me know when you've done that."

I pull on the door again, but it doesn't budge. Because he's so fucking strong and it pisses me off too.

"Ellie, I'm—"

"Let me out! I should be able to go if I want." My voice rises. "You don't get to keep me here just because you can!"

When I try the door again, his hand is gone. It opens and I'm flying across the porch, down the steps.

"Wait." Logan's hand grips my arm, not hard, but insistent.

And then James's steely voice comes from where he's standing by the car.

"Let her go."

Logan's head snaps up, and his eyes ice over.

"What'd you say?"

James moves nearer to us. "I said, let her go, Logan. Now."

Logan doesn't. And I suddenly feel like a gazelle wedged between two very pissed-off lions, just itching to rip each other's throats out.

"Are you fucking serious, mate? You honestly think I'd hurt her?"

James's tone is calm, but forceful—leaving no room for argument. "I think you've been hittin' the bottle and you're upset. And you're grabbing her arm. If you were anyone else you'd be on the ground right now with my foot on your throat. I know you, Lo, I know you'd never want to hurt her. But I'm tellin' you now, you need to back off, cool down and *let her fucking go*."

Logan stares at his friend—his brother in arms—for a few long moments. Then he shakes his head and without another word or glance my way, he drops my arm, turns around and walks back into his house—slamming the door behind him.

CHAPTER 22

Logan

There's a pounding, pounding, fucking *pounding* in my head. It knocks around, echoing inside my skull like a bullet. There's warm sunlight on my face, and when I finally creak my eyelids open, it feels like a laser beam shooting through my eyeballs, frying my brain.

I'm on the floor. And the morning sunlight has found me from the window above the sink. I should've hung Ellie's bloody kitchen curtains.

After she left last night I drank myself stupid . . . stupider . . . in the kitchen. Apparently, I slept here too. I rub my hand over my aching face, remembering my argument with Ellie, almost coming to blows with James, how she left because of what I did—didn't do.

Christ, how'd I turn into such a cunt so quick? It's like magic.

The pounding sound comes again . . . more of a knocking now . . . and I realize it's not coming from inside my head—it's coming from the front door.

Who the fuck would come see me? Now, at—I check my phone—six in the morning? With my tongue feeling like sandpaper, I pull myself up and take the long, painful walk to the front door.

Why'd I buy a house that's so bloody big? That's right—'cause I'm a dickhead. Definitely.

I open the door and wonder if I'm dreaming. Or still drunk.

Because there's a prince on my porch.

"Morning, Logan," Nicholas says.

I consider bowing like I know I should—but no, not happening. I'll fall the fuck over or puke on him.

"Morning, Your Highness." I glance behind him and spot James standing beside the car. He waves jovially. I lift my chin in return, grateful that there are no hard feelings about my being an arse last night.

"What are you doing here?" I ask.

"I brought tea." He hands me one of the two lidded paper cups "James thought you could use a strong cup."

James was right.

"Thank you." I finger the edge of the lid. "If you've come to talk about Ellie—"

"Actually, I didn't. But . . . I would avoid Olivia if I were you. She brought her bat from New York and the growing belly hasn't affected her swing."

"Thanks for the warning."

The Prince looks up at the porch roof, then glances around my shoulder into the house.

"I wanted to see how the house was coming along."

"The house?"

He nods. "Yes. Ellie mentioned you're doing all the interior work yourself."

"Yeah."

"I thought I could come by and lend a hand."

No—too early. My brain does not compute.

"Lend a hand?"

Nicholas seems insulted. "I've built homes before, Logan. On three continents. I'm not totally helpless."

I shake my head. "No, I know . . . I just—"

"And putting up walls is a two-man job. Unless one of the other boys is coming by . . ."

"No." I shake my head, trying to clear the fog. "No . . . Tommy's mum still won't let him out of his room. Everyone else is working. So, I'm doing it myself."

Then Nicholas says, in that tone that doesn't leave any room for argument, "Not today, you're not."

After I give the Prince a tour of the house, we get to work. Hanging sheetrock and spackling isn't exactly light exercise—and with it being an usually warm day, I'm drenched by noon, sweating out all the poison from last night. We order sandwiches from the market a few blocks over and after rehydrating and a hot shower, I feel less like a heap of trash somebody pissed on.

There's a line from a movie—I forget which one—about how the perfect way to end a hard day's work is with a bottle of beer. Whoever wrote it knew his stuff. Because later, Nicholas and I sit in the back garden, each of us with a cold bottle of beer, watching the sun go down.

It glows deep pink and bright orange—like God struck a match and lit the sky on fire. And I think of Ellie . . . of how I want her here watching the sunset, all wrapped up in my arms, on my lap, every single night.

"I'm going to tell you something I haven't told anyone," Nicholas says, his eyes on the sky. "When I came home for the first time after abdicating, and attended my first event, it was . . . uncomfortable."

He braces his elbows on his knees, looking down at the bottle, picking at the label. "The way they looked at me had changed. You could feel it in the air. I don't think I fully understood the respect I commanded previously, the power I'd had—until that moment. Until it was less than it had been. I felt . . . neutered."

I nod, because that's it exactly—*less than*.

Even with the family I come from, I've never felt looked down on, not since I was fifteen years old. I work hard, I'm the best at what I do, and that matters to me. The idea of people thinking I'm trying to weasel my way under a door, take something—*someone*—that I don't deserve is . . . unpleasant. It lays in my gut like a rotten food—needing to be purged.

"Do you know how long it lasted?" Nicholas asks.

"How long?"

"About five minutes. That's how long it took for me to spot Olivia across the room. And then I thought—*I get to have her*. Keep her. Love her and be loved by her . . . forever. This astounding, brilliant woman. Then I asked myself: *Why do I give a shit about the opinions of people I've never given a shit about and still don't?*" He snaps his fingers. "And like that, the unpleasantness got knocked on its arse. And I felt like me again."

I take a pull of my beer. "So it's just that easy, then?"

Nicholas looks at me thoughtfully. "When you look at her, does the whole world just sort of . . . fade away? And she's the only thing you see? The only thing you ever *want* to see?"

I smile stupidly. "Yeah . . . yeah, it's just like that."

"Then yes, it's that easy."

Nicholas drinks his beer. "Besides, when it's all said and done . . . I'm still a prince and you can still kill anyone in the room with your bare fucking hands. So . . ." He taps his bottle to mine, "cheers."

CHAPTER 23

Ellie

After leaving Logan's house last night, I didn't go back to the party. I couldn't. Couldn't imagine having to slap on a smile and pretend that I was okay. That I didn't feel like my chest cavity was filled with concrete. But although I was sad, I didn't cry. Because it doesn't feel like Logan and I are done—like we're over—like I need to mourn. It's more like we're stuck, twisted up in vines that are holding us in place.

Olivia came to my room. She left the party early, because she was tired and even with the flats, her feet and ankles were swollen. Her toes look like ten overstuffed sausages—the kind that Bosco once ate a whole package of. Our dad's coming to Wessco next week, so he'll be here when the babies are born and he's bringing Bosco with him—the little demon. It'll be good to see them, to talk to my dad, hug him. I've missed him. He's good at reminding me that even when life is difficult, we can figure it out, make it better.

Liv and I talked about men. How stupid they can be, how stubborn. She said that change is hard for everyone—but for leaders like Logan and Nicholas, it's particularly difficult. Olivia made a lot of sense—she gave me sage, old-married-woman advice.

Then she offered me her bat.

I love her.

And now I'm in my room, lying on the bed, staring up at the canopy, my phone playing music from random playlists. "Collide" by Howie Day comes on—I've always liked this song. It reminds me of me and Logan. How our lives have woven around each other's through the years. So many memories and moments. We'd circle each other, watch one another, veer away or try to fight it . . . but we were always pulled back together. Colliding. Connecting.

There was never going to be anyone for me but Logan St. James.

And despite how things went down last night, I believe he feels the same way. I remember the caress of his hand on my face, the way he looks as me like I'm the only thing he sees. I hear his whispers in my head, worshipful words, because he cherishes me. I know it; I feel the truth of it deep inside.

The song lyrics make me think of what he must be feeling right now. He said he wanted to be a part of something, but now he's not a part of anything.

Logan's lost his place. His footing.

For someone like him, that must be awful. And because I love him, I should be patient and supportive. I was right to call him out for standing me up—that wasn't okay—but I should have listened more. I should help him find his new place.

Considering I want to be a psychologist, my empathy could use a little work.

I grab my phone and type a text to Logan:

I love you

But before I can hit send, someone knocks on my door. For a second I think it could be Olivia coming back to check on me. Then I start to smile as I imagine it might be Logan—coming to find me at the same time I'm reaching out to him. Wouldn't that be romantic?

I climb off the bed and go to the door, excited.

But when I open it, my excitement plummets, and so does my smile.

Because it's not Logan.

He tells me his name is Cain Gallagher. And it's clear he's an angry man.

It's in the hiss of his words and tight clench of his hand around the gun he's pointing at me. He's somewhere in his late thirties, medium height, with a thin but strong build, and his eyes are small and sharp like two poisonous darts. He's controlled, focused and wrathful.

He tells me his mother used to work in the palace, that he grew up here, was even an assistant gardener when he was younger. Then he moved away, got a job and got married, but his life never became what he wanted it to be.

What he deserved it to be.

His mother passed away a few years ago and he moved back to Wessco.

And that's when things really went south. He lost his house and his career, his marriage fell apart—but it wasn't because of anything he did. It was done *to* him.

And somehow, in his twisted rage . . . it became Nicholas Pembrook's fault.

Because Nicholas had everything, and deserved nothing.

So Cain Gallagher decided to fix things. To make it right, make it even.

It was Cain who set The Horny Goat on fire. It was Cain who sent the letters and left that sick box for my sister. And it will be Cain who takes Nicholas's wife and children away from him. Today.

I don't know why he tells me all of this, but I think he's

going to kill me, so it won't matter anyway. He seems to want someone to know that it was him, that he bested them all.

It would be too easy to say that Cain Gallagher is insane—I don't think he is. At least, not in the technical sense. He knows what he's doing. He knows that it's wrong. He just doesn't care.

Because he's so, so angry.

He shoves the gun closer and I smell the gun metal, almost feel the cold press of steel. A scream is caught in my throat—because it's terrifying. I want to put my hands up and cower, I want to pull out of his grip and run, but I don't. Because I'm so afraid of the end of that gun. Petrified that if I struggle or move the wrong way it will go off. It will end me.

So I don't scream or fight or thrash. When he tells me to sit in the chair I do, frozen and as still as possible.

I barely breathe.

There's a knock on my bedroom door and the gun jostles in Cain's hand. I squeeze my eyes shut and wait for the blast. But it doesn't come.

Instead, I hear Logan's beautiful voice.

"Ellie. It's me—open up, we need to talk."

Cain moves behind me and aims the gun at the door.

Oh no. Oh no. *No, no, no, no, no . . .*

"Go away, Logan."

"Ellie, please. I was a twat, I know . . . I'm sorry. Let me in."

And I want to shout to him that I understand. That I've already forgiven him, that I love him.

But that will only get him killed.

So I lie.

"No, you were right. The princess's sister and the East Amboy bodyguard don't make sense—we'll never last."

"Elle . . ."

"I've changed my mind, Logan. I want the fairy tale. I want what Olivia has . . . castles and carriages . . . and like you said, you'll never be able to give me that. I would just be settling for you. You'll never be able to make me happy."

And it's as if I can feel his shock. His pain. And I'm sorry. I'm so, so sorry.

The doorknob moves. "Ellie—"

I panic, screaming at the top of my lungs.

"Don't come in! I don't want to see you! Go away, Logan. We're done—just *go*!"

Please go, I beg silently. *Please go*, my soul cries.

Go and live an amazing life, Logan. Love deeply and truly. I wish that for him. I want that for him—a life of joy and beauty and laughter.

I hear his footsteps retreating. Leaving me. And I'm glad. My shoulders sag and my lungs deflate with relief.

Until Cain taps my temple with the gun. "Call your sister."

And the terror pulls my muscles tight again. I start to answer him, and then the door booms open . . .

Logan

One thought repeats in my head. One pledge, one promise:

I'm going to kill this man.

For touching her. For scaring her. For holding a weapon on her.

He will never leave this fucking room alive.

"Get that gun away from her," I growl, measuring the distance from me to him—calculating the seconds it'll take to reach him.

Ellie's eyes are wide with terror, her face bleached white.

"Whatever you're thinking," he hisses at me, "however fast you might be, I promise this bullet is faster. It'll tear a hole in her head before you lay a finger on me."

He punctuates his words by moving the gun closer to Ellie's temple, pressing it against her skin. "Shut the door."

I grind my teeth and shut the fucking door. Because I can't get to her in time.

Not yet.

He lifts Ellie by the arm, sticking the gun between her shoulder blades and backing up, keeping her in front of him like a shield.

She shakes her head, crying. "Why didn't you go, Logan? You would be safe."

"I'll never leave you." I swear to her. "Never."

"Very sweet." The man spits. He tells me to sit in the chair near the fireplace, to put my arms behind the back. I hear a rustle of plastic before he tells Ellie, "Tie him up. Tightly, or I'll shoot you both."

I feel her hands against my wrists, securing . . . zip ties. *Fucking zip ties.* Almost impossible to stretch or break no matter how much adrenaline and fury is pumping through me.

He yanks Ellie up and pushes her towards the desk, where the phone is. They're both in front of me now—which is better. If I can see them, it will be easier to make my move when the chance presents itself.

"There are too many guards around your sister's room. Call her—tell her to come here. Now."

"And you're gonna do what, exactly?" I ask, wanting to keep his attention on me. "You think they're just gonna let you walk out of here with the Duchess?"

"They'd better. If not, I'll put two shots in her belly. It may not kill her, but it'll take care of the bastards she's carrying."

"You're not getting anywhere near my sister, you sick fuck," Ellie hisses.

He lashes out to backhand her, but Ellie lifts her forearm, blocking the strike like I taught her years ago.

That's my girl.

He grips her by the hair, twisting her neck up to look at him. "Call her!"

"No!" Ellie shouts, even as a tear leaks from her eye.

I'm going to rip his head off his fucking shoulders, I swear to God.

But then suddenly he gets real calm. Thoughtful. He releases Ellie's hair, raises his arm and points the gun at my head.

"Call her, or I'm going to blow his brains out all over that wall. I don't need him; I'll still have you."

A strangled whimper comes from Ellie's throat, and then more tears. "No . . ."

"You have ten seconds. I'm counting."

"Logan . . ." Ellie whispers. And it's tortured. Because she can't call.

We both know it.

"Listen to me, Ellie. It's okay. It's all right, love."

She shakes her head, sobbing. "What do I do?"

I look into her perfect blue eyes and in my mind I'm holding her, comforting her, giving her my strength. "You know what I want you to do."

And my gaze drifts over her beautiful face, memorizing every curve and angle.

"I love you, Ellie," I choke out. "I should've told you sooner and more, but I do. These last weeks have been the best of my life. More than I ever dreamed, and I dreamed of you so often. Thank you, my sweet girl, for loving so well."

Her pretty face crumples. "I love you, Logan. Please don't leave me . . . please . . ."

"*Shhh* . . . it's all right. Everything will work out, I swear, Ellie. I promise you."

And I believe that, truly. Because there has to be a God—a

woman like Ellie Hammond doesn't happen by accident. My girl was made by design. And if there is a God, he'll take care of her, protect her.

I hate that it won't be me. I want to be the man who holds her and keeps her. But even if I don't get to have that honor, when this ends, however it does . . . she'll come out the other side unscathed.

I believe that with all my heart—the one that has only ever belonged to her.

She reaches for me. "Logan."

"Close your eyes now. Close your eyes, Ellie, and know that I love you."

She doesn't close her eyes. Ellie falls to the ground, sobbing.

Then a moment later she's throwing herself at me. She covers my body with hers, wrapping her arms around the chair and hugging me.

"Ellie, stop!" My blood curdles with the horror that he could shoot her.

But he doesn't shoot. And she doesn't stop.

Not until she presses the cold, steely weight of the knife I strapped to her leg years ago into my hand, behind the chair—where the fucker can't see. When she looks into my face, her pupils are tighter and focused; she's calmer now, almost relieved.

She turns her head, staring at the gun that's pointed at her head.

"I'll call. I'll call my sister now."

"Get up!" The soon-to-be-dead bastard yanks Ellie off me and tosses her towards the desk. She makes a show of fumbling with the phone, dropping the receiver, giving me time to cut the plastic ties around my wrists.

I wait for him to lower the gun, just a bit to his side, so it's not trained on Ellie directly. And then I move. Spring up and grab him.

A shot echoes in the room, blasting my eardrums, then another . . .

Then, with the firm, harsh twist of my hands and the sound of a snapping neck—it's over. The man drops in a dead heap at Ellie's feet.

I take her in my arms, weak and heavy-limbed with the knowledge that she's safe. I scan her body, skim my hand over her, checking for injury. "Are you hit? Did he hurt you?"

She shakes her head, then cries, "Logan, you're bleeding!"

"It's just a scratch." I guide her towards the door, my shoulder throbbing.

Ellie grabs a shirt off the bed as we walk out into the hall. I lean against the wall, sliding down to the floor. She yells for help, and there's commotion as people rush to us and into the room.

Ellie tears her shirt into two pieces and presses one to my shoulder and one to my arm, and I groan—because it fucking stings.

"You're bleeding a lot."

Huh. So I am. The white cloths are quickly turning red.

I shrug. "Two scratches. Don't worry."

But she is worried. Her full little mouth is set in a tight frown and her brows are puckered.

I tilt my head at her. "You're looking very pretty today, Ellie."

Her eyes spark brightly and her eyes flare.

"Seriously? Are you high?"

I grin, feeling a bit high. "Kiss me, love."

She yells at me instead. "You've been fucking shot, Logan!"

I crook my finger at her, drawing her closer. And I wink. "That's the very best time for kissing."

Then I pull her to me with my good hand and cover her rosebud mouth with mine, kissing her deep and long.

And then . . . I black out.

CHAPTER 24

Ellie

Two weeks later

Logan is going to be knighted by the Queen. For outstanding sacrifice to the Crown. We got the official proclamation today. He's going to be "Sir" Logan soon.

I haven't thought of the details yet, but I have a feeling the title will be part of some titillating bedroom role-play in our future.

The story's been in all the papers. How he saved the day—protected Princess Olivia and her babies and her sister too. He's a hero. Not that that's news to me, he's been my hero for years, but now he gets to be Wessco's hero as well.

When it comes to recovering from the gunshot wounds in his shoulder and arm, however . . . he's a big fucking baby.

Typical. *Men.*

I think he acts that way on purpose. *My bandage itches, my soup is cold . . . My cock is hard—how about you come over here and help me out with that, lass?*

The doctor said no strenuous activity, but Logan's idea of strenuous and mine are two different things. He hasn't ripped his stitches, but it's not for lack of trying.

He's a terrible patient. Sexy and broody and too sweet for his own good.

He tells me he loves me every day. Every. Single. Day. First thing in the morning, last thing before we drift off in each other's arms. And it thrills me, makes my heart throb every time.

Logan's accepted having security around the house—because the day he got out of the hospital, I moved in with him. Being the protected as well as the protector no longer eats at him like it did in the beginning.

Seeing a gun held to my head changed that for him.

Now, Logan's okay having a small army surrounding me, guarding the house and the new life we're building together. He's gotten friendly with the guys on detail—telling them when they're doing something wrong, calling them out when he catches them looking at my ass.

He hasn't made any big employment moves yet, but he's leaning toward starting his own security consulting firm. It's something he's good at, something he knows—it's his calling, his duty, he says. For now, he's okay money-wise, living off savings and focusing on finishing the house and recovering.

Whatever Logan decides to do, he'll be successful—he doesn't have it in him to be anything less.

The Queen was right. Love isn't a cure; it doesn't magically solve every problem. But it makes solving those problems worth it. Love is our inspiration, our motivation . . . and our reward.

Two weeks later

"Fucking Christ, do I love you."

Logan's voice melts against my ear, his breath tickling, his strong chest pressed against my back, his words making me wetter, where he's hot and hard, inside me. My head lolls against his good shoulder and my arms rise to wrap around his neck behind me.

"Logan . . ." I sigh.

His fingers trace my lips and I suck one into my mouth, scraping the pad with my teeth. Then he slides his hand down, caressing my breast and pinching my nipple. It sends a jolt of sensation between my legs and my pleasure builds and builds. I turn my head, seeking his mouth—wanting his lips on mine.

And he kisses me, because he knows that's what I need.

His hand slides lower, finding my clit, petting me in perfect time to the thrusting of his cock.

"Yes . . . yes," I breathe against his mouth, my voice reedy.

I climb and climb and then I peak—soar. My back arches and everything tightens and contracts as waves of hot, blissful sensations tear through my body. Logan holds me to him with his strong arms as I spasm around him.

Then when I'm weak and chasing my breath, he gently guides my upper body down to the bathroom vanity counter. Resting my cheek against the cool marble, tenderly running his fingers through my hair.

Then, he fucks me.

Grasping my hips, hard and fast, he lets go, losing himself to how good it feels, grunting as he pounds into me. I love it when he comes—I can feel it, the hot pulse of his cock as his semen fills me, so deep inside. His rough, harsh gasp against my shoulder blade when he folds over me, thrusting and jerking one final, glorious time.

Then it's all feathery kisses, soft and sweet and adoring. This is how we start our day.

Not too shabby.

After he slips out of me, I turn in his arms and kiss him fully on his minty-fresh mouth. And then I see the time on his watch.

"Shit! We're going to be late. We can't be late."

I slip away from him and turn the shower on full blast.

Logan gives me a teasing grin. "So that's how it is, huh? You got what you wanted from me."

I giggle, turning back towards him to peck his lips. "Yeah, I really did."

His pinches my ass, playfully. "I'm just a piece of meat to you."

"No—you're a sexy piece of meat to me. And I love you."

His mahogany eyes go warm and light, almost golden. It's how he gazes at me whenever I say those words.

After one more quick kiss, I hop in the shower—because we really do have to hurry. If we're late, I'll never hear the end of it from Livvy.

She wanted us to sleep at her and Nicholas's apartments last night, but I wanted to stay here, in Logan's house—*our* house. It's my favorite place to be, even more favorite than a palace.

In record time, I'm out of the shower, hair dripping, my T-shirt sticking to my still-damp body, running out the door to the SUV in the driveway. My dress and Logan's tux are waiting for us at the palace, where the glam squad will make me presentable.

Harry, a young, carefree security guard with shoulder-length brown hair, argues with Bartholomew, a bulkier bodyguard, in the driveway.

"You don't have it in you, mate."

"Oh, I have it in me—you can believe that."

I have no idea what their pissing contest is about, but I don't have time for it.

"You're both gonna have my foot in your asses if somebody doesn't drive me to the palace right now!" I yell.

They both look shocked.

And then they move their asses.

"She's kind of a violent little thing, isn't she?" Harry says to Logan as he climbs in the backseat with me.

Logan just laughs. And looks at me. "You're going to make a good mum one day."

I shake my head at him. "That's what you got out of my statement? Really?"

"Sure—you sound just like Tommy's mum and she's the best one I know."

And something occurs to me—something we haven't talked about yet.

"Do you want that one day?" I imitate Logan's accent. "To be a da?"

"I do." His face softens. "As long as you're the mum, I'd like very much to be the da."

My stomach gets warm and fluttery. "Me too. Should probably make me a Mrs. first, though."

Logan kisses my palm, smiling. "That's the plan."

Good to know.

But for today, there's only one wedding that matters: the royal one.

Lady Sarah sits at the vanity table, in the private bridal rooms in the back of St. George's Cathedral, looking unbelievably stunning in a short-sleeved white lace wedding gown with a two-tiered tulle skirt and cathedral-length lace veil. She's the image of the perfect bride. A dark-haired Bridal Barbie.

She stares at her reflection in the mirror, chanting, "It'll be fine. It will be fine. It will be fine."

"Is she on drugs?" Penelope Von Titebottum, Sarah's sister asks, pointing with the lily-and-lilac bouquet that matches her lavender maid-of-honor gown. "Did you take drugs, Sarah?"

"I wish." Sarah closes her eyes and breathes deep and cleansingly. "It's a calming technique Mother's meditation specialist taught me. 'Say it until you believe it.' It'll be fine. All fine. Very, very fine."

She really does sound like she's on drugs.

My poor sister waddles out of the bathroom, looking uncomfortable in a pretty lilac maternity-styled dress with an adorable white bow above her ginormous belly.

I'm not in the wedding party. I'm just here to look pretty. And help Sarah stay calm if I can. And . . . catch Livvy's babies, if needed.

"You feeling okay, Liv?" I ask her. "You look kind of pale."

She rubs my arm. "It's my only color these days." Then she lets out a slow breath . . . just like Sarah's.

"It will be fine . . . It will be fine . . ."

"It *will* be fine," my sister tells Sarah firmly. She's the only one in the room who's walked the royal green mile before, so I'm hoping Sarah will take her opinion to heart.

Sarah stands and nods. "You're right. Weddings happen every day." She shrugs. "I mean, truly, how many people are even out there anyway?"

Olivia closes her eyes and rubs her lower back.

Penelope tries to be helpful. "Not many. Only a few . . . thousand."

Slowly, Liv sinks down into the chair along the wall. Inhaling deeply.

"Thousands—child's play." Sarah scoffs—not convincingly. "And the total watching on television can't be more than a couple . . ."

"Million." Penelope waves her hand. "Tens of millions. *Pfft.*"

Sarah nods.

And then she collapses onto the vanity bench, covering her face with her hands. "Oh dear God, help me! Please . . . send me a miracle."

That's when Liv starts to pant. "Hee, hee, hee, hoo. Hee, hee, hee, hooooo."

Oh boy.

Sarah spins around. "Olivia, . . . are you . . . in labor?"

Holding her stomach, my sister nods. "I'm sorry. I'm sorry, I know this is—"

"—amazing!!" Sarah yells, throwing her arms up to heaven. "Thank you, Lord! Yes!"

"You're not upset that I'm stealing your thunder?" Olivia asks, panting.

"Take all the thunder, and the lightning, too! If anyone even suspects you're in labor no one will look at me. It's perfect." The future queen sobers. "Will you be able to make it through the ceremony, though? I don't want you to take any risks."

My sister grimaces. "I should be able to make it down the aisle. But I want to get to the hospital soon, so if the Archbishop starts droning on, I'll give you a signal. If I'm moaning in agony—you'll know."

My sister's spunkiness has returned to her.

And then a thought occurs to me. "Hey, the babies aren't just going to share a birthday with each other, they're going to share Henry and Sarah's wedding anniversary. Lenora's gonna be *pissed*."

Just before the ceremony is set to begin, I find Logan out in the main Cathedral. It's beautiful. Light streams through the windows, depicting saints and biblical scenes in richly-colored stained glass. When my eyes finally land on Logan, it's like the wind is knocked out of me—because I haven't seen him since we parted ways to get dressed at the palace. And now, he's wearing his tuxedo.

God damn, he is *fine*.

The cut of his jacket shows off his broad, strong shoulders.

The charcoal grey cravat accentuates his masculine throat and gives him a sophisticated but roguish look—like he stepped out of the pages of a romance novel. His dress pants hug him perfectly, highlighting his powerful legs, his hard, gorgeous ass, and his thick, impressive "endowments." I've seen Logan wearing a tuxedo before, but this time is different.

Because now, he's all mine.

And the way he stares at me—how his eyes drag up from my silver, strappy heels, over my curves beneath the snug, satin pale pink gown, to the blond curls piled high on my head—it seems like he's lost his breath too.

He swallows hard. "You look like an angel, Ellie." He lowers his voice and bends his head nearer. "Like a scrumptious dessert . . . and I'm going to eat you the first chance I get."

Heat spreads low in my stomach—I'll never get enough of him, or his wicked, adoring words. But then I blink, remembering why I sought him out, and that any eating will have to wait a while.

Aware of the guests wandering to their seats, I rise up and whisper in Logan's ear that Olivia is in labor.

He wants to get the car, take her to the hospital immediately. But I talk him out of it—even while he insists that my sister is "fucking batty" to wait. Then he covertly makes his way up to the altar, where Nicholas stands as best man beside Henry, both of them looking regal and elegant in their military uniforms.

"*What?*" Nicholas shouts. His face goes rigid and a little pale.

The whole church freezes—staring at the prince—like the greatest mannequin challenge ever.

I hike up my dress and my heels click on the stone floor as I run up the side aisle, passing the dozens of marble columns that rise to the high arched ceiling. I scoot between Nicholas, Henry and Logan who are talking like a football team huddle planning the next play.

"It's fine, guys. Everything's fine. All fine."

Now I sound like I'm on drugs.

Nicholas's green eyes are wide and wild. "No—none of this is fine."

"Olivia knows what she's doing. She would never put the babies at risk," I insist. "Please follow her lead on this, Nicholas." I give him an encouraging smile. "Happy wife, happy life."

He's unmoved—his face grumpy—his jaw like granite.

"How's Sarah?" Henry asks.

"She's okay. Calmer, now that there's a distraction to take some of the attention off of her."

"Good." Henry sighs, rubbing his hands on his slacks nervously. "That's good."

"And wait until you see her, Henry. You're going to lose it."

He chuckles. "I always do."

Henry rests his hand on his brother's arm. "The sooner we start, the sooner you can get on to the baby business. Yeah?"

Nicholas hesitates, but finally, he stiffly nods.

And everyone takes their places as Logan and I slide into our spots in the third pew. The music starts to play, and the wedding begins.

The Queen is escorted first, by her nephew, stoic and oblivious to what's going on behind the scenes. The entire congregation bows and curtsies.

After the bridesmaids and tiny adorable flower girls, Livvy walks alone. Waddling and smiling. But the aisle is so damn long she has to stop twice to breathe through her tightening stomach—while still smiling. Whispers roll through the crowd like a killer wave, and you can almost hear the news stations shifting into royal-baby-watch level: hysteria.

Nicholas steps forward when she gets to the altar, taking her hand and helping her into a cushioned chair, which he ordered an usher to place on the right side of the alter. They speak quietly . . . argue quietly for a moment, then Olivia gently kisses his knuckles, soothingly placating her handsome prince.

Nicholas rubs his jaw, but with a tight expression, takes his place to Henry's right.

And then the bridal march begins.

The crowd glances at Sarah, nodding at how lovely she is—but then they return to chattering about the crazy princess who's in labor. Sarah doesn't take her eyes off Henry as she walks to him—and she doesn't look even a little terrified.

She looks like a bride in love.

Henry steps close to Sarah as she approaches, gazing down at her tenderly.

"Hello."

Sarah grins up at him impishly. "Hello."

"This is madness," he whispers.

"It suits us though, doesn't it?"

Henry offers her his arm and, elegantly, Sarah takes it.

And then, they get married—and it's more wonderful than all the Disney Princess wedding ceremonies combined.

After the Archbishop pronounces them man and wife, when they're supposed to turn and walk down the aisle together, Henry gestures to Olivia. "Women in labor and children soon-to-be born, first."

Nicholas mutters under his breath, "About bloody time."

Then he walks over to my sister, swoops her up into his arms and carries her down the aisle.

The sight is one for the history books.

Logan grabs my hand and we chase after them. Nicholas slides Livvy into the back of one of the Rolls-Royces and Logan tells the guard at the wheel, "Move over. I'm driving."

On the way to the hospital, the hardest contraction, yet, hits. Olivia scrunches her eyes and breathes through it. After it passes, she collapses against the seat.

"Oh my God...this *suuuuucks*," she says, like a true lady.

Because that's my sister; the Royal Duchess.

Queens don't wait in maternity waiting rooms. Neither do Crown Princes or their newly minted princesses or any royals. It would cause chaos. It's not tradition.

The sister waits in the waiting rooms, with her boyfriend, and dad. I called my dad from the car, on the way to the hospital. There was a bunch of security—special badges, guards at every door. This hospital has delivered every royal since Nicholas's father, so they know what's up.

For the next eleven hours, we drink bad coffee, eat cold sandwiches . . . and wait. At one point, I fall asleep against Logan's chest and I dream that he asks my dad's permission to marry me.

I mean to tell Logan about it when I wake up. But before I can, Nicholas is there—walking through the hospital doors from the maternity ward, not looking like a prince at all. He looks young and exhausted, with a ten-o'clock shadow on his chin and joy in his eyes.

He looks like a new father—ecstatic and amazed—with unicorns and rainbows practically dancing in his eyes.

"It's a boy!" he tells the three of us—we're the first to know. "And a girl!"

Logan shakes his hand and pounds his back, and he gets hugs from me and my dad.

The perk of actually being on the front lines of the maternity waiting room is that you get first crack at the babies. You see them, hold them, know their names before anyone else.

I hold Lilliana Amelia Calista Ernstwhile Pembrook first. And she's perfect. Logan stands next to me and together we gaze down at her little round face, her patch of black hair, eyes shaped just like my sister's, though it's still too early to tell what color they'll be—gray green or dark blue.

Then my dad and I switch.

And I fall in love with Langdon Henry Eric Thomas Pembrook. He's just as perfect as his five-minutes-younger sister. His hair is just as black, but I think I see more of Nicholas in him around the eyes.

Olivia is sleepy, but so happy. She can't stop looking at them, and I can't blame her.

While my dad and I sit next to Olivia on one side of the bed, Logan and Nicholas move to the window and start talking about where the press will stand when they leave the hospital in a few days. The photographs that will be taken, the no-fly zone over the hospital. Because as perfect and beautiful and innocent as the twins are, these aren't just babies.

They never will be.

Already, everyone wants a piece of them.

"I don't like it." Logan crosses his arms and shakes his head. "It's too difficult to tell who's there, who can get close."

He was protective before, but Cain Gallagher's breach of security has made him even more ferocious about protecting us, even though it's technically not his job anymore.

"This is how it always goes," Nicholas laments. "Leaving the hospital is a publicly viewed event. It's tradition."

"Start a new tradition. You've got a knack for that."

My brother-in-law sits down in the chair next to Olivia's bed, holding her hand.

"Invite them to the palace," Logan suggests. "The guards can check their credentials, pat them down at the gates, and they can take their pictures of you bringing the babies out of the car, into their new home. It'll be safer."

Nicholas and Olivia look at each other, then Nicholas kisses her hand.

"Looks like we've got a new tradition."

Queen Lenora is not a hugger. She's not even an air kisser. She's more of a head patter, a shoulder tapper.

But babies are . . . well, they're fucking babies.

They're beautiful. Adorable. So cute it's almost painful to look at them. They're like kittens . . . but human.

But Queen Lenora is *really* not a hugger. Olivia, however, thinks she's a holder.

Which is why two weeks later, when the new prince and princess are first presented to Her Royal Great-Grandmama Queen Lenora, at the palace my sister places Lilliana right in her unsuspecting regal arms.

"Oh. Well . . . uh . . . all right." The Queen handles Lily like she's a bomb that could go off at any moment. Stiffly and distantly. Then Her Majesty smiles a little down at the baby. "It's very nice to make your acquaintance, Princess Lilliana."

And the baby cries.

Loud and heartbroken. And *loud*.

When Olivia moves to take her, Queen Lenora lifts her chin. "Leave her."

And she looks down at the bundle of cute in her hands, talking to her . . . like she's a dog. An upper-class dog.

"No. No-no, that won't do at all." She lays Lily on the couch beside her and claps her hands twice—quick and sharp. And miraculously, after one more little squawk, Lilliana stops crying and blinks up at the Queen.

"Thank you, much better."

She's like a scarier, meaner Mary Poppins.

"Now that you've composed yourself, you and your brother and I will take a stroll in the gardens together."

She motions to the nurse, who swaddles the baby and puts her in the pram.

"It's a bit cold for a walk, don't you think?" Nicholas asks.

"Nonsense. Fresh air is good for babies. I walked with you and Henry every day and look how well you both turned out."

"I didn't know you did that," Nicholas says softly.

"Yes, well, I'm full of surprises." The Queen slides on a pair of light brown leather gloves. "We'll make sure they're bundled adequately. I'll walk with them on the grounds every morning. Christopher—mark it in the schedule. This will be my time with them."

Guards open the double French doors and Queen Lenora pushes the twins in their pram out into the cool, overcast day. She talks to them as they stroll, and her voice floats inside for all to hear.

"I was born in Landlow Castle, during a snowstorm. The midwife was unable to reach us because the roads were impassable. So my grandmother delivered me. And she was a horrid woman, very strict and rigid. Not warm and delightful as I am . . ."

Logan puts his arm around me and whispers.

"It's official. I've now seen it fucking all."

EPILOGUE

Logan

Five years later

I wake to the soft sounds of music playing from the kitchen.

And that's how I know where Ellie is. It started about three years ago—her rising before me. Most times she's in the kitchen, sometimes in the den, but almost always, she's got one of her favorites playing low from the speakers. Today it's "Say You Won't Let Go."

It was our wedding song.

I look up through our skylight ceiling—it's dark, not yet dawn, and pouring cold rain. It's Sunday, and while every day is a workday when you own your own business, I won't be working for S&S Securities today. That stands for St. James and Sullivan—or Sullivan and St. James, depending on which one of us you ask. Tommy went in on the venture with me and we busted our arses to make it successful. It's good work, honest work.

We have a technical team that installs home security systems, but the main business is training and contracting personal bodyguards, as well as security details to guard and monitor property. Even the palace has contracted our guys—because we have a reputation for being the best, and it's well deserved.

We're not a fight club—we don't take just anyone. Our

people have to have a natural skill for it, they have to want it, they have to earn it.

I roll out of bed, slip on a pair of black running pants and walk down the hall. I finished the house in the first year we lived there, and it turned out even better than I'd imagined. The brick makes it solid and sturdy, the gleaming wood touches and earthy colors make it beautiful . . . and having Ellie here makes it a home. She hung curtains in every room, framed pictures on the walls. I pass one of the bedrooms on my right—the room we painted blue together.

When I make it down to the kitchen, she's at the counter, placing warm baked scones on a rack to cool. Stealthily, I move up close behind her and lay my hands across her cotton pajama-clad hips, pulling her against me, rubbing the length of my stiff cock between the cheeks of her perfect arse.

Her head tilts back on my shoulder and her hair tickles my chest. "Aren't you tired from last night?"

I kiss her temple and smell her skin. "I'll never get tired of fucking you, Ellie."

My hands slide to her front, resting on the small, firm swell where our baby sleeps. Ellie's so lovely when she's carrying. Something about watching her grow with the baby I put inside her turns me into a bit of a savage. I can't keep my hands off her when she's like this.

Though I suppose that's also true when she's not like this.

And it turns out, when we decided to start a family and forgo birth control, lots of fucking . . . makes lots of babies. She's four months gone with this latest one—our third.

"Come on, Declan! Jump. I'll catch you."

The little voice pipes up from the baby monitor on the counter.

"Like this, Declan, look!"

That would be three-year-old Finn urging one-and-a-half-year-old Declan to escape his crib.

I laugh into Ellie's shoulder and she giggles.

A clap of thunder booms over us and I nuzzle Ellie's neck. "It's raining. Miss Princess Jane is going to be quite put out that she can't ride her pony."

We're going to the palace today, for Henry and Sarah's oldest daughter Jane's fourth birthday. It's not the public celebration; this one's small and private—just family.

"Henry will just bring the pony inside for her," Ellie says.

"The Queen will love that," I say sarcastically, shaking my head. "Princess Jane has Henry wrapped around her little finger."

"Like you wouldn't do the same if it was Finn," Ellie teases.

"Finn doesn't want a pony. He wants a bazooka for Christmas—he told me so the other day. Haven't figured out yet how Santa's elves are going to manage that request."

Ellie laughs, pointing at me. "He's definitely your son."

I rub my eyes. "Yeah, he's mine all right. But I think the bazooka idea comes from your dad. He was playing army-man with him last week."

Ellie's father comes to Wessco every other month—he's been doing it for years now. He's still sober, still lives in New York, managing the charitable Amelia's restaurants that bear his beloved wife's name. I believe it's part of how he was able to finally make peace with her passing—by honoring her, keeping a part of the quaint coffee shop that was her dream, alive and thriving.

There's a scuffling sound from the monitor, a thud and then cheers of triumph.

"Mummy, Daddy—he did it! Declan jumped out of his crib. He jumped!"

I kiss my wife sweetly on her pretty mouth.

"And our fearless jumper Declan is all *your* son."

I'm about to head up to get the boys, but the gate at the top of the stairs will keep them safely contained for a bit longer. I wait because Tommy Sullivan lumbers through our backdoor, taking a seat at the kitchen counter, looking like a sack of sad.

Like many students who take a gap year, Ellie never went back to finish her advanced psychology degree. If she ever wants to, I'll support her 100 percent, but for now she seems content—happy—to take care of our boys and our home. And to let me take care of her.

But even without the degree, she's a listener, a helper and a counselor to our family and friends. Ellie slides a cup of tea in front of Tommy, and hands a steaming mug to me.

"I think this might be it," Tommy says. "It might really be over."

He's talking about Abigail Haddock. *Doctor* Abigail Haddock—the stunning, auburn-haired physician Tommy met in the hospital five years ago while he recovered from that gash on his head. The woman he stole a kiss from, while pretending to be delirious.

And it's been a roller coaster ever since. A sordid tale of lust and love, hiding and seeking—both of them too fucking stubborn to admit they care for each other more than they're willing to let on.

"Abby says she's going on a date with that doctor she works with." He looks at me. "We may have to take this guy out."

I blow the steam from my mug and shrug.

"Okay."

Ellie frowns back and forth between us.

"No. No, there will be no *taking out* of anyone."

I flash Tommy the okay sign. Ellie spots it, then smacks my arm. And I smirk, because she's still really cute when she's pissy.

When I hear the boys rattling the gate, I head for the stairs, leaving my wife with her elbows on the counter, prodding my best friend to tell her all about it, so she can save him.

Like she saved me.

Like we saved each other.

Despite the rain, Princess Jane's birthday party was lively and fun. Ellie was right—Prince Henry brought the pony inside for his daughter, and they'll probably never get the stink out of the ballroom.

The Queen sniffed and scowled, but I could tell she enjoys the antics of her offspring more than anything in the world. She's a wily one, hides it well—but I could still read it in the twinkle of her eye, the occasional quirk of her mouth and quick nod of her head, when she thought no one was looking.

And while Princess Jane is not Her Majesty's twin, she is her little shadow. Even at just four years old, the girl idolizes her Great-Granny, follows her, imitates her, does her best to be as royal and regal as her. The Queen takes pride in that too.

Just as Ellie chose not to go back to school, Prince Nicholas and Olivia chose not to go back to New York. Olivia's feelings about the palace softened, and she views it more as a safety net than a cage. And with the sweetness of his young family surrounding him, Nicholas doesn't think of his royal duties as the burden he once did. He enjoys them now, enjoys teaching his children about their lineage and gently preparing them for the royal roles they'll one day play, if they choose. Their decision to stay in Wessco was a joyous one for Ellie and for Tommy and me. Nicholas isn't my employer anymore—but he is my friend. Family. And that's even better.

And Ellie and I aren't the only ones popping out babies like it's going out of style. In addition to five-year-olds Prince Langdon and Princess Lilliana, they added baby Theo to the mix six months ago. Along with Princess Jane, Henry and Sarah have three-year-old Prince Edward—he and my Finn are the best of friends, thick as little thieves—as well as their sweet newborn, Margaret.

Life changes us, with its twists and turns, in ways we don't always see coming. It changes what we want, what we dream, lays blessings in our hands better than anything we could've imagined. These days, I no longer think about wanting to be a part of something bigger than myself. Because I already am. The home Ellie and I have, the family we've created—it's the most noble, lasting and precious thing I could ever imagine. I don't need anything more.

By the time we make it back home from the party at the palace, it's after dark and still raining. Ellie and I give the boys a bath, then we all snuggle together on the sofa in the den, me shirtless in sleeping pants, the three of them in sweet cotton pajamas. We lie under the soft blanket, with a fire glowing in the fireplace and the wind and rain howling outside.

While Declan pounds and climbs on me like I'm his personal jungle gym, Ellie reads Finn a bedtime story—about evil dragons and a hero who rescues the damsel . . . and a damsel who rescues him back.

"And they lived *happily ever after*." Ellie and Finn chime the last words together, closing the storybook.

Our oldest son gazes at his lovely mummy, like she's the all-knowing and all-beautiful Queen of the Universe. "Is it because they're a prince and a princess? Like Auntie Liv and Uncle Nick? Is that why they beat the dragon and get to live happily?"

Ellie rubs her nose against our son's button one and strokes his dark hair.

"No, baby. Happily ever after isn't just for royalty." My darling girl looks at me with all the love and adoration a woman can have for a man.

"Happy endings are for all of us."

BOOKS 1 & 2 IN
THE ROYALLY SERIES
AVAILABLE NOW!

Royally Screwed

Nicholas Arthur Frederick Edward Pembrook, Crowned Prince of Wessco, aka "His Royal Hotness," is wickedly charming, devastatingly handsome, and unabashedly arrogant—hard not to be when people are constantly bowing down to you.

Then, one snowy night in Manhattan, the prince meets a dark haired beauty who doesn't bow down. Instead, she throws a pie in his face.

Nicholas wants to find out if she tastes as good as her pie, and this heir apparent is used to getting what he wants.

Dating a prince isn't what waitress Olivia Hammond ever imagined it would be.

There's a disapproving queen, a wildly inappropriate spare heir, relentless paparazzi, and brutal public scrutiny. While they've traded in horse drawn carriages for Rolls Royces and haven't chopped anyone's head off lately—the royals are far from accepting of this commoner.

But to Olivia—Nicholas is worth it.

Nicholas grew up with the whole world watching, and now Marriage Watch is in full force. In the end, Nicholas has to decide who he is and, more importantly, who he wants to be: a King . . . or the man who gets to love Olivia forever.

Royally Matched

Some men are born responsible, some men have responsibility thrust upon them. Henry John Edgar Thomas Pembrook, Prince of Wessco, just got the motherlode of all responsibility dumped in his regal lap.

He's not handling it well.

Hoping to help her grandson to rise to the occasion, Queen Lenora agrees to give him "space"—but while the Queen's away, the Prince will play. After a chance meeting with an American television producer, Henry finally makes a decision all on his own:

Welcome to Matched: Royal Edition.

A reality TV dating game show featuring twenty of the world's most beautiful blue bloods gathered in the same castle. Only one will win the diamond tiara, only one will capture the handsome prince's heart.

While Henry revels in the sexy, raunchy antics of the contestants as they fight, literally, for his affection, it's the quiet, bespectacled girl in the corner—with the voice of an angel and a body that would tempt a saint—who catches his eye.

The more Henry gets to know Sarah Mirabelle Zinnia Von Titebottum, the more enamored he becomes of her simple beauty, her strength, her kind spirit . . . and her naughty sense of humor.

But Rome wasn't built in a day—and irresponsible royals aren't reformed overnight.

As he endeavors to right his wrongs, old words take on whole new meanings for the dashing Prince. Words like, Duty, Honor and most of all—Love.

ROYALLY SCREWED

Nicholas

One would think, as accustomed as I am to being watched, that I wouldn't be affected by the sensation of someone staring at me while I sleep.

One would be wrong.

My eyes spring open, to see Fergus's scraggly, crinkled countenance just inches from my face. "Bloody hell!"

It's not a pleasant view.

His one good eye glares disapprovingly, while the other—the wandering one—that my brother and I always suspected wasn't lazy at all, but a freakish ability to see everything at once, gazes towards the opposite side of the room.

Every stereotype starts somewhere, with some vague but

lingering grain of truth. I've long suspected the stereotype of the condescending, cantankerous servant began with Fergus.

God knows the wrinkled bastard is old enough.

He straightens up at my bedside, as much as his hunched, ancient spine will let him. "Took you long enough to wake up. You think I don't have better things to do? Was just about to kick you."

He's exaggerating. About having better things to do—not the plan to kick me.

I love my bed. It was an eighteenth birthday gift from the King of Genovia. It's a four-column, gleaming piece of art, hand-carved in the sixteenth century from one massive piece of Brazilian mahogany. My mattress is stuffed with the softest Hungarian goose feathers, my Egyptian cotton sheets have a thread count so high it's illegal in some parts of the world, and all I want to do is to roll over and bury myself under them like a child determined not to get up for school.

But Fergus's raspy warning grates like sandpaper on my eardrums.

"You're supposed to be in the green drawing room in twenty-five minutes."

And ducking under the covers is no longer an option. They won't save you from machete-wielding psychopaths . . . or a packed schedule.

Sometimes I think I'm schizophrenic. Dissociative. Possibly a split personality. It wouldn't be unheard of. All sorts of disorders show up in ancient family trees—hemophiliacs, insomniacs, lunatics . . . gingers. Guess I should feel lucky not to be any of those.

My problem is voices. Not *those* kinds of voices—more like

reactions in my head. Answers to questions that don't match what actually ends up coming out of my mouth.

I almost never say what I really think. Sometimes I'm so full of shit my eyes could turn brown. And, it might be for the best.

Because I happen to think most people are fucking idiots.

"And we're back, chatting with His Royal Highness, Prince Nicholas."

Speaking of idiots . . .

The light-haired, thin-boned, bespeckled man sitting across from me conducting this captivating televised interview? His name is Teddy Littlecock. No, really, that's his actual name—and from what I hear, it's not an oxymoron. Can you appreciate what it must've been like for him in school with a name like that? It's almost enough to make me feel bad for him. But not quite.

Because Littlecock is a journalist—and I have a special kind of disgust for them. The media's mission has always been to bend the mighty over a barrel and ram their transgressions up their aristocratic arses. Which, in a way, is fine—most aristocrats are first-class pricks; everybody knows that. What bothers me is when it's not deserved. When it's not even true. If there's no dirty laundry around, the media will drag a freshly starched shirt through the shit and create their own. Here's an oxymoron for you: journalistic integrity.

Old Teddy isn't just any reporter—he's Palace Approved. Which means unlike his bribing, blackmailing, lying brethren, Littlecock gets direct access—like this interview—in exchange for asking the stupidest bloody questions ever. It's mind-numbing.

Choosing between dull and dishonest is like being asked whether you want to be shot or stabbed.

"What do you do in your spare time? What are your hobbies?"

See what I mean? It's like those *Playboy* centerfold interviews—"*I like bubble baths, pillow fights, and long, naked walks on the beach.*" No she doesn't. But the point of the questions isn't to inform, it's to reinforce the fantasies of the blokes jerking off to her.

It's the same way for me.

I grin, flashing a hint of dimple—women fall all over themselves for dimples.

"Well, most nights I like to read."

I like to fuck.

Which is probably the answer my fans would rather hear. The Palace, however, would lose their ever-loving minds if I said that.

Anyway, where was I? That's right—the fucking. I like it long, hard, and frequent. With my hands on a firm, round arse—pulling some lovely little piece back against me, hearing her sweet moans bouncing off the walls as she comes around my cock. These century-old rooms have fantastic acoustics.

While some men choose women because of their talent at keeping their legs open, I prefer the ones who are good at keeping their mouths shut. Discretion and an ironclad NDA keep most of the real stories out of the papers.

"I enjoy horseback riding, polo, an afternoon of clay pigeon shooting with the Queen."

I enjoy rock climbing, driving as fast as I can without crashing, flying, good scotch, B-movies, and a scathingly passive-aggressive verbal exchange with the Queen.

It's that last one that keeps the Old Bird on her toes — my wit is her fountain of youth. Plus it's good practice for us both. Wessco is an active constitutional monarchy so unlike our ceremonial neighbors, the Queen is an equal ruling branch of government, along with Parliament. That essentially makes the royal family politicians. Top of the food chain, sure, but politicians all the same. And politics is a quick, dirty, brawling business. Every brawler knows that if you're going to bring a knife to a fistfight, that knife had better be sharp.

I cross my arms over my chest, displaying the tan, bare

forearms beneath the sleeves of my rolled-up pale-blue oxford. I'm told they have a rabid Twitter following—along with a few other parts of my body. I then tell the story of my first shoot. It's a fandom favorite—I could recite it in my sleep—and it almost feels like I am. Teddy chuckles at the ending—when my brat of a little brother loaded the launcher with a cow patty instead of a pigeon.

Then he sobers, adjusting his glasses, signaling that the sad portion of our program will now begin.

"It will be thirteen years this May since the tragic plane crash that took the lives of the Prince and Princess of Pembrook."

Called it.

I nod silently.

"Do you think of them often?"

The carved teak bracelet weighs heavily on my wrist. "I have many happy memories of my parents. But what's most important to me is that they live on through the causes they championed, the charities they supported, the endowments that carry their name. That's their legacy. By building up the foundations they advocated for, I'll ensure they'll always be remembered."

Words, words, words, talk, talk, talk. I'm good at that. Saying a lot without really answering a thing.

I think of them every single day.

It's not our way to be overly emotional—stiff upper lip, onward and upward, the king is dead—long live the king. But while to the world they were a pair of HRHs, to me and Henry they were just plain old Mum and Dad. They were good and fun and real. They hugged us often, and smacked us about when we deserved it—which was pretty often too. They were wise and kind and loved us fiercely—and that's a rarity in my social circle.

I wonder what they'd have to say about everything and how different things would be if they'd lived.

Teddy's talking again. I'm not listening, but I don't have

to—the last few words are all I need to hear. "... Lady Esmerelda last weekend?"

I've known Ezzy since our school days at Briar House. She's a good egg—loud and rowdy. "Lady Esmerelda and I are old friends."

"*Just* friends?"

She's also a committed lesbian. A fact her family wants to keep out of the press. I'm her favorite beard. Our mutually beneficial dates are organized through the Palace secretary.

I smile charmingly. "I make it a rule not to kiss and tell."

Teddy leans forward, catching a whiff of story. *The* story.

"So there is the possibility that something deeper could be developing between you? The country took so much joy in watching your parents' courtship. The people are on tenterhooks waiting for you, 'His Royal Hotness' as they call you on social media, to find your own ladylove and settle down."

I shrug. "Anything's possible."

Except for that. I won't be settling down anytime soon. He can bet his Littlecock on it.

As soon as the hot beam of front lighting is extinguished and the red recording signal on the camera blips off, I stand up from my chair, removing the microphone clipped to my collar.

Teddy stands as well. "Thank you for your time, Your Grace."

He bows slightly at the neck—the proper protocol.

I nod. "Always a pleasure, Littlecock."

That's not what she said. Ever.

Bridget, my personal secretary—a stout, middle-aged, well-ordered woman, appears at my side with a bottle of water.

"Thank you." I twist the cap. "Who's next?"

The Dark Suits thought it was a good time for a PR boost—which means days of interviews, tours, and photo shoots. My own personal fourth, fifth, and sixth circles of hell.

"He's the last for today."

"Hallelujah."

She falls in step beside me as I walk down the long, carpeted hallway that will eventually lead to Guthrie House—my private apartments at the Palace of Wessco.

"Lord Ellington is arriving shortly, and arrangements for dinner at Bon Repas are confirmed."

Being friends with me is harder than you'd think. I mean, I'm a great friend; my life, on the other hand, is a pain in the arse. I can't just drop by a pub last minute or hit up a new club on a random Friday night. These things have to preplanned, organized. Spontaneity is the only luxury I don't get to enjoy.

"Good."

With that, Bridget heads towards the palace offices and I enter my private quarters. Three floors, a full modernized kitchen, a morning room, a library, two guest rooms, servants' quarters, two master suites with balconies that open up to the most breathtaking views on the grounds. All fully restored and updated—the colors, tapestries, stonework, and moldings maintaining their historic integrity. Guthrie House is the official residence of the Prince or Princess of Pembrook—the heir apparent—whomever that may be. It was my father's before it was mine, my grandmother's before her coronation.

Royals are big on hand-me-downs.

I head up to the master bedroom, unbuttoning my shirt, looking forward to the hot, pounding feel of eight showerheads turned up to full blast. My shower is fucking fantastic.

But I don't make it that far.

Fergus meets me at the top of the stairs.

"She wants to see you," he croaks.

And *she* needs no further introduction.

I rub a hand down my face, scratching the dark five o'clock shadow on my chin. "When?"

"When do you think?" Fergus scoffs. "Yesterday, o'course."

Of course.

Back in the old days, the throne was the symbol of a monarch's power. In illustrations it was depicted with the rising sun behind it, the clouds and stars beneath it—the seat for a descendent of God himself. If the throne was the emblem of power, the throne room was the place where that sovereignty was wielded. Where decrees were issued, punishments were pronounced, and the command of "bring me his head" echoed off the cold stone walls.

That was then.

Now, the royal office is where the work gets done—the throne room is used for public tours. And yesterday's throne is today's executive desk. I'm sitting across from it right now. It's shining, solid mahogany and ridiculously huge.

If my grandmother were a man, I'd suspect she's compensating for something.

Christopher, the Queen's personal secretary, offers me tea but I decline with a wave of my hand. He's young, about twenty-three, as tall as I am and attractive, I guess—in an action-film star kind of way. He's not a terrible secretary, but he's not the sharpest tack in the box, either. I think the Queen keeps him around for kicks—because she likes looking at him, the dirty old girl. In my head, I call him Igor, because if my grandmother told him to eat nothing but flies for the rest of his life, he'd ask, "With the wings on or off?"

Finally, the adjoining door to the blue drawing room opens and Her Majesty Queen Lenora stands in the doorway.

There's a species of monkey indigenous to the Colombian

rain forest that's one of the most adorable-looking animals you'll ever see—its cuteness puts fuzzy hamsters and small dogs on Pinterest to shame. Except for its hidden razor-sharp teeth and its appetite for human eyeballs. Those lured in by the beast's precious appearance are doomed to lose theirs.

My grandmother is a lot like those vicious little monkeys.

She looks like a granny—like anyone's granny. Short and petite, with soft poofy hair, small pretty hands, shiny pearls, thin lips that can laugh at a dirty joke, and a face lined with wisdom. But it's the eyes that give her away.

Gunmetal gray eyes.

The kind that back in the day would have sent opposing armies fleeing. Because they're the eyes of a conqueror . . . undefeatable.

"Nicholas."

I rise and bow. "Grandmother."

She breezes past Christopher without a look. "Leave us."

I sit after she does, resting my ankle on the opposite knee, my arm casually slung along the back of the chair.

"I saw your interview," she tells me. "You should smile more. You used to seem like such a happy boy."

"I'll try to remember to pretend to be happier."

She opens the center drawer of her desk, withdrawing a keyboard, then taps away on it with more skill than you'd expect from someone her age. "Have you seen the evening's headlines?"

"I haven't."

She turns the screen towards me. Then she clicks rapidly on one news website after another.

PRINCE PARTIES AT THE PLAYBOY MANSION
HENRY THE HEARTBREAKER
RANDY ROYAL
WILD, WEALTHY—AND WET

The last one is paired with the unmistakable picture of

my brother diving into a swimming pool—naked as the day he was born.

I lean forward, squinting. "Henry will be horrified. The lighting is terrible in this one—you can barely make out his tattoo."

My grandmother's lips tighten. "You find this amusing?"

Mostly I find it annoying. Henry is immature, unmotivated—a slacker. He floats through life like a feather in the wind, coasting in whatever direction the breeze takes him.

I shrug. "He's twenty-four, he was just discharged from service . . ."

Mandatory military service. Every citizen of Wessco— male, female, or prince—is required to give two years.

"He was discharged *months ago*." She cuts me off. "And he's been around the world with eighty whores ever since."

"Have you tried calling his mobile?"

"Of course I have." She clucks. "He answers, makes that ridiculous static noise, and tells me he can't hear me. Then he says he loves me and hangs up."

My lips pull into a grin. The brat's entertaining—I'll give him that.

The Queen's eyes darken like an approaching storm. "He's in the States—Las Vegas—with plans to go to Manhattan soon. I want you to go there and bring him home, Nicholas. I don't care if you have to bash him over the head and shove him into a burlap sack, the boy needs to be brought to heel."

I've visited almost every major city in the world—and out of all of them, I hate New York the most.

"My schedule—"

"Has been rearranged. While there, you'll attend several functions in my stead. I'm needed here."

"I assume you'll be working on the House of Lords? Persuading the arseholes to finally do their job?"

"I'm glad you brought that up." My grandmother crosses

her arms. "Do you know what happens to a monarchy without a stable line of heirs, my boy?"

My eyes narrow. "I studied history at university—of course I do."

"Enlighten me."

I lift my shoulders. "Without a clear succession of uncontested heirs, there could be a power grab. Discord. Possibly civil war between different houses that see an opportunity to take over."

The hairs on the back of my neck prickle. And my palms start to sweat. It's that feeling you get when you're almost to the top of that first hill on a roller coaster. *Tick, tick, tick* . . .

"Where are you going with this? We have heirs. If Henry and I are taken out by some catastrophe, there's always cousin Marcus."

"Cousin Marcus is an imbecile. He married an imbecile. His children are double-damned imbeciles. They will never rule this country." She straightens her pearls and lifts her nose. "There are murmurings in Parliament about changing us to a ceremonial sovereignty."

"There are always murmurings."

"Not like this," she says sharply. "This is different. They're holding up the trade legislation, unemployment is climbing, wages are down." She taps the screen. "These headlines aren't helping. People are worried about putting food on their tables, while their prince cavorts from one luxury hotel to another. We need to give the press something positive to report. We need to give the people something to celebrate. And we need to show Parliament we are firmly in control so they'd best play nicely or we'll run roughshod over them."

I'm nodding. Agreeing. Like a stupid moth flapping happily towards the flame.

"What about a day of pride? We could open the ballrooms to the public, have a parade?" I suggest. "People love that sort of thing."

She taps her chin. "I was thinking something . . . bigger.

Something that will catch the world's attention. The event of the century." Her eyes glitter with anticipation—like an executioner right before he swings the axe.

And then the axe comes down.

"The *wedding* of the century."

PLEASE ENJOY
THIS EXCERPT FROM
EMMA CHASE'S

ROYALLY
MATCHED

Sarah

Later, when the sun hangs low in the sky but there are still a few hours until sunset, the full cast of ladies and crew are down in front of the castle. Vanessa Steele, the executive producer, announced that all assistants and non-cast members must remain indoors or off set. Since it's an outdoor shoot, she doesn't want to chance any of us getting caught in the shot.

I've found the perfect spot to watch the taping—on the forested side of the castle, up a hill, near a tree for cover, just in case. I have a stellar view of the castle entrance down below, and in the meantime, I have my book for company. Sitting back against the tree, I sigh with contentment. This is going to be lovely. Then I open my book . . . and practically jump out of my skin when a cough sounds from behind me.

I didn't see anyone when I first walked up here.

Closing my book, I look out from behind the trunk cautiously. Just far enough . . . to see the unmistakable sight of His Royal Highness, Prince Henry, standing a few yards away.

With a gasp, I duck back behind the tree.

I grew up inundated with news stories of the royal family and posters of our handsome princes pinned to my bedroom walls—every girl in Wessco did. Nicholas was the serious one, staid and well-spoken, honorable—just like Mr. Darcy. Henry always seemed more like Fiyero Tigelaar from *Wicked: The Life and Times of the Wicked Witch of the West*—fun-loving, passionate, and thoughtless, focused only on the next party and his own pleasure.

I stand up and peep back out from behind my tree for another glimpse.

And my heart starts to gallop, my head goes fuzzy, and it feels like my throat is closing in on itself. Because—sweet baby Jesus in a manger—he's coming this way! His long, purposeful strides are aimed right at me. Which means when he gets here, I'll actually have to speak to him. Although we met that one brief time—last year in a pub when he was with his brother and Olivia Hammond, who is now Princess Olivia, the Duchess of Fairstone—and while I'm acquainted with the details of Prince Henry John Edgar Thomas's life, he's still just a handsome stranger. And I don't do well with strangers.

My eyes dart around for an escape. Curling up behind the tree like a snail in its shell is out—he's obviously already spotted me. *Damn.* I glance up at the branches—I'm an excellent climber—but even the lowest one is out of jumping reach. *Double damn.*

He's almost here. *Shit, shit, shit.*

I think I'm hyperventilating. I may pass out. Which would solve the problem of having to talk with him, but it'd be even more embarrassing—I'm speaking from experience.

Mentally, I shake myself. I just need to think of something to say.

And now the only thing filling my mind is *thinkofsomethingtosay, thinkofsomethingtosay, thinkofseomthingtosay*.

My hands turn sweaty and numb.

I could ask about his mother—always a safe bet. Except . . . his mother is dead.

Damn it all to hell.

And . . . he's here.

My eyes drop down and I freeze, like a deer caught in the biggest, brightest headlights. I stare at his boots, dark and shiny like black mirrors. I force my gaze upward, over his long legs clad in black . . . polyester pants? His hips and waist are covered by a white jacket with garishly shiny buttons, purple accents, and gold-roped tassels on each of his broad shoulders.

It's a ridiculous outfit—like a cheap Prince Charming costume—and yet he still manages to look fantastic.

The top button is clasped at his neck, accentuating a sexy, masculine Adam's apple. He has a chiseled chin; a strong, slightly stubbled jawline; criminally full lips; a straight, regal nose; thick, wild dark-blond hair, and eyes so beautiful they'll steal your breath, words, and thoughts. They're a stormy shade of green, but warm like raw emeralds heated by the sun. I remember, the first time we met, thinking how none of the pictures I'd ever seen of him did his eyes justice. And, at this moment, I second that opinion.

If I weren't naturally speechless, I would be now.

Prince Henry's brow furrows, looking down at me in an almost disgruntled way.

"Did someone die?"

And it's such a ludicrous question, I forget to be panicked. "What?"

"Or are you a witch?" He clicks his tongue, shaking his

head. "Sorry—Wiccan? Pagan? Worshipper of the dark arts? What is the PC term these days?"

Is this really happening?

"Uh . . . Wiccan, I believe, is acceptable."

He nods. "Right. Are you a Wiccan, then?"

"No. Catholic. Not especially devout, but . . ."

"Hmm." He wiggles his finger at my hands. "What are you reading?"

"Oh . . . *Wuthering Heights*?"

He nods again. "Heathcliff, right?"

"Yes."

"So it's about a fat orange cat?"

My mind trips as I try to figure out what he's talking about. The comic! He thinks it's about Heathcliff the comic strip.

"Actually, no, it's about a young man and woman who—"

His eyes crinkle and his lips smirk, making my cheeks go warm and pink.

"Are you teasing me, Your Highness?"

"Yes." He chuckles. "Badly, apparently. And please, call me Henry."

My voice is airy, hesitant, as I try it out.

"Henry."

His smile remains, but softens—like he enjoys hearing the word. And then I remember myself, curtsying as I should have from the start.

"Oh! And I am—"

"You're Lady Sarah Von Titebottum."

Warmth unfurls in my stomach.

"You remembered?"

"I never forget a pretty face."

My cheeks go from pink to bright red. I change colors more often than a chameleon. It's a curse.

"I'm not usually good with names." His eyes drift down

to my hips, trying to look behind me. "But Titebottum does stand out."

When nervous, I typically go mute. This moment is the exception to that rule.

Just my luck.

"You would think so, although several of my uni professors had trouble with the pronunciation. Let's see, there was *Teet-bottum*, *Tight-butt-um*, and one who insisted it should be *Titty-bottum*. It's not everyday you hear a distinguished professor say the word *tit*. That one kept the class entertained for weeks."

He tilts his head back, chuckling again. "That's great."

My face is now approaching purple. I take a deep, slow breath. "Um . . . why did you ask if someone had died?"

He gestures to my clothes. "Both times I've seen you, you've worn black. What's that about?"

"Oh." I glance down at my long-sleeved, knee-length black dress with a crisp white collar and black ankle boots. "Well, black is easy; it goes with everything. And I'm not one for loud colors; I don't like to stand out. You could say I'm a bit . . . shy."

And the award for understatement of the year goes to . . .

"That's a shame. You'd look gorgeous in jeweled tones. Emerald, deep plum." His eyes wander, pausing at my legs, then my breasts. "In a clingy ruby number, you'd bring men to their knees."

I look at the ground. "You're teasing me again."

"No." His voice is rough, almost harsh. "No, I'm not."

My eyes snap up to his, and hold.

There are meetings in books that stand out, that alter the course of the story. Profound encounters between characters when one soul seems to say to the other, "There you are—I've been looking for you."

Of course, life isn't a novel, so I'm probably just imagining the slipping, sliding feeling inside me, like things are shifting around before finally snapping into their rightful place. And I think my mind is playing tricks on me—fancying that it's interest alighting in Prince Henry's eyes.

Heated interest.

My breath catches and I cough, breaking the moment.

Then I gesture to his jacket. "Do you really think you're qualified to give fashion advice?"

He laughs, rubbing the back of his neck. "I thought I looked like an absolute tool—now I'm sure of it."

"Did the producers pick that out for you?"

"Yes. I'm supposed to ride down to the castle on horseback. Make my grand entrance." Briskly, his long fingers unbutton the jacket. He shrugs it off, dropping it on the ground, revealing a snug white T-shirt and gloriously sculpted arms.

"Better?"

"Yes," I squeak.

The teasing smirk comes back, then he grips the back of his T-shirt, pulling it off. And my mouth falls open at the sight of warm skin, perfect brown nipples, and the ridges and swells of muscles up and down his torso.

"What do you think of this?" he asks.

I think this is worse than I thought.

Henry Pembrook isn't a Fiyero—he's a Willoughby. A John Willoughby from *Sense and Sensibility*—thrilling, charming, unpredictable and seductive. Marianne Dashwood learned the hard way that if you play with a heartbreaker, you can't be surprised when your heart gets shattered into a thousand pieces.

I shrug, trying to seem cool and unaffected. "Might look a bit too 'Putin' on the horse."

He nods, then puts his shirt back on, and my stomach swirls with a strange mix of relief and disappointment.

"Why aren't you down with the other girls?"

"Me? Oh, I'm not part of the show. I couldn't imagine . . ."

"Then why are you here?"

"Penelope. Mother wouldn't let her participate unless I tagged along to keep an eye on her."

"Every family has a wild child. Penny's yours?"

Takes one to know one.

"Yes, definitely."

He tilts his head, the sunlight making his eyes a deeper green, almost simmering. "And what about you? Is there any wild in you, Teet-bottom?"

My cheeks go up in flames. "Not even a little. I'm the boring one. The good one."

His teeth scrape his lower lip and it looks . . . naughty.

"Corrupting the good ones is my favorite pastime."

Oh yes, definitely a Willoughby.

I hug my book to my chest. "I'm not corruptible."

His smile broadens. "Good. I like a challenge."

A crew member suddenly appears, trailing a large white horse behind him. "They're ready for you, Prince Henry."

Keeping his eyes on me, he places one foot in the stirrup and smoothly swings up onto the saddle. With his hands on the leather reins, he winks.

"See you around, Titty-bottom."

I cover my face and groan.

"I never should have told you that."

"Can't blame me. It makes you turn so many lovely shades. Is it just your cheeks that blush?" His gaze drags down my body, as if he can see beneath my clothes. "Or does it happen everywhere?"

I fold my arms, ignoring the question.

"I think you might be a bully, Prince Henry."

"Well, in grade school I did enjoy pulling on the girls' braids. But these days I only tug on a woman's hair in a very specific situation." His voice drops lower. "Let me know if you'd like a demonstration."

His words cause images of slick, entwined limbs and

gasping moans to flare in my mind. And as if on cue, the blush blooms hot under my skin.

Henry laughs, the sound deep and manly. Then he spurs his horse and rides away, leaving me glowing like a damn Christmas tree. I open *Wuthering Heights* and press the pages against my face, cringing.

It's going to be a long month.

CPSIA information can be obtained
at www.ICGtesting.com
Printed in the USA
BVOW03s1046040817
491169BV00001B/4/P